An Orphan's Dream

ALSO BY JUDY SUMMERS

The Forgotten Sister
A Winter's Wish
A Daughter's Promise

Judy Summers

An Orphan's Dream

MLP

Copyright © 2025 Judy Summers

The right of Judy Summers to be identified as the Author of the Work has been asserted by her in accordance with the Copyright, Designs and Patents Act 1988.

First published in Great Britain in 2025 by
Mountain Leopard Press
An imprint of HEADLINE PUBLISHING GROUP

1

Apart from any use permitted under UK copyright law, this publication may only be reproduced, stored, or transmitted, in any form, or by any means, with prior permission in writing of the publishers or, in the case of reprographic production, in accordance with the terms of licences issued by the Copyright Licensing Agency.

All characters in this publication are fictitious and any resemblance to real persons, living or dead, is purely coincidental.

Cataloguing in Publication Data is available from the British Library

ISBN 978 1 0354 2121 3 (Paperback)

Typeset in 12/17pt Sabon LT Std by Jouve (UK), Milton Keynes

Printed and bound in Great Britain by Clays Ltd, Elcograf S.p.A.

Headline's policy is to use papers that are natural, renewable and recyclable products and made from wood grown in well-managed forests and other controlled sources. The logging and manufacturing processes are expected to conform to the environmental regulations of the country of origin.

Headline Publishing Group Limited
An Hachette UK Company
Carmelite House
50 Victoria Embankment
London EC4Y 0DZ

The authorised representative in the EEA is Hachette Ireland, 8 Castlecourt Centre, Dublin 15, D15 XTP3, Ireland (email: info@hbgi.ie)

www.headline.co.uk
www.hachette.co.uk

Chapter 1

Liverpool, July 1864

Jemima stared down into the rich, steaming cup of chocolate and tried not to cry.

It just wouldn't do, not while she was here in a crowded public place, and particularly not when she was sitting on her own. She would make a sad spectacle of herself, and if word got back to Mrs Silverton that she'd done anything less than rigidly respectable, there would be trouble.

Being by herself wasn't helping. Normally, of course, Betty would be here too, because this was where they always came on a Saturday afternoon after they'd been paid, spending a small portion of their wages on a weekly treat before taking the rest home. When Jemima had first been employed, she'd been more than happy to bring her entire pay packet back to Pa as her contribution – the wages paid to a fifteen-year-old female assistant teacher not being great, in any case – and proud to do so. But dearest Pa had insisted that she spend a little on herself first. After all, he'd pointed out, working men always kept some of their earnings back, so why shouldn't she?

So, since last September, Jemima and Betty's Saturdays had taken on a familiar and enjoyable routine. School in the morning, with Betty often rushing in late due to her family commitments, but Jemima having done Betty's early chores as well as her own, to cover for her. Then lessons, recess, more lessons, and bidding farewell to the excited children as they ran off for their day and a half of holiday before Monday came round again. Then tidying up and sweeping the classrooms to the accompaniment of a lecture from Mrs Silverton on what they could have done better that week, then pay and an escape to Hopkins' tea room for a drink of chocolate and a bun. Jemima was so grateful that Pa had—

She only just succeeded in choking back a sob. Because it was all going to end. This would be the last time she would ever sit at one of these tables, covered with their pretty cloths, the last time she would drink the chocolate and eat the macaroons for which Mrs Hopkins was famed. In fact Jemima shouldn't be here today, even, not when Pa needed her; but he'd insisted, had said he'd be all right resting until she got back. She needed her treat, he said. She was a young thing and shouldn't be cooped up in a sickroom when she could be out living her life. Still thinking of her, even at such a time: that was just like Pa.

And so Jemima sat, as a kind of farewell to old times. When her cup and plate were empty she would, again with great finality, pop into the grocery in the other half of the building and buy Pa a bag of his favourite barley sugar to bring home, even though he . . .

She really *must* compose herself. She picked up the chocolate and took a tiny sip. It was as delicious as ever, but she hardly tasted it. She needed to think of something else, or she would collapse in a heap, here with all these cheerful people around her.

Jemima tried to distract herself by looking around the room. It was crowded, as it always was on a Saturday afternoon. Naturally there were some people she didn't recognise, but others she knew by sight, as they were post-wages regulars like herself and Betty. A sprinkling of other girls and young women in twos and threes, employed in the local shops; a few courting couples, the boys in tight white collars and the girls in their best hats; and the single elderly lady who always occupied the same table in the far corner, from where she could survey the room, and who was always treated with extreme deference by the staff.

The place was owned by a married couple – he running the grocery shop while she did the cooking and baking for the tea room – and between them they also seemed to manage a baby and a dog. Despite the establishment's modest air, the quality of the Hopkins pies, pastries and delicacies was renowned among Liverpool's lower middle classes, and business was thriving. And, of course, it served no alcohol, so it was an entirely respectable establishment in which two young assistant teachers could drink tea or chocolate without risk to their reputations or positions.

Jemima rarely saw Mrs Hopkins herself, except for a glimpse of her flying about the kitchen whenever the door opened, as most of the serving was done by a cheerful woman called Sally and a girl, Hannah, who was two or three years younger than Jemima. The sole exception was that Mrs Hopkins would always personally bring out the tray for the elderly lady in the corner, stopping to exchange a few words before she went back to her ovens and pans.

With a sigh, Jemima realised that she'd managed to take her mind off everything for about one minute, but now the weight was settling heavily on her shoulders again. Despite her best efforts, a tear splashed into her cup. There was no point in staying here. It had been a mistake to come, especially when Betty had been obliged to rush straight home after work today, needed to look after some of her many younger siblings while her mother went out. But somehow Jemima had convinced herself that as long as she continued with her usual routine, as long as she collected her wages and walked to the tea room and had her chocolate and her macaroon, that everything would still be normal. But it wasn't, was it? And nothing would ever be the same again.

'Excuse me, dear, do you mind if I join you at this table?'

Jemima looked up and found, to her surprise, that she was being addressed by the elderly lady. She glanced over to the table in the corner to see that it was already being occupied by someone else, so she could hardly refuse; besides, it would be bad manners to do so. 'Of course, ma'am.' Politely, Jemima stood and pulled out the opposite chair, waiting until the woman was comfortably seated before she took her own place again.

Given the way in which she was always so carefully waited on by the staff, Jemima had assumed that the woman would be stern, but now she had the chance to observe her at close quarters she could see a kind face with smile lines around the eyes.

It was absolutely necessary to try to appear normal, so with a huge effort Jemima prepared herself for a bit of small talk. 'I do believe,' she said, pushing the crumbling remains around her plate, 'that Mrs Hopkins must make the best macaroons in Liverpool, if not in England.'

By complete chance, this seemed to be exactly the right thing to say; the woman beamed. 'That she does. She was a talented cook from the first moment she stood at the range as a girl, and she's only gone from strength to strength since then.'

Comprehension dawned. The pride in the voice, the reference to Mrs Hopkins as a child, the way she always made time to come out personally: this must be her mother. Thank goodness Jemima had said something positive rather than putting her foot in it!

She sat up straighter. 'I'm so glad we agree, Mrs . . . ?'

'Roberts, dear. Mrs Roberts.' There was a slight pause before she continued. 'Now, you might call me a nosy old woman, and if you prefer then I'll go away again. But I've been able to give a sympathetic ear to many, many girls over the years, and if it helps you to talk to a stranger, please do. One thing is plain, and that's that you're not your usual self today. I see that your friend isn't here, but if you're upset because you've fallen out, there's surely a way to put things right.'

Jemima couldn't help but correct the mistake. 'Oh no, ma'am, that's not it at all. She just had to go home early today to help her mother.'

Mrs Roberts nodded, and Jemima understood she hadn't actually thought that was the problem at all; she'd only used it to get Jemima to talk. But now she'd started, she somehow wanted to continue, and what was the harm in speaking to someone she would, in all probability, never see again? It wasn't as if she had anyone else to confide in, except Betty, who had plenty of concerns of her own, and the relief of having an older, wiser woman at hand was suddenly irresistible.

Fighting back against a renewed threat of tears, Jemima managed, 'It's my Pa.'

Mrs Roberts made no reply, but her mouth set in a line.

Jemima was flustered at the implication. 'Oh no, not that! He could never be— no, he's the dearest Pa in the world. But . . .' She forced herself to say the words out loud over the heaving of her chest and the lump in her throat, the words she could hardly bring herself to think, never mind speak. 'He's dying.'

She heard a sharp intake of breath. 'Oh, my dear, how terrible for you.'

Jemima's hand was lying on the table next to her cup, and she felt it being taken in Mrs Roberts's own. The warmth of the touch, the kindness of it, was what really made her tears flow, and with her other hand Jemima groped for her handkerchief.

'Now, my dear,' continued Mrs Roberts, with great compassion in her voice, 'I'm sorry that there's nothing I can do or say that will take that pain away from you. It will be a very difficult time for you and for all your family. But the rest of you will be able to support each other, so I hope you can take comfort from that. Your mother, your brothers and sisters?'

Jemima shook her head and lowered her face, scrubbing it with the handkerchief. Slowly she allowed it to be coaxed out of her that she would be completely alone once Pa was gone: Ma had died when Jemima was a little girl, and there were no other siblings.

Mrs Roberts's face assumed a greater expression of concern as the sad tale continued and Jemima belatedly realised that she had no business – no right – to be burdening a stranger with her problems. What on earth was she thinking? And people would be staring by now.

'I really must go,' Jemima said, standing up so abruptly that the dregs of the chocolate nearly slopped out of the cup. 'Pa absolutely insisted that I should come here today, just like normal, but I've been away from him too long.'

Mrs Roberts retained Jemima's hand just for a moment. 'I know that I'm nothing to you, my dear, just some stranger in a tea room. But if you ever need a sympathetic ear, or a cup of tea – or both – then you'll find me here most afternoons.'

Jemima nodded.

'And . . . may I know your name?'

Had she not mentioned it when Mrs Roberts had introduced herself? How ill-mannered of her. 'It's Jemima, ma'am. Jemima Jenkins.'

'Well, I wish you nothing but the best, Jemima Jenkins, and remember that Hopkins' tea room will always be a place of sanctuary.'

'Thank you, ma'am, and thank you for listening. I'm grateful, I really am. But I must get back to my Pa.'

Jemima just about managed a collected walk out of the tea room, rather than a full-scale flight, but it was close. She stopped in the vestibule for a moment to take a few deep breaths and then entered the grocery.

Mr Hopkins was busy with another customer, chatting in his normal calm and kindly manner as he helped her to pack her purchases, but the boy who was his assistant spotted Jemima and gave a grin. 'Afternoon, miss! Quarter of barley sugar, is it?'

'Yes please, Charlie.' He was a bright lad, who must have been a pleasure to teach when he was at school. Jemima wondered which one he'd attended, and whether his work in the shop had helped with his arithmetic.

As it happened, he was a little *too* bright and

perceptive today. He handed over the twist of paper, took her coin and peered closely at her. 'You all right, miss? Do you need to sit down? Glass of water?'

Jemima stowed the sweets in the little shoulder bag she carried everywhere. 'No, no, I'm fine, thank you. Just some dust in my eye and a slight headache. I'll walk it off on the way home.'

'If you're sure, miss. You go carefully, now.'

Everyone was being so kind. How could she bear it?

Jemima paused once more in the vestibule, looking back through the glass window of the door to the tea room. The efficient Hannah was clearing away the plates and cups from the table where Mrs Roberts still sat, and was evidently making some remark about her change of seat. They chatted for a moment and then the girl returned to the kitchen. Mrs Roberts began to stand, and Jemima hurried away so it would not seem as if she were waiting for the elderly lady in order to waylay her.

As she walked out of Williamson Square and along a crowded Duke Street, Jemima's mind was in so much turmoil that she didn't even stop to look properly in the windows of the many book- and print-shops that lined the road, her gaze merely sliding past their wares. John Gore's was advertising bound volumes of the latest poetry by Browning and Tennyson. Hughes and Shaw was partly a bookbinders, but also displayed prints and papers, including the first part of a new monthly serialisation by Charles Dickens. George Perry's window boasted a brand new plan of Liverpool and some fine engravings. Normally Jemima would have found all of this fascinating, and lingered in front of each, but today none of it held any interest.

Even if it did, it was an interest she would have to learn to do without, because what she'd been far too proud to mention to Mrs Roberts was the impending downturn in her financial situation. Not only was she about to lose her dearest Pa, to become an orphan, but she would have to survive on the pitiful wages paid to a single girl. There was a little money saved up, because Pa had always been so careful about it, but that wouldn't last forever and she certainly had no scope to be extravagant. There would be no more chocolate or macaroons, to be sure, nor books or papers, but the situation was even more serious than that. Their boarding-house accommodation, in a well-kept establishment on a reasonably reputable street, would have to be exchanged for something much cheaper once she was on her own. It wasn't 'home', not exactly, for they hadn't had a proper one of those since Ma died, but the surroundings were at least familiar, comforting and safe, and she was going to lose all of that, too.

As Jemima walked on, in an almost dreamlike state, she had the strangest feeling that someone far behind her was calling out her name. She made a vague and half-hearted attempt to turn, but the street was packed and most of the tide was going in the same direction she was, and anyway she was surely imagining things. Was it due to her distress? The last thing she needed was to lose the ability to think clearly, even if she did have to put up with the tea-room fare sitting uneasily in her stomach. She resolutely ignored the voice and continued on her way.

Soon Jemima had turned off on to the not-quite-so-smart Suffolk Street, and a hundred yards after that into the shabbier Pitt Street, which was just about holding on to respectability by the tips of its fingers. The boarding house did at least front on to the street, and wasn't hidden away down a back alley, and it boasted a scoured white step and a brightly polished door-knocker. Jemima didn't need to knock or to ring the bell; as trusted long-term residents she and Pa had been honoured with a key to the front door.

Inside, the hallway was quiet, and Jemima paused for a moment in front of the small looking glass to take off her bonnet. Smoothing her hair, she saw a pale face with sad, reddened eyes staring back, so unlike the blooming reflection that used to greet her. Her chief concern was that Pa would notice and that it would upset him further, although he was so far gone by now... Just in case, she dabbed at her eyes with the rather damp handkerchief and pinched her cheeks to bring a little colour to them. Then she exhaled slowly before she climbed the stairs, bracing herself for what she might find.

The house was divided into rooms and apartments of varying sizes and rents. Thanks to Pa's careful financial management over the years, they were able to afford to live in the best situation it had to offer: two rooms on the first floor, with a view over the street to the front. It wasn't quite like renting a house of their own, as Jemima remembered from her earliest years; but it was convenient, and their meals were included in the rent, so she didn't even have to cook when she got home each evening.

At first Jemima's key wouldn't turn, and because she still wasn't thinking properly it took her a moment to realise that this was because the door was already unlocked. She pushed it open to find that Mrs Lewis, the landlady, was sitting by Pa's side, where his bed was placed over by the window. Bless him, he'd always insisted that Jemima should have the apartment's bedroom to herself, so she had her own private space in there while he slept on one side of the sitting room. The creak of him settling on the narrow single bed, long after Jemima was safely tucked up under her own blankets, was one of the most familiar and comforting sounds of her childhood. This arrangement made the actual living space a little cramped, but there was still room for a couple of chairs and a kettle by the fire, along with a small table and some shelves for their few plates and cups and Pa's little collection of books. It wasn't much, but it was *theirs*, hers and Pa's.

Mrs Lewis turned as she heard the door, putting down her sewing so she could bring a finger to her lips. 'He's asleep,' she whispered. 'I had mending to do, so I thought I might as well keep him company until you got home. He was awake for a while, and knew me, but then he dropped off.' She stood up, still keeping her voice low. 'I'll go now that you're back. I've tonight's tea to get ready.'

Jemima thanked her. She heard the door close but paid little heed to the sound of footsteps on the stairs, because all her attention was fixed on the pale wreck of a man who lay in the bed.

Years ago, when life was full of sunshine, the name of James Jenkins had been a byword down at the docks for size and strength. He could lift more weight, carry more loads and keep going for longer than any other man there. He'd been a coal heaver, one of the most demanding jobs imaginable: these workers unloaded huge, heavy, filthy sacks off the barges that docked continuously, all day every day, and then carried them on their broad shoulders and bent backs across to the wagons that would take them out into the fuel-guzzling city. Only the very strongest and fittest men were employed for the task, because the weight would crush anyone less able, but it was so demanding that the working lifespan of a coal heaver was only about ten years. It couldn't be started until a man was in his twenties – nobody younger had the strength – but it was all over by the time he reached his mid-thirties, because by then he'd be twisted with pain, coughing, exhausted and broken. This didn't bother the employers, who could simply choose from among the ready supply of younger, fitter men looking for work, but it meant the start of a slow decline for the heavers themselves.

Such had been the case for Pa, and as Jemima had grown up, he'd been on his way down. First he'd slipped from his coveted full-time and well-paid position to queuing up for casual daily-paid labour unloading lighter goods. After a while the aches and pains had caught up with him, the wheezing in his chest had got worse, and he sank into lowlier and lighter work which paid less and less. And then, within the last year, some kind of illness had struck him. It was difficult to know what it was – he'd had no specific accident and hadn't fallen into a fever – but it was like something was eating him up from the inside. He'd become gaunt and then skeletal, struggling at work and eventually being let go entirely. His pride had kept him upright a little while longer, as he attempted to make himself useful by doing odd jobs round the house for Mrs Lewis, but soon he'd got so weak that he'd been forced to take to his bed. He would never leave it again; Jemima had known that for some while, as she nursed him and watched his skin stretch ever more tightly over his bones. Her beautiful Pa was an emaciated ruin, a man not yet forty-five who looked ninety.

There was no real need for a fire at this time of year, but Pa did get so cold these days that Jemima lit one. There was already water in the kettle, so she set that to boil, hoping she might be able to get him to sip a little tea when he awoke. There wasn't much else to do: the room was clean and Mrs Lewis had obviously been doing a bit of dusting while she'd been there, judging by the few bits and pieces that had been knocked askew.

Jemima straightened the books on their shelf, managing the ghost of a smile as she remembered each one and what they'd meant to Pa. He'd never been to a proper school, having been sent out to work at a young age, but he'd learned his letters at Sunday school and then continued practising as much as he could when he was older. Liverpool was a wonderful place for working men who wanted to improve themselves: thanks to various rich benefactors there were public lectures, and even a library where books could be borrowed by anyone who was a member. Pa had attended every free event he possibly could, eager to learn anything new whatever the subject. After Ma had died he'd sometimes taken Jemima with him, if no neighbour was available to mind her, and when she was little she'd been treated as a novelty, patted on the head by the other men and sometimes given sweets or a farthing. But as she grew older she'd been aware of an undercurrent of hostility, murmurs of how this wasn't the place for a young woman, who ought to be at home seeing to domestic matters.

Pa had ignored all this and encouraged Jemima to learn, as well as himself; not just so he would have someone to talk to about it all, but genuinely for her own sake, because 'learning is never wasted'. He'd also insisted that she attend a proper school, paying the pennies to keep her at it even as his earnings shrank, so she could make something of herself. 'You're my Jemima,' he used to say, 'and I believe in you.' And his belief and support had paid off: the day Jemima had come home to say she'd been offered her present position had been one of the proudest of Pa's life. He, a dock labourer, a working man since the age of eight, was now the father of an assistant teacher! He'd taken her hands and spun her around the room, laughing and saying how proud her Ma would have been.

It had been suggested to Jemima more than once, by jealous fellow schoolgirls and scornful boys, that she was lucky to get all this attention from Pa, and that it was probably because she had no siblings, and specifically no brothers. If Pa had been the father of sons he might have saved those precious pennies for them rather than educating a mere girl, they told her, but Jemima knew in her heart that he would have encouraged her anyway. He loved her, and that knowledge was a constant in her life.

It was, however, unusual to be an only child, and Jemima often wondered how this had come about, especially when Pa liked children so much. Obviously Ma had died young, but Jemima had been five and a half at the time, so she might well have been left with two or even three younger siblings, judging by the size and shape of other families. And there were no older brothers or sisters, either, for all that Ma and Pa must have been married for some while before Jemima came along. But she'd been too young to wonder about all this while Ma was alive, and she hadn't liked to ask Pa after their loss in case it caused him upset. They just went on together: she being everything to him just as he was to her. Privately, though, Jemima did sometimes feel the lack of siblings and wished that she had at least one sister. But that was never to be, so there was no point in dwelling on it. Ma had a favourite saying, one of the few things Jemima could remember properly about her: 'If wishes were horses, beggars would ride.' Life, she said, was what you made it.

Pa's books were now all neat on their shelf, properly lined up and grouped according to subject area. The collection was small but wide-ranging, including a few novels and volumes of literature as well as factual works on engineering, farming and history. When he woke up he might be lucid for a little while, as he still sometimes was in the afternoons, so Jemima would pick something out to read to him.

She heard him stir just as she was running her hands along the lettered spines, so she moved to the vacant chair next to the bed and took his hand. 'Pa? Pa, can you hear me?'

He made a vaguely coherent sound, and she felt her hand being lightly squeezed by the gaunt fingers.

'Do you think you could drink some tea for me? The kettle's on.'

He didn't reply, but he did lick his lips, which Jemima

took as meaning yes. She sat stroking his hair until the water boiled, then made tea and poured him half a cup. She knelt by the bed and slipped one hand under his head to support it while he managed a few sips.

'There now, Pa, that'll do you good.' This close to him, she could hear the terrible wheezing and groaning noises coming from his chest as it rose and fell. 'Are you in pain, Pa? There's a few drops of that laudanum mixture left, enough for today and tomorrow, and I can get some more from the dispensary on Monday.'

Pa shook his head. 'Makes me sleepy,' he whispered. 'Just now . . . want . . . awake . . . see you.'

'All right, if you're sure.' She put the cup aside and tucked the blankets around him more closely. 'You shouldn't talk too much, though: you'll wear yourself out. Would you like me to read to you?'

He nodded.

'Anything in particular? Not *The Future of Farming*, surely. The Shakespeare extracts? Poetry?'

Pa mumbled something, and Jemima leaned in close to hear. 'The one with all the sisters. Your Ma always liked . . .'

Jemima knew the one he meant, and she went to draw it out from the shelf. It was an odd thing for a working man to have in his collection: an old novel from about fifty years ago, called *Pride and Prejudice* and set in a world so alien that she could hardly imagine it. A world where a family could live in a large many-roomed house in the country, which they had all to themselves, and walk miles across open fields – a feature Jemima had only seen once or twice – and where they had servants, carriages, trips to London, multi-course dinners and visits from friends and relations. But it was witty and funny, and Jemima had read and enjoyed it many times despite the strange setting and the totally unfamiliar way of life. Given her own situation, she'd always particularly liked the idea of a family of five sisters – just imagine! – but when she'd picked it up most recently, what had struck her most was the theme that the girls' entire future livelihood depended on every breath that their father took, and that they would be thrown out of house and home as soon as he died. That had soured the work for her, and she'd put it away and hadn't picked it up since. But if it was what Pa wanted to hear, it was what he would get. He used to read it out loud to Ma of an evening while she got on with her sewing or knitting, and Ma always enjoyed it, so hopefully it would take his mind back to happier times.

Jemima settled herself on the chair.

Pa's eyes were open now, she saw, and he seemed alert. 'You're a good girl.'

'I try to be, Pa, for you.'

'Sisters...'

'Yes, Pa, I've got the book with the sisters. Shall I start from the beginning, or is there a particular part you want to hear?'

'Sisters,' he repeated, a little wistfully, and Jemima wondered if he was about to doze off again. But his voice, although weak and wheezy, was coherent. 'All those sisters. Just like you.'

Chapter 2

Jemima felt tears prick at her eyes at this new manifestation of Pa's illness. He'd spent much of his time asleep in the last week or so, but when he did wake he'd still known who and where he was – or, at least, he had done up until now. So where had this confusion come from? He was surely mixing her up with someone else. With Ma? Did he think Ma was beside him? But no, she'd never had any sisters either; only several brothers who were all now dead.

'And you've got brothers, too,' rambled Pa. 'How many? Three or four, at least, though there was that one who died – I was there, I saw it . . .'

'Pa, stop it, please!' begged Jemima. 'You're not yourself; you don't know what you're saying. I'm here: it's me, Jemima. Your daughter, your only child. I don't have any sisters or brothers.'

'But you do.' His hand reached out for hers, and the grip was surprisingly firm.

'Pa...'

'Flowers!' he said, suddenly. 'The flower book.'

Jemima didn't know what to do. There was no volume relating to flowers among the collection on the shelf. Was he raving? Was he about to fall into a delirium that would make him a danger to himself?

His head, which he'd managed to raise an inch or two, fell back on to the pillow. 'Sister... flowers... the book.' He took a hoarse breath and dropped to a whisper. 'In the table... drawer... kept it separate... your Ma...'

Jemima followed his gaze to the table on the other side of the room. It was the type that had a drawer under the tabletop, and they always kept a few coins in there. If she ever opened it, it was only to find a penny or two at the front, so she didn't need to pull it right out. She went over and did so now, finding to her surprise that there was a small book tucked away at the back. She fished it out and looked wonderingly at the green marbled cover and the lettering on the spine: *Flora Domestica; Or, The Portable Flower-garden.*

She carried it carefully back to the bed and held it up where Pa could see it. 'This one? Was it another one of Ma's favourites?' Jemima wondered why Pa had never shelved it with the others, but perhaps he liked to keep it as a private reminder of his lost but still beloved wife.

It now struck Jemima that it was unusual that Pa had never married again. Most widowed men did, because they needed a wife to keep their house for them and look after their children. And Pa had only been in his early thirties when Ma died, so there would surely have been plenty of takers if he'd decided to look about him for someone new. A strong man, earning good money, who didn't get drunk, get into fights or beat his wife? Who rented his own house and only had one child to provide for? There would have been a queue of widows and unmarried women beating a path to his door. But he'd remained single for Ma's sake, and her own, all that time.

If it were even *possible* to love him more, Jemima would.

'Yes,' Pa was rasping. 'First, from the library, for her, and then . . . bought one for Ma. To remind us of . . . You read that, and you'll be all right when I'm gone.' He paused, wheezing again and unable to catch his breath to continue.

Jemima had no idea what he was talking about, or why learning about flowers should be of importance to her future, but she certainly wasn't about to waste any precious minutes on it while he was awake and still with her. 'Later, Pa – I'll look at it later, I promise. Now, could you sip a bit more tea for me? And I'll read to you, and we'll have a nice cosy afternoon together.'

The curtain was already open, but she pulled it back further so he could see out into the clear sky over the roofs opposite. She even considered opening the window a little, in case they could catch the sounds of the docks, about half a mile distant, but she decided against it in case the draught made his chest worse.

He hadn't asked for any particular part of *Pride and Prejudice* so Jemima opened it at a favourite passage – one far removed from the subject of impending penury after a father's death – and began to read.

* * *

Jemima remained at Pa's side all the rest of Saturday, dropping off occasionally while he was asleep, and then through a restless night and into Sunday morning.

She was supposed to go down to the kitchen for her meals, along with all the other residents, but she didn't want to leave Pa for any length of time, and besides, she wasn't hungry. So she only made one very quick trip down to refill the kettle, so she could make him more tea in their room when he woke up properly, and then resumed her place by his bedside.

At around noon there was a tap at the door and Mrs

Lewis entered, followed by Sarah, the maid-of-all-work, carrying a tray. 'I know your Pa's a bit far gone for a proper meal,' said the landlady, 'but you need to eat and you've paid for this with your rent.' She moved to the table, pushed in the still-open drawer, and gestured for Sarah to place the tray. On it were a bowl and a spoon plus a generous slice of bread, and Jemima could smell a decent meat stew. She was so light-headed by now that she wasn't sure whether the scent made her feel hungry or sick.

Sarah managed to touch Jemima's hand in silent sympathy before Mrs Lewis shooed her out and came over to the bed. 'Still going, is he? Good for him.'

Jemima remembered what day it was. 'I'm so sorry, Mrs Lewis, I should have paid next week's rent when I saw you yesterday, and I forgot. Why didn't you remind me? I'll get it now.'

The few pennies that they kept in the drawer wouldn't be enough, so Jemima disappeared for a moment into her bedroom so she could extract some of what was hidden there. Thank goodness Pa had foreseen that there would come a day when he would cease earning, and had saved accordingly.

When she returned Mrs Lewis was still by the bed, straightening the blankets, and Jemima handed over the coins.

There was a pause while they both looked at the money in Mrs Lewis's hand, neither of them voicing the thought that Pa might not be with them for a whole further week.

'Well,' said the landlady, briskly. 'I'll leave you to it. You eat that while it's hot and I'll send the girl up for the tray later.' She left.

Pa was still asleep, so Jemima forced herself to sit down at the table and eat. To start with she thought that the sensation of nausea was uppermost, but by the time the bowl was nearly empty she was feeling much better. Mrs Lewis was kind to look after them with these little extra attentions. Of course, she had a character to keep up, because she only wanted a certain class of people to aspire to board with her, but still. She'd visited their rooms almost every day since Pa had taken to his bed, sometimes when Jemima was there but mainly to keep Pa company while Jemima was out at work.

A tap on the door sounded, and at Jemima's invitation Sarah inserted herself into the room. Given their relative situations she and Jemima weren't really supposed to be friends, but they were, after a fashion. Sarah had arrived in the house when both girls were twelve, and Jemima the only child resident; Jemima had therefore thought it only right to try to make her as welcome as possible. But

Sarah was both painfully shy and greatly intimidated by the strict Mrs Lewis, so Jemima acceded to her wish that she would only pop down to chat or to help out a bit when the landlady was out. She'd also given up on trying to persuade Sarah to call her by her name, instead of 'miss', as she understood that the maid would get into trouble if anyone else heard her being so familiar with a resident.

Sarah crept across the room and gazed down at Pa for a few moments. Jemima took her hand, not sure whether she was giving or seeking comfort.

'He's been so kind to me,' whispered Sarah, 'ever since I've been here. Never shouted, like some of the other residents, and smiled and told me I was a good, hard-working girl.'

That was just like Pa.

'And when he was working downstairs for a while, fixing things, he even asked me about myself, asked could I read, and what I wanted to do with my life. Me! It was almost like having my own P—' She swallowed the end of the sentence and stared at the ground, worried she'd given offence, but Jemima didn't mind at all.

Sarah tip-toed out with the tray, as well as the untouched packet of barley sugar that Jemima pressed on her, knowing that she had very few treats, and Jemima put the kettle on in case Pa should wake again during the afternoon. He did, and she had some tea ready, but today he could hardly get it down. He was wasting away before her eyes, and there was nothing she could do.

He spoke as she was wiping his mouth. 'The money. Have you checked the money?'

'I did the other day, Pa, and it was all still there, don't worry.'

'Make sure.'

To humour him – because she hadn't spent anything except the rent, and how else would the coins disappear? – Jemima went round the various hiding places. Pa had always been very careful: not just about saving, but about making sure they could hold on to what they'd accumulated. The Liverpool police would do little more than laugh if a person of their class tried to report stolen money: the poorer sort might just about get justice for a murder, if they were lucky, but the investigation of theft was only for those of substantial property. So, as Pa had said, they needed to look after themselves.

When they'd moved to these rooms, he'd set up the same sort of arrangement as they'd had at their old house. The few pennies and halfpennies in the table drawer were loose there deliberately; not just because it was easy to get at them when a small purchase needed to be made, but also as a blind. It was the obvious place to keep coins, so if anyone did manage to get in and start pilfering it might fool them into thinking that this easy gain was enough, and that there wasn't any more or that it wasn't worth looking for it.

But there was: a decent stash of shillings, florins and half-crowns, the earnings of Pa's years of hard labour, carefully put away instead of being spent at the public house or the gin shop, where so many dockers' wages ended up. These were divided into three bags, each of which was hidden in a different place. One was tucked in the far corner behind the books on the shelf in the sitting room, and one lay in a drawer in Jemima's bedroom, under her spare petticoat – this was the one from which she'd extracted the rent money. The final, emergency, bag, also in her bedroom, was sewn into the lining of an old coat of Pa's that was hanging in the wardrobe.

She sat down by the bed. 'It's all there, Pa, don't worry. Now, what shall we do? More reading? Or shall I just sit and hold your hand if you're too tired to listen?'

'I'll talk.'

'But Pa—'

He shook his head. 'While I still can. You need to know.'

'Know what?' Jemima wondered if this was going to be a repeat of yesterday's ramblings.

Pa took the deepest breath she'd seen him inhale for

some while, and it cost him some effort. 'You made us so happy. When you came into our life.'

'When I was born, you mean?'

'Yes. But . . . you weren't born to us.'

Jemima froze. He was wrong. He was ill, he was confused, he didn't know what he was saying. She wished he would stop this; it was just too upsetting. 'You don't mean—'

He took in another wheezing breath. 'Neighbours. Neighbours had lots of children, we had none. When you were born . . .' He tailed off into a cough.

He really did sound as though he meant what he was saying, and, despite the warmth of the summer's day, Jemima's hands and feet were cold. 'Pa?' She resisted the urge to shake him and tell him to come round properly and stop talking nonsense.

Because something deep down told her that he wasn't.

'They couldn't feed you. Their Ma – your Ma's friend. Took you in.' He paused. 'Loved you. Always.'

Jemima's eyes were stinging. 'Stop it! You were always my real Ma and Pa. I'd feel it if you weren't. I'd *know*.'

He groped for her hand. 'Listen. Find them, so you're not alone.'

This time it was Jemima's turn to shake her head. 'No. I don't want anyone except you. And when – *if* – anything happens to you, I'll manage.'

Pa lay back, his energy running out. 'Name. What was their name? Can't... Something common.'

Jemima gripped his fingers. 'Pa, this can't be true. And even if it is, how would I find them? They don't still live next to our old house?'

'No. Gone. Long time... before we did. Couldn't pay the rent. Evicted.'

'If it'll make you happy then I'll do whatever you want. But I think you're just confused. Please don't tell me you're not my Pa, I can't bear it.'

His papery, emaciated hand squeezed hers. 'Always your Pa. Forever. But find them. You can't be alone. Eldest girl... your sister... unusual first name. Bible. *Flowers*. Find...'

This was getting worse by the moment. But the effort of saying so much was beginning to tell, and Pa fell silent as he collapsed back on to the pillow. It wasn't long before he drifted off into sleep, leaving Jemima to stare at the familiar walls and wonder why they were spinning.

* * *

On Monday morning Jemima had no choice but to go to school. The absolute last thing she needed was to lose her job, so she would have to get through the day as best she could and then hope that Pa was still alive when she got home – the thought of him dying alone, with her not there to comfort him, was just too terrible to contemplate. At least she would have Betty's robust and comforting presence to support her during her time at work, so she would feel less empty and isolated as she counted down the hours and minutes until she could rush back to Pa.

Everything was blurred as she left him sleeping and went out. It was only a short walk to St James's Road, a route so familiar that Jemima didn't even need to think about it, and she was surprised to find herself suddenly in front of the building without having noticed how she'd got there. Fortunately she appeared to be early and there was plenty of time before the start of morning lessons.

Betty hurried up as Jemima stood in the porch, unusually punctual. 'Jemima! I've been thinking about you non-stop since Saturday. I wanted to come and see you were all right, but there was so much to do at home, and our Bert and our Molly were . . . well, anyway. How are you, and how's your Pa?'

Jemima found that she couldn't speak over the lump in her throat.

Betty took her hand in sympathy. 'Oh, you poor love. I'll help you through the day as best I can. Maybe Mrs

Silverton will let me come over to the older girls to be with you today . . .' She tailed off, as aware as Jemima was that Mrs Silverton, a stickler for routine and discipline, would allow no such thing. 'Well, in any case, I can do your chores at the end of the day as well as my own, so you can leave as soon as the children do.'

Their conversation was halted by the sound of the key turning in the school door from the inside. Mrs Silverton appeared, and they both bobbed a curtsey before slipping past her into the schoolroom. It was a single, wide room divided into three distinct areas, with desks and benches in rows facing the long wall on the far side and a teacher's desk and blackboard opposite each section. Light entered from two rows of windows, plenty of it at this time of year, but they were too high up to allow anyone to see outside.

To their left as they entered was the infants' space, where boys and girls were taught together up until the age of seven by Miss Robinson. She was a nice young teacher who wasn't all that much older than Jemima and Betty, and who was just as petrified of the headmaster and his wife. Betty was her assistant, having had plenty of practice dealing with young children at home, and the infants loved her.

The older children were strictly segregated by sex, with the girls taught in the middle of the room by Mrs

Silverton, aided by Jemima, and the boys at the far end by Mr Silverton and his male assistant. The swishing, smacking sound of the cane emanated regularly from their side, accompanied very occasionally by a stifled cry of pain, but most of the bigger boys prided themselves on making no noise when they were struck, even though it made some of the girls flinch and the infants cry when they heard it. Jemima knew, like everyone did, that riotous and naughty boys needed to be kept in check, or they'd never learn anything, but she couldn't help wondering whether Mr Silverton needed to use the cane *quite* so often for minor infractions such as poor spelling and ink blots. One day she might even summon up the courage to voice this thought out loud.

The pupils at the school were all nice children; or, at least, nice in the sense of coming from respectable homes with parents who could afford the weekly fees. No really rich families sent their sons and daughters to St James's, but Jemima's charges were the children of shopkeepers and clerks, with starched pinafores and proper shoes, not the ragged offspring of daily-paid and precarious labourers who needed every penny they earned for rent and food. There were many youngsters in Liverpool who were from classes even lower than that, of course – the beggars, ne'er-do-wells and criminals – and Jemima knew as well as anyone else which streets to avoid in order not to be surrounded by swarms of bare-footed and hard-faced tiny ruffians.

However, Jemima did sometimes have another wildly heretical thought, which was that these poor children's lives might be improved if they had the chance of an education. She *had* once made the mistake of saying this out loud, and had been roundly derided and scolded by both Mr and Mrs Silverton as a result. The very idea, they said, was ridiculous, and even assuming that such children were even capable of learning, all that would result was a class of slightly better-educated criminals. The poor were poor because they were feckless, and there was nothing anyone could do about it, except possibly offer occasional charity to the more deserving among them and point them towards the workhouse. *The rich man in his castle, the poor man at his gate, God made them, high and lowly, and ordered their estate*; that was one of the hymns they sang in school, and it was the truth.

Jemima moved mechanically, filling the older girls' inkwells with care and watching Betty set out slates and slate pencils in the infants' section. She herself had by far the less pleasant job of the two, working with Mrs Silverton rather than Miss Robinson, but she was glad to spare Betty the additional trouble that her liveliness would cause over here. They were both lucky to be in the school at all, given their family backgrounds. Jemima's status as the daughter of a dock worker would normally have prevented the head and his wife wanting to employ her at all, but she'd been such a model pupil during her own time that she was partly redeemed, backed up by the fact that if anyone asked, Mrs Silverton could say that her assistant's father was 'retired, and living on his own means'.

Betty's father, Mr Whiting, meanwhile, was a builder with thirteen children, but he earned enough to send all of them to school for a few years each, the girls as well as the boys, and indeed five of the younger members of the family were current pupils. Today Jemima would see Albert in his usual place among the older boys, while Ralph and Sid fidgeted with the infants. The twins Molly and Maisie, who were eight, were in Jemima's section, but they would be absent today, along with several of the other girls, because Monday was wash day for most families, and those who didn't send their clothes out to laundries needed every daughter they could find at home to help.

This was merely another sign for Mrs Silverton that the Whiting family were not *quite* of the class she would want in her school, neither as pupils nor as staff. Betty's position was therefore, if anything, even more insecure than Jemima's, particularly given her propensity to talk back and argue, the inevitable result of being a member of such a large family. But Jemima had lobbied as vigorously as her limited influence would allow for her friend's employment once she was secure of her own, and since then she'd kept Betty away from Mrs Silverton as best she could, even if it meant diverting the mistress's wrath on to herself from time to time. And the fudging of Betty's home address as being in Colquitt Street – rather than its true Back Colquitt Street, the yard behind the main road – gave just enough respectability to be acceptable.

Once the big ink bottle was safely stoppered and stowed away, and the pens set out on each desk, there wasn't much else to do, because Jemima had already swept the floor and written *Monday, July 11th, 1864* in painstakingly neat copperplate handwriting on the blackboard before she'd left on Saturday. She was just flicking some imaginary dust from Mrs Silverton's desk when Miss Robinson arrived, coming over to ask Jemima how she was, in a sympathetic tone, before she went to the infants' section.

At the sound of the school bell Jemima and Betty went out into the yard and watched the three rigidly straight lines of children forming up. They all trooped inside in strict silence and stood beside their seats, each teacher saying 'Good morning, class,' in turn and receiving a reply in varying degrees of unison. Jemima's emotions, tightly controlled for the last half-hour, now inconveniently wanted to burst out again, but she absolutely *could not* start crying here, not in front of the children and certainly not in front of Mrs Silverton.

The usual morning routine of prayers, handwriting and arithmetic began. Jemima patrolled the girls' section in order to help anyone who needed it, and guided many a small ink-stained hand around the complexities of a copperplate lower case *r* or *s*. Performing these familiar tasks should have helped, but she found that she just couldn't settle. There was so much going on inside her head that it ached and she felt dizzy, and this only got worse as the morning went on. Her existing worries about Pa were overwhelming enough on their own, but when added to the possibility – which she still couldn't quite bring herself to believe – that she was adopted, and that her whole life had been a lie, she couldn't see straight. It affected her work, and when, shortly before the children's morning recess, she told a confused little girl that the change from a shilling after spending fourpence was sixpence, she had to step back and rub her eyes, wishing for a cool cloth to put on her forehead.

Fortunately Mrs Silverton hadn't noticed anything wrong, though Miss Robinson had, and she held out a

AN ORPHAN'S DREAM

hand to stop Jemima following the children outside for her supervision duties. 'You really don't look well, and I think you should go home. I'll have a word with Mrs Silverton on your behalf.'

The mistress had already left the room, because the standard procedure for recess was that the teachers had a short break and a cup of tea while the assistants watched over the children in the yard, but it wasn't long before she returned, displeased at Jemima's being even a minute late.

She surveyed the scene. 'What's going on here?'

Miss Robinson was braver than she looked. 'I wonder, ma'am, if Jemima might be permitted to go home. She's not well this morning, and with her family situation . . .'

There was silence for a moment as Mrs Silverton looked Jemima up and down. 'Your father's condition has deteriorated, I gather?'

'Yes, ma'am,' Jemima managed.

'Significantly?'

Jemima swallowed. 'Yes, ma'am. I don't think he's going to . . .'

The words *live much longer* wouldn't come out, but Mrs Silverton understood. 'Very well. If we've reached that stage then you'd better go. You needn't come back.'

Jemima was struck by such unexpected kindness. 'Thank you, ma'am, I'm so grateful to you.'

Mrs Silverton opened her mouth again, but Jemima was already halfway to the door. On her way through the yard she paused only to tell Betty where she was going, and Betty promised to visit after the end of the school day. Then Jemima was rushing the short way back to Pitt Street.

The door to their rooms was unlocked again, so Jemima wasn't surprised to see Mrs Lewis inside, although the latter was startled to see her. 'I didn't expect you back until this afternoon. I was just—'

Jemima rushed to the bed. 'Is he . . .?'

'He's still with us, for now. But you should prepare yourself for the idea that it won't be long.'

Mrs Lewis slipped out, and Jemima began what was to be her last vigil. All through the rest of the morning she sat by Pa, holding his hand and speaking to him in a comforting tone, although she wasn't sure he could hear her. She hoped that he was at least aware of her presence, aware that he wasn't spending his last hours alone. Once or twice he stirred, not waking completely but mumbling words that were sometimes identifiable. Jemima caught her own name as well as 'Ellen' – that was Ma – and, again, something about sisters and flowers.

By the middle of the afternoon Pa had sunk into a deeper sleep. Jemima knew she wouldn't be able to get him to drink anything, but she used a handkerchief and some of the water from the kettle to moisten his lips every so often. The sounds of the working day outside, the noises of cleaning from other parts of the house . . . all of it faded away, and there was nobody in the world except Jemima and Pa. Just the two of them, as it had been since she was a little girl. She kept up the soothing flow of words for a little longer, then ended it with a whispered 'You'll be with Ma soon,' and fell silent.

Still holding his hand in both of her own, Jemima gazed down at Pa's dear face, peaceful now and showing fewer signs of the pain that had racked him for so long. She listened to his breathing, the only sound on earth that mattered, and willed it to keep going.

At four o'clock, the breathing stopped.

Chapter 3

Jemima leaned forward to kiss Pa's forehead, but otherwise she didn't move. As long as she sat here, as long as she had his hand clasped in her own, he was still here, he was still with her. She wasn't alone, not yet.

At some point there was a tap at the door, and Betty put her head around it. 'Jemima?'

'It's all right, you can come in,' said Jemima, calmly. 'Nothing will disturb him now.' With no warning, she burst into huge, uncontrollable sobs.

'Oh, Jemima!' Betty rushed in and embraced her, holding her while the storm broke. Jemima could see nothing, hear nothing, feel nothing, except Pa's loss. In theory she had known for some while that it was going to happen, but that was very different from the actual event. While he was still with her, however tenuous his hold on life, she could tell herself that there was still hope, but now he was gone, and the finality of it was terrifying.

Eventually the heaving and sobbing subsided enough for her to breathe more easily, and the real world started to return. Jemima saw that she had soaked the front of Betty's dress, and she pulled back with an apology, wiping her eyes.

'Never you mind that,' said Betty. 'I'm here to look after you, not the other way round. I've told Ma she'll just have to manage for this evening. Henry and Rob are here too, but they're out in the street; they didn't want to come up and disturb you.'

There was another knock at the door and Jemima turned to see Mrs Lewis on the threshold.

The landlady took in the situation at a glance. 'My condolences, Miss Jenkins.'

The formal tone brought Jemima back into some semblance of consciousness. She would have to be in charge from now on, not only of her own life but also of the immediate arrangements. There was nobody else: Pa would not be buried unless Jemima organised it herself, she would have no black to wear unless she went out and bought it herself, and she would find nowhere new to live unless she searched, signed and paid for it herself. She would have to be an adult.

Jemima wiped her eyes, not having the faintest clue where to start.

'You've never had to do this kind of thing before, I take it,' said Mrs Lewis, brusquely. 'It's not the first death we've ever had in the house, so if you have the funds then I know a woman who can be fetched for the laying-out, and a decent funeral service that will see everything done respectably.'

'He was in a burial club. I have the letter somewhere.'

'Good.' Mrs Lewis turned to Betty. 'Are those your brothers outside?'

'Yes, ma'am.'

'I'll go down and give them directions so they can have the necessary people summoned; it's much more suitable to send men on such an errand.'

'They'll be glad to help, ma'am.'

Mrs Lewis bustled out again, leaving Jemima alone with Betty and Pa. His hand lay on the outside of the covers, where she'd been holding it, and she reached out to tuck it under the blankets. 'Don't want you to get cold, Pa,' she murmured.

'You look pretty white and cold yourself,' said Betty. 'It'll take a while to light a fire here and boil your kettle. I'll go down and find the kitchen and see if I can't get you some tea.' She hesitated. 'Will you be all right while I'm gone?'

'Yes. And in any case, I'll have to get used to it, won't I? Being alone.'

* * *

Jemima sat, automatically swallowing some sweet tea when a cup was put in her hand, and watching in a detached kind of way while people she didn't know came and went. Sarah crept up to hold her hand for a few minutes, but had to rush away when an impatient 'Now *where* has that girl got to?' sounded from downstairs.

It was getting dark by the time the strangers had all left. Pa was washed and dressed in his Sunday best, still on the bed, but the funeral man had said he'd bring a coffin first thing and arrange for the burial later in the morning. 'Can't be too quick, in this warm weather,' he'd added, rather tactlessly.

Betty popped out of the room again and engaged in a whispered conversation with her brothers, who were now on the landing.

She came back in. 'I suppose it's no good asking you to come back to ours overnight?'

Jemima shook her head. 'I can't leave him alone.'

'I thought you'd say that. I'm sending the boys home, but Henry will come back with some bits of black crape for you – Ma kept the ribbons she had when her sister died – and I'll stay right here with you.'

'But you'll have school in the morning!'

'I've been to school having stopped up all night before, when some of our littl'uns were poorly, and I can do it again. And Henry's out of work at the moment, so he can stay too – he says he'll sit outside the door here if your landlady will let him.'

Jemima was too tired and numb to argue.

The sense of unreality returned as the evening wore on. The trappings of death were all around her now: the closed window curtains, the black ribbons pinned to her bodice and the armband on her sleeve, the black crape draped over Pa's tiny shaving mirror on the washstand and on the outside handle of the door. And, of course, Pa himself lying cold and still on the bed. But it wasn't real, it couldn't be real. She couldn't have lost him forever. Tomorrow morning she would wake up and find it had all been a bad dream, and that Pa was happy and well and ready to take her to the library, or to talk about the latest lecture he'd attended.

As the night became cooler, the stark truth penetrated more and more deeply into Jemima's mind. She shivered, and then somehow a shawl was around her shoulders, placed there by Betty's silent care. Jemima might not have any family left, but she was grateful for such a friend.

The question of whether she did, in fact, have a family was one Jemima didn't want to think about, not now. Pa and Ma had been all that mattered to her. Even if this other family did exist, and wasn't just the product of Pa's wandering mind during his illness, what were they to her? She'd clearly meant nothing to them if they'd been prepared to give her away without a second thought. She would put them from her mind entirely.

Dawn light was visible around the closed curtain before Jemima would have thought it possible. She forced her stiff and aching limbs to move, thinking that the least she could do was to find Betty something to eat and drink before she had to go to school. Sarah would be at work in the kitchen by now, and would surely be able to spare some bread and jam, or a boiled egg, in lieu of the breakfast that was included in the rent. She didn't want anything herself, and Pa—

Jemima stopped, winded, in the very act of reaching for the door handle. But she had to go on. She had to get used to this.

Quietly, so as not to disturb any of the other residents, Jemima opened the door. Then she gave an almighty start as a figure not two yards away got to its feet.

She couldn't help a little squeak, but calmed herself when she saw that it was Betty's eldest brother, Henry, two or three years older than herself, whom she'd met a couple of times but didn't know very well.

He was immediately alert, all quiet attention. 'Are you all right? And Betty? Is there anything you need that I can get for you?' He was slim, neat and dark-haired, and in the light slanting out through the open doorway Jemima could see that his eyes were kind and full of compassion.

'Thank you, no. I was just going down to the kitchen to find something for Betty to eat before she has to go out – and for you too, of course, now I've remembered that you were here – sorry – you must forgive me—' She had no idea what she was saying, and stopped.

'It's all right, really.' He started to reach out a hand and then hastily drew it back before it could touch her. 'I really am very sorry about your Pa. I never met him, but Betty's spoken about you and about him, and he sounds like one of the best of men.'

Jemima nodded. 'Thank you. He was. And thank you for staying – it's very kind.' She noticed that Henry was wearing a black armband, and was struck by his thoughtfulness for a man he didn't even know.

'Anything to help, at such a time.' He cleared his throat. 'Now, shall I go downstairs for you?'

'Best not. Sarah doesn't know you and you'd probably scare her half to dea—half out of her wits.'

'Yes, yes, of course. I should have thought of that.'

'I'll see what I can find and bring it up. Betty just dozed off about an hour ago, but if she wakes up, please tell her where I've gone so she doesn't worry. I'll be straight back.'

Jemima went down to the kitchen with her request, and was supplied by a tearful Sarah with bread, jam, tea *and* eggs, as well as hesitant condolences. Jemima took the tray back upstairs, refusing Henry's help to carry it into the sitting room; partly because she was almost there anyway by that time, and also to spare him any possible embarrassment, because she knew that he walked with a limp and the teapot was very full.

'Do come in,' she said, as she passed. 'Normally Mrs Lewis would be horrified at me having a male guest in the room, but she can hardly object under the circumstances and with Betty here too.'

She placed the tray on the table and made them both eat, resolutely standing between them and the cold, still form of Pa on the other side of the room. None of this was their fault, and their kindness needed to be appreciated.

Eventually Betty stood and engulfed Jemima in an embrace. 'I'd stay with you if I could,' she began, awkwardly, 'but . . .'

'You have to go,' said Jemima, firmly. 'Mrs Silverton

would never forgive you for staying away for my Pa's funeral. I'm still astonished she was so sympathetic to me, giving me some time and saying not to come back until it was all over.'

'That was a surprise,' agreed Betty. 'But who knows? Perhaps we've misunderstood her all this time and she does have a heart in there somewhere.' She kissed Jemima on the cheek. 'I'll come back when I can, but it might not be today as I can't be out two evenings in a row – Ma hasn't got anyone else to help her in the house.' Then she turned to Henry. 'You look after her today, you hear?'

Jemima looked on in confusion, not entirely sure how Mrs Whiting could have nobody else to help her when the family was so numerous.

Betty misunderstood Jemima's expression. 'Henry's out of work at the moment, until he recovers from his accident,' she explained. 'He's going to stay with you through the funeral.'

'I'm a poor substitute for Betty, I know,' he said. 'But it's not right to leave you to do this on your own if any of our family can help. That's what friends are for.'

Jemima turned away and wiped her eyes.

Betty clattered down the stairs. Henry courteously returned to his post on the landing, in order to leave Jemima alone with her Pa and her thoughts.

Jemima moved one of the chairs from the table back

to the bedside, but she didn't attempt to take Pa's hand this time. His arms were folded across his chest under the blanket, and she didn't like to disturb him, but it wasn't just that. He was already *not there*, not Pa. The still form on the bed wasn't him.

Sounds from the front door and the stairs indicated that the undertakers were on their way up, so Jemima stood and attempted to retain her composure. It was going to be a difficult day, having to deal with the funeral so soon, but she could face it. She could face it because Pa himself had brought her up to have the courage and the confidence that would get her through it. *You're my Jemima, and I believe in you.*

'Thank you, Pa. Thank you for everything.' She kissed his cold, waxy forehead one last time and then managed to call 'Come in' when she heard the knock.

The soberly dressed men who entered were experienced in this kind of thing, and it was all achieved with dignity. Pa was placed in the coffin, the lid of which was then nailed down, and he was conveyed down the stairs and out to the waiting cart. Two of the men bowed to Jemima and left, while the other two walked by the horse's head as they set off, Jemima and Henry following behind. There was certainly nothing extravagant or fancy about the arrangements, but Pa's assiduous payments to a burial club over the years meant that he had a coffin rather than a mere shroud, and that he would have a proper paid service spoken by a clergyman, and his own grave with a marker for his name. It was all decent – respectable, as both Mrs Lewis and Mrs Silverton would say – and much, much better than the undignified, unmarked and communal paupers' graves that awaited so many of Liverpool's citizens.

The church they were going to was only a few minutes' walk away: St Thomas's, the nearest one to the docks and the burial site of many dock workers. Jemima's eyes were glazed as she put one foot in front of the other to follow the coffin through the gate, past the grand tombstones near the church and then along a path that led around the building and further away. Here the graves were simpler and meaner, and at the end of a row there was a gaping hole in the ground.

* * *

Man that is born of a woman hath but a short time to live, and is full of misery. He cometh up, and is cut down, like a flower; he fleeth as it were a shadow, and never continueth in one stay.

Jemima tried to let the clergyman's words wash over her as she stood in the graveyard, cool on this shadowy, unfashionable side of the church, but one of them jarred. *Flower.* A word Pa had repeated several times before his death, and in the context of the other family that Jemima might or might not have.

Now was not the time to think of that. She wished she had a flower, a real one, with her now so she could throw it into the grave to lie on top of the coffin, but she didn't. At the appropriate moment she took a handful of soil and dropped it so it sprayed out on the wooden lid, and then she stood back as the diggers began to fill in the grave. Pa's body would now be under six feet of earth while she stayed on the surface and wondered how she would face the rest of her life.

As the coffin disappeared, Jemima felt increasingly young, alone and scared, and by the time all was done, and a small piece of wood with JAMES JENKINS 12-VII-1864 scratched on it was pushed into the mound at the end where his head lay, she could hardly breathe.

She tried to calm herself by staring at the grave and forcing through some practical thoughts. It was too early for a larger marker – she knew that, didn't she? Because the earth needed to settle before one could be installed. She didn't think that the burial club money would run to anything in stone, nor that she would be able to afford the extra cost of paying for it herself, but a wooden cross would do well, and she promised herself that she would plant some flowers to grow permanently, rather than just bringing cut ones that would fade and die.

She stared into the distance for some while, and then belatedly became conscious of the fact that Henry was still standing by, waiting for her at a respectful distance with his cap in his hands. She moved to join him, and they made their way back along Pitt Street.

For a while they walked in silence. He was evidently unwilling to break in on Jemima's thoughts, but she wanted to have them broken into; she needed to think of something else other than Pa lying in the cold ground and separated from her forever. 'May I ask,' she said, eventually, 'how your recovery's going?'

'I'm on the mend, slowly,' he said. 'Thank you for asking.'

There was another silence.

'It was an accident at work, wasn't it?' Jemima continued, aware that it probably wasn't the best topic, but hoping that if she at least got him talking they might eventually be able to find a subject that didn't cause either of them pain.

'Yes. We were working out to the south of the city, where they're building all those new streets of terraced houses. I was halfway up one when the scaffolding gave way and I fell. Lucky to get away with just a broken leg, really.' He paused. 'And luckier still it was me, and not Pa or Rob.'

'Why do you say that?'

'Well, Pa's our main earner, and Rob's bigger and stronger than me, for all he's younger. He was already getting more work, and in line for better pay.'

Jemima knew exactly how old Rob was, because he and Betty were twins: sixteen, the same as she was, though they'd be seventeen this October and she not until next May. But despite his youth Rob had not only the height but also nearly the strength of a grown man, as many of the girls who lived nearby had already started to notice. Jemima found him pleasant enough, whenever she'd spoken to him, but he didn't have a great deal of conversation.

'So, anyway,' Henry was continuing, 'with them both still working, Betty's pay, Matthew running errands on the site and Harriet and Anna sending back some of their wages from service, we're able to make do until I can find something else.'

'Something else? You won't go back to the building site with the others?'

He shook his head. 'They wouldn't take me.'

'But surely your leg will heal enough . . .?'

'Even a hint of a limp is enough to put paid to that, when there's so many fit men looking for work. Besides, builders are superstitious, and they won't want me back now I've had an accident, in case there's another one.'

'That's hardly fair!'

'Fair or not, it's the way of the world.' He shrugged. 'I could spend my whole life wishing things were different, or I can accept it and move on.'

Jemima considered this sentiment for a few moments.

'Sorry,' said Henry, suddenly. 'Here I am talking about myself, with all that you've had to deal with recently—'

'Oh no, please, don't apologise! I brought the subject up, and honestly it will do me good to talk about something that isn't . . .' Jemima paused, knowing that her voice was starting to wobble. She made an effort. 'So, if not building, then what?'

'Well, I was always pretty good at school. We couldn't afford for me to stay on, what with me being the eldest and needing to get out to work with so many children to feed, but during the weeks when I couldn't walk at all I started reading and studying again, to have something to do. Pa says builders and sites always need accounting clerks – for ordering materials, sorting out wages, that sort of thing – so if I could qualify as one of them then it's good steady work and I could still be in the trade.'

'Qualify?'

'There's an examination, if you want to work with money and accounts. You don't have to have it, especially if you've got the right connections who can get you a job without, but it's a great advantage and Pa says he doesn't know anyone who's got the certificate who's out of work. So I'm studying for it.'

Jemima caught something in his tone. 'You don't sound all that enthusiastic about it?'

'Well, of course, it's much better than trying to get labouring work, which I was never really cut out for even before the accident.' He indicated his slight frame, so different from his brother's. 'And I'm not finding the studying too hard. I think I'll be able to pass the examination, when the time comes. But . . .' he hesitated, as if unsure whether to continue or not. 'What I'd really like to be is a teacher.'

'A teacher?'

'Yes.'

'Well, why not?'

'Because it's too late,' Henry explained. 'I had to leave school when I was twelve, and to be a teacher you've got to stay on and then train as an assistant or a pupil teacher – as you know yourself, of course. I suppose I could go back to school, or one of these places where they give lessons in the evenings, but it would mean far too long without proper pay, and we can't afford it. I'm the oldest, and I've got a responsibility.'

'Well, even if you don't do that, I think it's wonderful

that you want to learn more. You can go to those evening lectures and things anyway, you know, and join the library. Why, Pa—'

She came to an abrupt halt on the pavement.

'I'm so sorry,' he said, again. 'I shouldn't have— I didn't mean—'

'It's all right,' she managed. 'It wasn't your fault.'

They were nearly back at the boarding house as this was said, and they walked the short way to the front door in silence.

Mrs Lewis appeared just as they were approaching, coming down the street in the opposite direction with a loaded shopping basket over her arm. She halted when she saw Jemima and stood waiting by the door.

Henry paused. 'I'll leave you here, then. Betty will be round whenever she can make it.'

'Thank you,' said Jemima, simply. 'To both of you. For everything.'

Henry touched his cap to Mrs Lewis, and Jemima followed the landlady into the house. She expected that Mrs Lewis would take her shopping through to the kitchen, but she stopped in the hallway and put the basket down. 'That's strange.'

'What is?'

The landlady pointed up the stairs. 'There's light

coming through there. Did you leave your door open when you went out?'

'No, I locked it.' Had she, though? Jemima couldn't remember one way or the other. It was such a habitual action that she'd probably done it without noticing. She tried to think back. Yes, she was sure that she'd locked the door. She remembered because she'd been thinking that she'd have the keys all to herself as long as she remained here, with no need for Pa to have them any more.

Mrs Lewis was halfway up the stairs. 'Well, it's open now.' She made it to the top, and then gasped as she looked into the room.

Jemima hurried up to join her. 'What . . .?'

Then she, too, was taken aback by shock. The door was thrown wide and the sitting room was in a state of chaos.

Trembling, Jemima pushed past Mrs Lewis and stepped inside. Her and Pa's belongings were strewn around. All the sheets and blankets from his bed were twisted on the floor, the table drawer had been wrenched out, and the precious collection of books was scattered everywhere. From what she could see through the open door of the bedroom, it was the same in there.

A sudden, sickening fear came over Jemima.

She looked at the broken drawer where it now lay at the foot of the table. It was empty.

She looked at the shelf where the books had been, and where one of the bags of money had been hidden. It, too, was empty.

She ran into the bedroom. There was no purse to be found in the empty drawer or among any of her items of clothing that were now scattered around the floor.

Slowly, she turned to the wardrobe. Surely . . . but Pa's coat had been pulled out, and the lining was ripped and empty.

Somebody had known that Jemima would be out of the house all morning as she buried her father. And someone had taken advantage of that fact in order to break in and steal every single penny he'd left to her.

The room began to spin, and then everything went black.

Chapter 4

Henry berated himself all the way home. He'd admired Jemima right from the first moment Betty had introduced them, ages ago, but he'd never really managed more than a few words with her, either because the situation didn't warrant it or because he'd been too tongue-tied. Now, today, he'd had the chance to be genuinely useful to her, and what had he done? Rattled on about himself at a time when everything should have been about her and her comfort, and then ended up by upsetting her. *Well done, Henry.*

There was no excuse for staying longer once he'd escorted her back to her door, and he certainly didn't want to give her any kind of reputation by delaying her out in the street for a chat, especially not with that suspicious landlady's beady eye on them. Besides, why would a pretty, clever girl like Jemima Jenkins want to talk to him? Girls preferred big strong men, didn't they? Men like the ones who were in plentiful supply on building sites and other workplaces. A weedy fellow who was more interested in books and learning could hold no attraction. She'd only chatted to him on the way back because it was useful for her to take her mind off her own troubles, until he'd managed to mess that up as well.

His leg was hurting rather a lot by the time he got home. The morning had involved more walking than he'd been used to recently, and the long periods of standing still hadn't helped much, either. But it was all in a good cause, and at least he could console himself with the thought that it would eventually heal completely. The idea of being crippled for life, a burden on his family, didn't bear thinking about. He was the one, after Pa, who was supposed to step up and look after everyone.

The normal gaggle of small children were playing in the shared yard as he passed through. With a practised eye, he spotted three-year-old Benjy among them, tagging along with some of the older neighbouring girls who didn't go to school.

And there was dear Ma, her usual industrious self as he stepped into the steaming downstairs room that served as kitchen and parlour in one. Henry kissed her on the cheek, picked the squalling baby Tilly out of her cradle and bounced her up and down on the knee of his good leg to lessen the noise while Ma cooked, cleaned, boiled a pot of napkins and started on a pile of mending, most of which she seemed able to manage simultaneously.

He thought of Jemima, sitting in silence in her empty rooms, and sighed.

* * *

The sharp tang of smelling salts jerked Jemima back into the land of the living.

She was lying on the floor of her bedroom, she found, and the bottle was being waved under her nose by Mrs Lewis.

In her half-stupefied state Jemima was attempting to mumble some words of gratitude when she was shocked into full awareness by an unexpectedly harsh tone. 'Good, you're awake – a sudden death in the house wouldn't do my name any good. Now, get up and get out.'

Jemima raised her head off the floor. 'What? I mean – I beg your pardon?' She couldn't have heard that correctly.

'I said, get out,' snapped Mrs Lewis. 'Look at the state of this place – you've been letting bad company in, and look what they've done to my best rooms!'

'I haven't!' protested Jemima. 'Of course I haven't. Someone's broken in while I was at Pa's funeral.' Hot tears filled her eyes. 'How *could* they?' She began to cry, like a helpless, bullied child who couldn't understand why the world was so unfair. 'How could anyone be so *cruel*?'

Mrs Lewis shook her head. 'If someone had broken in, they'd have had to bash in the front door, and you saw yourself there's no damage to that. No, you've lent someone the keys I trusted your Pa with.'

'But I haven't!'

'Anyway, you can't stay here. This is a respectable house.'

Jemima was still not entirely sure that the conversation she was having was real. 'But we've been here years.'

'A young girl living with her widowed father, that's one thing. But an orphaned miss who keeps bad company and lets the rooms be ransacked like this? Why, you've already had a gentleman caller, and so soon after you lost your Pa, too – you should be ashamed of yourself.'

'A gentleman? Oh no, you've misunderstood. That was—'

'I know what I saw and what the girl told me, in all her innocence. Breakfast in your rooms, no less! *And* you were late with the rent this week. Any of those is a good enough reason to throw you out, and when you put them all together, well . . .'

Jemima was weeping in real earnest now, unable to believe that this was really happening. 'But where will I go?'

'That's not my concern. To the workhouse, for all I care, or the streets. As long as you're away from here and not giving my house a bad name.'

Jemima tried to marshal her thoughts. 'But the rent's paid until the end of the week.'

'I'll be keeping that in lieu of the damage done here. I'll let you stay until tomorrow,' Mrs Lewis continued, in a tone that implied this was some kind of great favour, 'so nobody can say you had to leave on the very day of the funeral. That will give you a chance to pack up. But tomorrow morning you're out.'

Struggling to her feet, Jemima attempted to maintain a few shreds of dignity, although she wasn't quite sure whether what she really wanted to do was scream or run away or vomit. 'Very well. I was intending to move out anyway once Pa was gone – I'll just have to do it sooner.' And then the recollection landed on her with all the blackness and crushing weight of a sack of coal: *But I'll have no money to rent anywhere else.* She was penniless.

No, worse: she was a penniless orphan. A penniless *female* orphan.

She looked around the room, still nauseous at the idea that someone could have taken advantage of her being at a funeral to steal the money Pa had saved up for her. What sort of person . . . ?

And then, as she continued to survey the damage, Jemima noticed a few odd details. A number of items had been pulled out of the wardrobe, but among them only Pa's coat had been torn. Several drawers had been jerked out from the dresser, but only the one that had contained the money had been ransacked.

She went into the sitting room. The books had been swept from the shelf but the cups and plates had not.

Someone had known exactly where the money was hidden.

And then a suspicion so monstrous entered Jemima's mind that at first she couldn't even believe it herself. Mrs Lewis had kindly spent time sitting with Pa while he'd been bedridden these last few weeks. She'd been alone in here with him while Jemima was at school. And he'd spent at least some of that time asleep.

Mrs Lewis emerged from the bedroom, and Jemima turned wide, horrified eyes on her.

The landlady seemed to read her mind. She darted forward, seized Jemima's arm in a painful grip and hissed, 'If you so much as *think* of making an unfounded accusation about me, I'll take you for slander, and you'll lose anything you've still got, including your good name. You'll never get another place to live.' Her fingers dug in more deeply. 'Do you understand me?'

And, suddenly, Jemima *did* understand. A single girl with no father, no family, no protector at all: anyone who wanted to could take advantage of her and get away with it. She had no recourse to justice. She'd already known that even Pa could never have gone to the police if their money was stolen; how much less likely was it that they'd accept a complaint from an orphan girl, and one against a respectable landlady, at that? She'd be laughed out of town, if not worse.

As soon as the fragile thread of Pa's life had broken, Jemima had fallen. It was not her fault, and there was nothing she could do about it, but she was now no longer 'respectable'; she was on the wrong side of the all-important dividing line between layers of society. She had nothing and nobody, and if she was going to survive, she would have to rely on her own wits.

There was a moment of silence, as the course of Jemima's future life hung in the balance. She was all at sea, but was she going to give up and sink, slipping down through the waves into a life of poverty and despair, with all that entailed? Or did she have the courage to at least make an attempt to strike out for the shore?

Jemima came to a decision, and when she spoke, her voice was steady. 'Very well. I'll leave tomorrow and make it known that this was what I'd always intended. In return, you will write a note of reference saying that I've been a good tenant, and I will have the meals tonight and tomorrow morning that I'm entitled to as part of the rent.' She stared Mrs Lewis unflinchingly in the eye.

After a moment Mrs Lewis dropped her gaze. 'Agreed.'

'Good. Now,' continued Jemima with dignity, 'please leave me alone while I tidy up and sort out Pa's belongings and my own.' She swept Mrs Lewis out as though she were a hostess and the landlady an unwanted guest, shutting the door behind her and then locking it from the inside.

Then she collapsed on the bed and cried. She cried for Pa, for herself, for her future, and for the utter sickening dejection of knowing that Mrs Lewis could do this and get away with it.

It was that last thought that finally made Jemima pull herself together. She needed to start work on sorting these belongings, these trappings of the life she was going to leave behind. Nobody else was going to do it for her – not ever again – so she would just have to face up to her situation and get on with it. And if, at the same time, she nursed the small, flickering flame of injustice that had begun to burn inside her, then so much the better.

Nothing had been stolen except the money, which

just rather proved her suspicions, as any normal robber who had gone to the trouble of breaking in would have taken anything that could have raised even a few pennies. There was no point in dwelling on this now, however, not after the bargain Jemima had made with Mrs Lewis, so she needed to cut her losses and focus on what she *could* do, on what she *did* have. Justice would have to wait.

Contrary to Jemima's first, black thought, she didn't quite have nothing. There was no money, but Pa's clothes were decent and would fetch something, and she could also sell or pawn the cups and plates – she wouldn't be able to carry them away with her, in any case. There would be no hiring of a cart to move several boxes of possessions; she would take only what she could fit in the old carpet bag of Pa's that was collecting dust on top of the wardrobe.

Her little roll of needles and thread had survived, so she set to work mending the rip in Pa's coat, and then folded it neatly and laid it on his bed in the sitting room along with his other clothes. The heavy work trousers would serve another man, somewhere, as would the shirts and all the rest of it. But it all reminded her of him, it *smelled* of him, and it was causing her so much pain to part with everything that she thought her heart would break. But Jemima had to be ruthless: what use were his clothes to her now, when set against the need for a roof over her head?

She limited herself to keeping one of his handkerchiefs, the one that had always been something of a family joke, because Ma had stitched the initials 'JJ' on it, as though he were a fine gentleman and not a coal heaver bending his back so that the fine gentlemen might have fires to warm themselves by. It wouldn't take up much room; Jemima put it in her shoulder bag.

The sight of the books scattered across the sitting-room floor caused her another pang. Every line of every volume was dear to her – how could she get rid of them? But they were heavy, and they also represented food and shelter for days or even weeks. Until she could get back on her feet again, she would just have to harden her heart.

Jemima picked them up one at a time, stroking the covers and storing away a memory associated with each one: something Pa had read out to her, or a discussion they'd had about the contents. She wondered what the difference in money would be between selling the books and merely pawning them; if she could manage the latter, she could hold on to the hope that one day she would be able to get them back. But for now . . .

Volumes on farming and engineering went on the

bed next to the clothes without too much of a qualm, along with a few of the other drier factual works. Then they were joined by the histories of England and its kings and queens, which she would never need to teach; her girls learned the basics of the three Rs together with sewing and household management, not history or geography.

After a few minutes, just three books remained on the floor. Jemima's hand hovered over the extracts from Shakespeare. She had no doubt that it was her rather surprising ability to quote from his poems and plays that had secured her the favour of Mr Silverton when she was being considered for her post at the school, over and above Mrs Silverton's doubts about her social background.

But it had to go, adding to the heap on the bed.

Jemima sat for some while with *Pride and Prejudice* in her hand, remembering the many times they'd read it either separately or out loud to each other, and what Pa had said about Ma enjoying it so much. She stared at the cover with its embossed title. Could she possibly bear to part with it?

Her emotions were still all over the place, and she couldn't make up her mind, so she decided to let fate take a hand. She would close her eyes, open the book at a random page, and then look down to see if the first words that she saw were able to tell her anything or sway her decision. If it was something about the enjoyment of reading, or any thought at all that induced happiness, she would keep it.

It was possible, of course, that her hands knew what they were doing even if her mind did not, and that it wasn't mere coincidence that the page opened on a passage in which the mother was lamenting that all the women in the family would be thrown out of the house once the father was dead, because they would be penniless.

Jemima snapped the book shut and placed it resolutely with the others. The girls in the story had managed to escape penury in the end; she knew that from her multiple re-readings. But this had been partly because their father had survived and mainly because they had married rich men, neither of which applied to Jemima. She would dearly love to be able to say the first of those about herself, but she had no interest in the second. She almost snorted as she thought of it. It was 1864, for goodness' sake, and Liverpool was thriving enough to offer plenty of opportunities for women: Jemima was going to work hard in her job to support herself, not rely on any man.

So that just left the flower book.

It lay forlorn on the rug, thrown down with no regard

for it either as an object or for what it represented to her. Jemima's eyes began to sting again. She hadn't even known of the book's existence until a few days ago, and now it was one of the most precious things in the world. Pa had been so insistent that she should read it, and she still didn't know why, but she couldn't bring herself even to open it, not yet. It was all tied up with him and Ma and some kind of mysterious past, and she just wasn't ready to face all that right now.

She ought to be stern with herself, and put it with the others. She should, she really should.

She would. She would do it any moment now.

And yet the book remained on the floor. It had been so roughly treated that the spine was cracked and some of the pages had come loose. That would lessen its value, surely. There was no point in pawning or selling it if it didn't raise any money to put towards the things she needed. She wasn't being sentimental; of course not. It was purely a practical decision. She would keep it for now, and she could always let it go later if she really needed to, perhaps even fixing it first.

Flora Domestica; Or, The Portable Flower-garden was taken into the bedroom and stowed safely at the bottom of the carpet bag.

* * *

It wasn't difficult to find a pawn shop. There were plenty of them all over Liverpool, displaying a variety of goods depending on the area in which they were situated and the class of their clientele. There was no need to cross town to find one that was full of rags; Jemima was able to find a place on Pitt Street itself, one that gave off an air of genteel poverty rather than destitution. There was a suit in the window, along with a clock and a few items of plate.

A bell rang as she opened the door and entered with Pa's neatly folded clothes in her arms. Today had already been an object lesson in being taken advantage of, so when the proprietor came bustling forward to meet her Jemima had the wit not to explain the true situation, having already removed the telltale signs of mourning from her person. Instead she said that her father had sent her because he had some clothes he could do without, just while he was temporarily short of funds. In shaking out the clothes and holding them up for inspection she casually noted how large they were, so the pawnbroker would think that a big, strong man might be coming his way if he attempted to cheat her.

Either that worked, or Jemima proved better at haggling than she'd thought she would be, because she secured enough money to be sure of immediate relief – a couple of days' worth of rent and food, at least, assuming she could find somewhere more modest than her current rooms – along with the promise that he would consider the rest of her goods if she brought those down as well. Jemima thus made several more trips in the long summer twilight, bringing down the plates and cups, some few clothes of her own that wouldn't fit in her bag, and finally the books. Fortunately there was nothing that was too big for her to carry, because the furniture and bedding in the rooms belonged to Mrs Lewis.

By the time this was all over the pawnbroker had surely seen through her, but he said nothing and Jemima guessed that a certain amount of tact was one of the requirements of his job. She stowed the coins carefully, deep in the pocket inside her dress, and paused for one moment outside the shop window as he placed her books in a prominent position. She would be back for them one day, she vowed, before the date on the ticket expired.

Then Jemima turned and walked briskly back to the boarding house, not wanting either to loiter or to catch anyone's eye, just in case. She felt more danger around her than ever before, as though she were carrying a large sign about her neck that said *I am carrying every penny I own in the world and can be robbed without consequence.*

Jemima kept the money on her person all through the evening meal in the boarding-house kitchen, during which she looked the other residents in the eye and accepted their condolences while dropping the occasional mention of moving on voluntarily, being in possession of settled future plans, and other such lies. She also ate as heartily as she could force herself to do, aware that she'd hardly eaten anything recently and not sure when she would next get a proper cooked meal. Nobody around the table seemed to be in the least aware of the robbery, or of anything that had happened earlier, and Jemima kept her own counsel, exchanging an occasional mutually suspicious glance with Mrs Lewis.

The rooms were bleak and empty when she went back up to sleep in them for the last time.

Jemima forced herself to lie down properly on her own bed, though she didn't undress. She didn't *think* she would be disturbed during the night – Mrs Lewis would be hard put to maintain her house's reputation if it became known that a resident had been attacked and robbed in her own room in the small hours – but she'd locked the door and put a chair against it, and she checked in her pocket for the money every time she stirred.

She was exhausted, but she couldn't sleep. Either her mind would wander back to happier times, which only ended in her being upset, or she was faced with the blankness, the abyss, of not knowing what her life was to be after tomorrow. Where would she live? What would it be like? How would she afford rent and food, and clothes that were smart enough for her job? She had no doubt that Mrs Silverton would soon let her go if she started to turn up at school in rags.

Mrs Silverton. Now, there was a thought. The schoolmistress had been unexpectedly kind when Jemima had told her that Pa was dying, letting her have as much time off as she needed. Jemima would certainly be able to show that she didn't intend to milk it; she would be back first thing tomorrow morning, the very day after Pa's funeral. She would take her carpet bag and hide it under the bench in the porch, so that she didn't look homeless, and she would be as efficient as ever. And then, whenever she could find the right moment during the day – perhaps Mr or Mrs Silverton would express sympathy for her situation at some point – she would ask if she might temporarily lodge with them, in the schoolhouse that came with the post of headmaster. They had no children of their own, or at least none who were still young enough to live with them, so they would have a spare room, and surely this was the most 'respectable' (to use Mrs Silverton's own favourite word) solution? It needn't be for long, but it would tide Jemima over while she looked for somewhere else close to the school, and the money she'd got from the pawn shop would be enough to offer as advance rent.

She touched the coins again. They were still there.

With this crumb of comfort in her head Jemima was able to fall into a doze, but she still got no real rest, disturbed by jagged dreams and visions of flowers, of graves, of unknown sisters with no faces . . .

It was still only just dawn when she woke properly, sweating with terror after a nightmare she couldn't quite remember.

Jemima lay still for a moment, unwilling to get up. Perhaps if she just lay here forever, all her troubles would go away. But that was no way to think, so she got up, washed, and made sure that everything she was taking with her was packed in her two bags. She stripped the covers from both beds and folded them, leaving them unmistakeably visible in a pile, so that Mrs Lewis couldn't take any further vindictive action by accusing her of theft. Then she looked around the rooms that had been her home with Pa since she was nine years old, said a silent but heartfelt goodbye, and walked out.

She took the keys with her down to the kitchen, so she could hand them over to Mrs Lewis in public, and narrowly avoided the temptation to ask the landlady in front of everybody if she wanted to search her bag.

Then Jemima stood and held out her hand for the promised letter of reference, which she opened and read before putting it away. It was barely adequate – *Miss Jemima Jenkins and her father lodged at my boarding house in Pitt Street from August 1857 to July 1864, they always paid rent on time and did not cause any trouble*, plus a signature – but it would do.

Jemima still had little appetite, but she forced down some breakfast before standing, wishing everyone a brisk good morning, giving Sarah what she hoped was an encouraging smile, and striding down the passage to the front door.

She wavered once she was out in the street, but she overcame it by giving herself a stern lecture, and the walk up to St James's Road was made without incident. None of the strangers who passed her on the way could possibly know how much her life had changed in just a couple of days, and she was determined to keep it that way. Her job, her wages, her determination, would keep her on the straight and narrow.

Jemima was in very good time at school, and was able to tuck the large bag far back under the bench in the porch, where it would lie unnoticed until she came back for it. The coins were still in her pocket, though; she didn't think she'd ever trust anyone or any hiding place with money again.

To her surprise, she heard the key turning almost as soon as she'd arrived, although it wasn't nearly time for school to start yet. She curtseyed as Mrs Silverton appeared in the open doorway, but couldn't step past her, as she didn't move.

Instead, the schoolmistress was staring at her with an expression of mingled puzzlement and distaste. 'What are you doing here?'

Jemima was confused. 'I beg your pardon, ma'am?'

'I said, what are you doing here?'

'I'm here for work, ma'am, just as usual. I know it was only yesterday that my Pa was—'

'Ah. You misunderstood me, I see. I thought you might have done.'

'I know that you said I needn't come back until I was ready, ma'am, and it was very kind of you to let me have the time off to be with Pa in his last moments but I can assure you—'

Mrs Silverton cut her off. 'As I said, a misunderstanding. When I spoke to you on Monday, I meant that you needn't come back at all.' She looked down at Jemima with an expression that held not one shred of sympathy. 'You are dismissed.'

Chapter 5

Jemima was still standing with her mouth open, trying to take in Mrs Silverton's words, when Betty arrived.

'Jemima! Oh, it's good to see you back. I couldn't come round yesterday, but Henry said...' She tailed off, looking from Jemima to Mrs Silverton. 'What?'

'I'll forgive you that grammatical infelicity just this once,' said the schoolmistress, severely, 'if you go straight inside. You'll have to set up the girls' class today, as well as the infants', and the same every day until I can engage a new assistant.'

Betty looked at Jemima in horror. 'You've never handed in your notice! What are you going to do?'

Jemima was still incapable of speech.

Mrs Silverton wasn't. 'Jemima will no longer be working here,' she said, acidly. 'She is no longer a suitable person to be employed by the school. Now, go inside.' She moved to leave space for Betty to pass her.

Betty stayed where she was and folded her arms. 'You can't do that.'

Mrs Silverton was so taken aback that she actually responded. 'Of course I can.'

'Jemima hasn't done anything wrong.'

'I'm not saying she has. It's not what she's done that makes her unsuitable – it's who she is.'

'She's still the same person that she ever was.'

'Who she is *now*,' amended Mrs Silverton. 'Or, rather, her position in society. As an orphan, a single girl with no family, Jemima is—' She suddenly realised that she was debating the subject with one of her minions. 'This is none of your business,' she snapped. 'Now, do as you're told and go inside, if you don't want me to be looking for *two* new assistants.'

Betty opened her mouth, but it was Jemima who spoke. 'No!' she squeaked, the sound coming out at a much higher pitch than she'd expected. 'Please don't! I couldn't bear it if Betty lost her job. I'll go, I promise, and I won't make a fuss, just let Betty stay, please.'

Mrs Silverton gave a curt nod.

'Please, Betty, for me,' said Jemima, turning to her friend. 'Please just go in and work as normal. I'll be all right. I'll find something else.'

Betty looked absolutely torn, but eventually she nodded. 'All right. Because it's what *you* want. But I'll be round to see you straight after school so we can talk about what's what.'

Jemima watched her friend enter, and then remained standing where she was as Mrs Silverton shut the heavy school door in her face.

No job, no home, and very little money. That was what Jemima had, as she pulled her bag out from its now redundant hiding place. But all of those situations could be remedied if she only put her mind to it. What would Pa say, if he were here now? Of course, she wouldn't be in this situation if he were still here, but if he did know about this new state of affairs, he'd tell her not to be afraid. *You're my Jemima, and I believe in you.*

Jemima straightened her bonnet, picked up her bag and strode away from the school.

* * *

'We have nothing available, I'm afraid.'

Jemima knew that there were several other boarding houses in the local area, because she walked past them every day on her way from ho—on her way from Pitt Street to school. These had seemed like good places to start, but they were all inexplicably popular just at the moment and there were no vacancies anywhere.

Or, at least, no vacancies for her. Despite her letter of reference, Jemima suspected that her status as a single girl was telling against her at every place she tried. If she'd been part of a family with parents, or half of a married couple, or a single man, things might have been different.

As she traipsed further and further away from the school – not that that mattered any more – Jemima wondered why and how women were so reluctant to help another female. Mrs Lewis had robbed and cheated her, and then thrown her out. Mrs Silverton, far from being sympathetic, had piled on the pain by sacking her. And everyone who had turned her away from the door of a boarding house this morning had been a woman. Why could they not show some solidarity?

The answer was obvious, of course, once she thought about it properly, as she had plenty of time to do while walking. They all knew that it could easily have been them in such a dire position, and the thought scared them. They held their own positions in society thanks to men – they were married or they were widows – and the only way they could stay above Jemima and others like her was to trample them down.

Jemima was in danger of falling into despair, so she

reminded herself that she had also received kindness and sympathy. From Betty, of course, and Betty's brother Henry, whose quiet and supportive presence had made the day of Pa's funeral less terrible than it could have been, but also from Mrs Roberts, at the tea room, and from Sarah in Pitt Street. And Sarah was in just as pitiable a state as Jemima herself: she had a roof over her head, granted, but she was trapped in a life of hard labour under a hard mistress, and with little chance of escape. Whereas Jemima still had hope.

She did wonder, for a few moments, about going back to the tea room and finding Mrs Roberts. But what would she be playing at, if she did? The elderly lady had offered sympathy and a kind ear, but she would hardly appreciate it if a girl she'd spoken to only once suddenly turned up asking for accommodation and a job. No, Jemima would make her own way.

It was at this point that Jemima became aware that she had not really been concentrating on where she was going, and while her head was thinking all this, her feet had taken her rather nearer to the docks than she had intended.

There would be no boarding houses here of the type that she was looking for. The street in which she currently stood was lined with terraces of small houses, of the sort she had once lived in with Ma and Pa, which meant that they were inhabited by families, likely to be numerous and crowded, and unlikely to be looking for a lodger. If she went even nearer to the docks she would find some bigger buildings, but they would be raucous public houses, and worse.

Jemima stopped for a moment to orient herself. She didn't know what road she was on, but all she had to do was turn around and walk back up the hill, keeping the docks behind her, and she would soon be on more familiar ground.

She was getting some strange looks, both from the many children who were playing in the street and from their mothers when their chores brought them outside. She supposed this was only natural; a stranger, an unaccompanied girl carrying luggage – who or what did they think she was?

Jemima decided it wasn't worth stating her business or asking for help, so she merely gave a general smile and turned back with as much dignity as she could summon. Her professional interest was caught by the many groups of children, and she wondered how many of them had ever gone to school, and whether any of them would like to, if they could afford it.

Just as she was setting off, a tot of no more than two or three cannoned into her legs, unable to stop as he hurtled down the slope. He bounced off her, fell flat on the road and began to cry, so Jemima put down her carpet bag in order to use both hands to pick him up and set him on his feet. 'There, now. No harm done.'

Almost immediately a girl of about six shouldered her way forward and took the tot. 'He's my bruvver,' she said, in a belligerent tone, 'and *I'll* look after him.'

'I'm sure you will,' said Jemima, smiling at both of them. She reached down for her bag.

It wasn't there.

Jemima's heart gave such a painful lurch that she nearly fell over, but it hadn't gone far; it was being held by a barefooted boy standing just a few feet away.

Jemima barely had time to consider how she might regain her meagre remaining possessions with least trouble when he held out the bag. 'Here you are, miss.'

He was thanked with much more effusiveness than he might have expected, and gave Jemima the sort of look that implied he thought her soft in the head. A lesson, she told herself as she made her way up the road, in not relying on first impressions, and not judging people by class. The boy with ragged trousers and no shoes had been far more honest than the supposedly 'respectable' Mrs Lewis, and kinder than Mrs Silverton.

It wasn't long before Jemima was safely back on familiar ground, although she still didn't have anywhere to stay and it was now heading for mid-afternoon. She'd already exhausted all the possibilities she knew of, so there was no help for it but to strike out elsewhere. Crossing Duke Street, therefore, she continued on, but once she reached the wide thoroughfare of Renshaw Street everything became unsuitable for the opposite reason: the shops here were very upmarket, displaying unaffordable goods, and the carriages of the rich bowled up and down. Truly, Liverpool was a city of extremes. It was not half an hour since she'd been surrounded by ragged children, and here she was outside the Adelphi Hotel, no less. If her situation wasn't becoming so desperate, she might have laughed at the prospect of walking in there and demanding a room. A soft, luxurious bed, a sumptuous meal of several courses, a bath of hot water filled on request by a servant . . . all things that had never been for her, and were now even more unimaginably out of reach. She'd settle for a place to sleep, some bread and tea, and a reasonable confidence in not being assaulted or robbed overnight.

Another half-hour and her arms were aching. She'd switched the carpet bag from one hand to the other many times, but it was getting heavier and heavier. And Liverpool had changed once more: now the shops and houses were becoming smaller and meaner again. A clothier selling second-hand shirts; a cobbler whose boots had been mended many times; a butcher displaying sheep's heads and a row of glassy-eyed dead rabbits. However, there were two places on this street that had cards in the window advertising rooms to let, and which Jemima guessed were probably around the price range she was looking for. She approached the first.

She took a moment to compose herself and make sure she didn't look like too much of a vagabond, straightening her bonnet in the reflection of the front window and tucking away a few strands of hair that had come loose during the course of her exertions.

Her knock was answered by a middle-aged woman. 'Yes?'

'I'm here to enquire about renting a room, ma'am.' Jemima pointed to the card.

'Oh yes?' The woman looked her up and down. 'On your own?'

'Yes, ma'am. I have a reference from my previous landlady . . .' Jemima began to reach into her shoulder bag.

'And what sort of business does a girl have, renting a room on her own?'

It was the same suspicious tone she'd encountered several times earlier today, and Jemima knew with a sinking heart that the conversation was going to head in the same direction. Still, she had to try. 'I'm an independent woman, ma'am, a schoolmistress.'

She was met with a sceptical look.

'Well, an assistant schoolmistress,' Jemima added.

'Where?'

'At Saint James's—'

The woman snorted. 'Well, you're a long way from there, aren't you? Get away with you. I don't know what sort of tale you're trying to spin, but there's no room for you here.'

Jemima was getting desperate. It was at least summer – if it were winter it would be dark already – but the light wouldn't last forever, and she really didn't want to be trudging round the streets after nightfall. 'Please,' she began.

'Unless,' interrupted the woman, her eyes narrowing, 'you're looking for a job as a maid? Mine left, and I'm in need of a new one. Four shillings a week, plus your board and lodging.'

Jemima was honestly almost tempted. It was a roof and food. But she knew nothing about this woman and very little about the duties of a maid, except what she'd learned from Sarah, which was hardly positive. Plus it would mean giving up on all her plans for a career as a teacher, wasting all the education Pa had provided for her. It would mean letting him down.

'Thank you for the offer, ma'am, but I'm not looking

for work in service. I'll try somewhere else for lodgings, if you have no vacancies.'

The woman shrugged and disappeared back inside, shutting the door behind her.

Jemima forced her aching arms to pick up her burden once more and made her way a few doors up, hoping that she wouldn't come to regret the decision she'd just made. But she wasn't quite that desperate, not yet, and she couldn't bear to give up on all that Pa had wanted for her.

Unfortunately, there was no answer at all at the second boarding house, so Jemima was forced to keep walking further up the road. And then she stopped, as a huge, forbidding building came into view over the lower roofs.

The workhouse.

The idea of having to seek admittance there was a constant fear for a large proportion of Liverpool's population, but, thanks to Pa, Jemima had always been cushioned against any such danger. But now... had fate brought her here? Had her feet taken this direction by overruling her mind, knowing deep down that this was where she was bound to end up eventually?

No. No, no, *no*. This was not for her. To walk straight into the workhouse on the very day she'd lost her rooms and her job was too much like giving up. Pa would never forgive her. *You're my Jemima, and I believe in you.* She had to keep going, keep trying.

Jemima's attention was caught by a man passing by with three small children. He carried a little boy in one arm while a second trotted along holding his other hand, and the eldest, a girl, clutched at the ragged hem of his jacket. All the children were crying, and the girl was pleading. 'Please, Pa, don't make us go there, not again!'

'There's no choice,' he was saying. 'It's just until I get more work, and you'll be sure of being fed, you know that. I'll come and get you as soon as I can, just like I did last time. Remember?'

'But we hated it!' wailed the girl, and the howls of the two boys intensified too. 'It was horrible, and they put us all in different places so I couldn't look after our Davey—'

'Stop it!' cried the man, in a more savage tone, halting and letting go of the boy's hand so he could grasp his daughter's shoulder and shake her. 'I told you, you're going and that's that. Now stop your whingeing, or I might well decide not to come back.' His eye caught Jemima's for a moment, and he looked quickly away. 'And, like I said, you'll get fed there, so it's not all bad.'

They moved on, and Jemima watched as they disappeared into the workhouse. How sad, how terrible for them all. Why, if her Pa had ever had to part from her like that, because he'd got to the stage where he couldn't feed her, he'd have been heartbroken. No doubt this man was the same, and he was disguising his shame and fear with anger.

She found one more house advertising rooms, but the door was opened by a girl who looked no more than ten and who had a black eye. A cloud of gin fumes hit Jemima so hard that she almost staggered backwards, and she hastily told the child that she'd made a mistake and turned away. Then she went back and knocked several times at the place where there'd been no reply earlier, waiting and waiting on the doorstep, but again to no avail. In the end she was forced to step back on to the pavement.

'Looking for somewhere to stay, are you?'

The man addressing her was the same one she'd seen a little while ago, though he was now alone. She didn't really want to engage in conversation, but she had every sympathy for his position, so she made a vague, non-committal reply.

'You can come with me, if you like,' he said. 'I've got a bit of money for a night out, and a room to go back to.' He jingled some coins in his pocket. 'Room all to myself, now, too, with the nippers out the way, and plenty of space for two in the bed, if you know what I mean.'

Jemima was revolted. Not just by his proposition, which was bad enough, but by the knowledge that he'd just dropped his weeping, pleading daughter and sons at the workhouse, saying he had no money to feed them.

She made the mistake of engaging.

'If you've got money and a room,' she said, tartly, 'I suggest you go and pick your children up and feed them.' She tried to brush past him.

It only took him half a second to move from affability to vicious malice. 'You watch your mouth, girl!' He grabbed at her arm. 'There I was, just having a nice bit of conversation, and you start nagging me. If you didn't want to talk to me, you should've said so to start with, not led me on like that.' His grip tightened. 'Now, you look like you're in need of somewhere to stay, and I'm offering. How about it?' His tone was threatening rather than inviting, and he began to pull her further along the pavement.

Jemima twisted her arm in an attempt to free herself, but with no success. She looked up and down the street. There weren't as many people out and about here: there were no shop windows to look in, and too many carts in the road for children to be playing out. But any drivers who passed were either concentrating on their horses, or they glanced at her and then looked away. Nobody would help her, she knew.

'Please let go of my arm,' she tried, hoping that civility might defuse the situation.

It didn't. 'And what if I don't want to? Come on, now, girl, don't make a fuss. You'd rather have a drink and some pennies and a good time, I'm sure, than have me take what I want without all that.'

Jemima should have been scared, but she wasn't: she was incensed. How *dare* this man – this stranger, this uncaring father – feel entitled to her attention, to her very person, in this way? Hadn't today been bad enough, with Mrs Lewis and Mrs Silverton and the 'no vacancies' everywhere? The world was doing its best to be unfair, and she wasn't having it. She opened her mouth and clenched her fist.

'Oh, there you are!'

The voice was female and loud, enough to make both Jemima and her assailant turn, and she saw that Betty and Henry were approaching.

'Been looking for you everywhere,' continued Betty, at an unnecessary volume. 'Pa said you'd probably get lost on your way to finding us, so we're all out looking for you.' She barged into them. ''Scuse me, but we must get home.'

The man's expression of surprise turned threatening, but Henry smoothly moved in between him and Jemima. 'Shall I carry your bag?'

Defeated, and only really having been opportunistic, the man slouched away.

Jemima was just about to speak, to thank them and to wonder how they'd found her, when Betty rounded on her furiously. 'What on earth do you think you're doing?'

'I was—'

'You never told me this morning that your landlady had kicked you out! I went round there straight after school to find you, only for that maid to tell me you'd gone. And no word where to! You could have been anywhere! It was only 'cos Henry happened to see you going past earlier that we knew you'd come up this way.'

Betty paused to take a breath, and Jemima took the opportunity to jump in. 'I'm sorry – I really am. It had only just happened when I got to school, and then after what Mrs Silverton said I was so shocked that I wasn't thinking straight, and then I was afraid she'd sack you too, and I knew I just had to get away . . .' She gulped and rushed to continue before Betty could start again. 'If I'd found somewhere else to lodge then I would have come back later, after school finished, to tell you. But it's turned out to be much more difficult than I thought it would be.'

A second thought struck Jemima, and she addressed Henry. 'How did you know where I was?'

'I saw you earlier. You were coming up Colquitt Street from the direction of Duke Street, so I knew which way you were going, at least. I was just coming home from the library.'

'The library?'

A faint tinge came to his cheeks. 'After what you said yesterday, I thought I'd go and see if I could become a member, and I did. I was just on my way home, and walking down Colquitt Street to turn off into our yard. You were on the other side of the road, and you looked like – well, you were concentrating, thinking about something, so I didn't like to disturb you. I didn't know anything about you losing your job or your rooms until Betty came home later, otherwise I would have said something.'

'And the point is,' said Betty, now with sufficient breath to launch another tirade, 'you didn't need to be traipsing round the streets. Why didn't you come straight to us? I had to stay at school, but Ma was at home.'

Jemima was confused. 'Well, I had no reason to drop in to see her, especially if you weren't there, and I thought I'd better get on with finding somewhere else to live.'

Betty rolled her eyes. 'That's what I'm talking about, you daft ha'porth! Why didn't you think to come and stay with us?'

Jemima was taken aback. 'Well, I didn't think . . .'

Betty snorted. 'No, you didn't, did you? Anyway, let's get you back there now.' She led the way, striding furiously ahead.

Henry paused politely to allow Jemima to go in front of him.

'Thank you,' said Jemima, simply. 'It's so kind of you, and you didn't have to come looking for me. I'm sorry Betty's angry.'

'She'll calm down, don't worry. She's just upset that something could have happened to you. And so am I – and when I heard, I was worried that you might have been heading for . . .' He threw a significant look in the direction of the workhouse.

'That's not why I came up this way,' was all Jemima said, as she turned her back on the fearsome building and followed Betty in the opposite direction. But what she was thinking was how kind they were to be looking out for her, when they had such a large family of their own to worry about. For what was she, to anyone?

'You're Betty's friend,' said Henry, and for a moment Jemima thought he'd read her mind. But he was merely continuing his previous subject. 'So of course she's upset. But I'd take it as a compliment if I were you.'

By the time they reached Back Colquitt Street the sun was setting, and Betty had indeed calmed down. She'd taken Jemima's arm a few minutes previously, and she patted it as they turned into the yard. 'I'm sorry I shouted. But I just didn't understand why you didn't come straight to us.'

'I suppose I didn't want to bother you with my problems, and it's not like I can offer anything in return.'

'Your problems are my problems, girl – that's what friends are for. How many times have you covered for me when I've been late, or got Mrs Silverton off my back? I wouldn't even *have* that job if it wasn't for you. And besides, never mind give and take: this isn't a business. We're friends, and that means I'm here for you whenever and whatever, just like I know you'd be for me.'

Jemima couldn't reply, but she squeezed Betty's arm.

'And now,' said Betty, as they reached the house, 'you'd better prepare yourself. You've always been used to things being pretty quiet, I know, living with just your Pa. It isn't like that here.' She pushed open the door. 'Welcome to the madhouse.'

Chapter 6

Jemima's first impression was one of overpowering noise and commotion. There were children crammed everywhere inside the room, and every face turned to her as Betty led the way in and called out greetings.

'You found her, then,' said Mrs Whiting, wiping her hands on her apron as she stepped away from the fire for a moment. Briefly she looked as though she might scold Jemima in the same way that Betty had done, but when she looked properly at Jemima's face her expression softened. 'You must be tired,' she said. 'You come on in and sit down. Molly, Bert, Maisie!' she shouted, without turning round to look at the table. 'You move so these three can have the chairs.' She addressed Jemima again in an almost apologetic tone. 'They're not often all in the house at the same time, only for tea and bed.'

Jemima smiled at her former pupils as they slipped

off to join some smaller children playing a game in the corner, Maisie pausing for a moment to whisper a shy, 'I'm glad you're here' in Jemima's ear. Rob and Mr Whiting were already seated at the table, along with a boy of about twelve.

'You know Rob,' said Betty. 'This is my Pa, and that's Matthew.'

Jemima immediately began to thank Mr Whiting for allowing her to join them, but he waved away her gratitude. 'Betty told us,' he said, simply. 'I'm sorry to hear about your Pa, and we can always fit another one in here for a while.' He surveyed the crammed room with smiling complacency. 'Besides, with Harriet and Anna living out, it's not so crowded these days.'

Jemima blinked.

'They're both in service,' explained Mrs Whiting, carrying a steaming bowl in each hand and putting them down on the table in front of her husband and second son. 'And good positions, too,' she added over her shoulder as she went back for the next two. 'Not maids-of-all-work. Anna works for a respectable businessman and his wife, and they've got a cook and another maid as well as her. And Harriet's in a house with twelve servants – fancy that! Oh, thank you.'

Jemima had followed her and picked up more bowls. 'Those for Betty and yourself, pet, then these for Henry and Matthew.' Mrs Whiting saw Jemima looking over at the mass of giggling children in the corner. 'Those who work get fed first; don't you worry about them, they'll get theirs after.'

'If these are for workers . . .' began Jemima, but Mrs Whiting stopped her.

'That includes you,' she said. 'You were employed right up until today and you'll soon find something else. And Henry, too – all that studying for exams is hard work, I don't doubt, and it'll pay off when he gets a good position.'

All the chairs were now occupied, and Jemima wondered where Mrs Whiting was going to sit herself, but she left them to it and returned to the cooking fire to check the progress of the largest kettle Jemima had ever seen.

'With Anna and Harriet gone,' she continued, 'there's room in the attic with the girls, so you can share Betty's bed.'

Jemima began to stammer out renewed thanks, but once again she was forestalled.

'Never mind any of that tonight. You get a night's sleep, and it will all be better in the morning and you can start to think of what to do next. I don't rate that Mrs Silverton as any kind of decent woman, letting you go when you'd done nothing wrong.'

Jemima turned her attention to the meal in front of

her. Henry had waited to start until she was ready, but the others were all halfway through theirs. It was mainly potatoes in broth, with a few bits of bacon and onion to flavour it, and Jemima – sinking into the warmth of kindness and friendship, of exhaustion and relief – thought she'd never tasted anything so delicious.

After everyone had been fed, Mrs Whiting shooed all the children outside while she and Betty did the dishes. Jemima, of course, offered to help; but as it was something she'd very rarely had to do before, she was ashamed to find she wasn't very good at it. The water was too hot for her hands, and she was slow with the scrubbing. In the end Mrs Whiting made the tactful suggestion that she should wipe up the table instead, which Jemima did, telling herself that she would learn how to become more useful around the house, even if she only ended up staying here a few days. It would be good practice, anyway, as she would need to be much more capable of looking out for herself from now on.

As darkness fell the children trooped back in, and soon every square inch of floor was filled as well as every chair and most of the adults' knees. Mrs Whiting was still working, somehow feeding the baby as well as getting on with some knitting, which she could hardly see now that the cooking fire had been allowed to die down, but the rest of the household was at rest.

Maisie looked hopefully at Jemima, and then at her brothers and sisters. 'Jemima tells stories to us at school, sometimes.'

It was true; if it was nearly the end of the day, and the girls needed to be kept quiet for just a few minutes after they'd tidied everything away, or sometimes if Mrs Silverton was marking or otherwise engaged, Jemima would seat herself in front of the class and make up a tale to amuse them. The girls enjoyed it, and so did she, although she was sometimes so captivating that it distracted the nearest infants as well.

At least half a dozen pairs of eyes were now fixed on her, and she tried to muster the dregs of her energy.

'Not tonight,' said Betty, amid a chorus of disappointment. 'Jemima's had a hard day, and she's tired.'

'Tomorrow, I promise,' said Jemima, to console them, before hastily adding, 'although, of course, I'll hope to have found lodgings of my own by then. But I can pop by whenever it's convenient to your Ma and Pa.'

'You stay as long as you need,' rumbled Mr Whiting, from behind the two small boys sitting on his lap. 'Until you find something proper and suitable. We don't want you going anywhere that's not right, just because you're in a hurry. Ain't that right, Ma?'

Mrs Whiting agreed. 'Girls need to be careful, and if you've no family of your own, you need someone to look out for you.' She put her knitting down. 'Now, bedtime for all of you younger ones – there's school tomorrow. You too, Matthew, if you don't want to be asleep on your feet at work in the morning.'

Amid yawns and the sounds of many feet on the stairs, the room was suddenly much emptier.

'Aaah,' said Mr Whiting, stretching his legs out now he had the luxury of a bit of space, and lighting his pipe. 'A bit of peace and quiet before we go up ourselves won't do any harm.'

Jemima was so exhausted after her long and trying day that she could barely keep her eyes open. She didn't want to get up and leave the room, though, in case it looked rude – and, besides, she didn't know where she was going.

Fortunately it wasn't long before Mr and Mrs Whiting began to stir. 'Betty'll show you everything, pet,' Mrs Whiting said to Jemima, quietly so as not to wake the baby now slumbering in her arms, 'and I'll see you in the morning. Tomorrow's another day, and you'll be all right.'

Betty pulled Jemima to her feet and led her to the back door. 'The privies are normally empty at this time, as children are in bed and men still at the pub.'

Once they were back inside Betty picked up Jemima's luggage and led the way up the stairs. There were two doors off a tiny landing. 'Ma and Pa, with Tilly,' whispered Betty, pointing at one, 'and the boys in the other. Not Henry and Rob – they sleep downstairs, 'cos there's already five of them in there and only the one bed. We're luckier.'

A second flight of stairs, so steep as to be almost a ladder, led up to an attic that was just large enough for two bedframes. The moonlight slanting in through a propped-open skylight allowed Jemima to see that Molly and Maisie were already asleep in one.

Betty pointed to the other, pushing Jemima's bag under it. 'See? Plenty of room.' She undressed to her shift and scrambled over to the far side.

Jemima did have a nightdress, but she felt too awkward to find and unpack it and get completely changed, so she followed Betty's example and then got into the bed.

'We won't need too many blankets,' said Betty, 'but there's a cotton sheet – here, pull it up.' Jemima agreed and did so; it was absolutely stifling in the attic, even with the skylight open.

Jemima hadn't shared a bedroom with anyone, never mind a bed, since she was tiny, and it was odd to feel Betty stirring beside her, and to hear the breathing of the other girls. But this was so much better than spending the night alone in an unfamiliar lodging house, possibly sharing with a girl or woman she didn't know, and listening out every moment for footsteps on the stairs or the sound of persons unknown trying to turn the handle of her door.

She was so comfortable that it was almost tempting to believe that she was just staying there overnight and that life was otherwise normal; Pa would be asleep in his bed in their sitting room half a mile away. But he wasn't, was he? He was slumbering permanently under six feet of earth in St Thomas's churchyard.

You've no family of your own, Mrs Whiting had said, which was both true and possibly not true. Did she have a family out there somewhere? Were there parents, brothers and sisters, related to her by blood, lying in beds elsewhere in Liverpool?

Parents, no. She would never have any parents except dearest Ma and Pa; and, in fact, now she came to think of it, Pa hadn't really mentioned them. He had talked instead of her having siblings. What had he said? Jemima was more than half-asleep by now, but some of his words floated round in her head. Their surname was something common. They were evicted and moved away before we did. There were brothers and sisters, though he hadn't said how many, except that a brother had died and he'd seen it. The eldest sister had an unusual first name, something from the Bible. And then there were all those tantalising and confusing references to flowers, and the book she'd never known they had.

Family. Even if they were her relations, they'd given her away. She only knew of one family, and that was all she wanted. She could still hear Pa's voice, now, but how long would it be until both the sound and the look of him faded? Jemima couldn't picture Ma's face any more; she was just a blur of disjointed impressions. Hugs, kisses, the smell of soap, the feel of Jemima's hair being brushed or her hand being held. How long before Pa went the same way?

Carefully, so as not to wake the now sleeping Betty or the other girls, Jemima reached one hand down out of the bed. She rummaged around in her bag until she found Pa's handkerchief, and then she drew it out and laid it under her cheek, so that something of his would be close by her while she slept.

* * *

The following morning was chaos, as a torrent of adults and children woke, dressed, talked, shouted, and made their way downstairs.

Mrs Whiting was already there, making cold tea with yesterday's boiled water so as not to have to light the fire this early in the day, and cutting chunks of bread which Betty began to spread with jam and dole out. Once everyone was eating, a second round was begun, this time the slices being wrapped for each working man to take with him for dinnertime, along with a piece of hard cheese. Mr Whiting, Rob and Matthew set off.

'I'd better go too, Ma,' said Betty. 'Best not be late today, after the mood Mrs Silverton was in yesterday.'

'Off you go, then,' called Mrs Whiting. 'Jemima, pet, just make sure all those children have clean faces and hands before they leave.' She held out a damp cloth.

Pleased to be treated so much as one of the family, Jemima lined up Albert, Molly, Maisie, Ralph and Sid and gave them a wipe, cleaning behind their ears so thoroughly that the two youngest complained. Then they, too, were off, though with no dinner to carry: they would come home for theirs in the middle of the day.

Mrs Whiting heaved a sigh as she looked around the room in the aftermath of the whirlwind. Only she, Jemima and Henry were left, along with the youngest boy – Benjy, Jemima recalled, wanting to be polite enough to remember who was who – and the baby, who was a girl called Tilly.

'Let me help you tidy up, Mrs Whiting, before I go out to start looking for lodgings,' said Jemima. 'They'll be doing breakfast everywhere now, and won't thank me for interruptions – I'll have better luck if I leave it an hour.'

Mrs Whiting paused in the act of wrapping up what remained of a four-pound loaf of bread, which wasn't much. 'About that,' she said, briskly. 'I talked it over with Pa last night, after we'd gone to bed, and we're happy for you to stay here if you want. It's not right, a girl living out on her own, and you'd be safe here while you look for another job. What d'you think?'

Jemima was overcome. The thought of not having to spend the day tramping round the streets, having doors slammed in her face, was . . . 'You're so kind, ma'am,' she croaked. She cleared her throat. 'I'd love to, thank you.'

'Well then, that's settled.' Mrs Whiting smiled. 'And don't be calling me ma'am, or I won't know myself.'

'You deserve it, Ma,' said Henry, looking both surprised and pleased with what he'd just heard, and coming over to drop a kiss on his mother's cheek. Jemima saw that his limp was more pronounced this morning, and felt another surge of gratitude at how much time he'd spent walking on her behalf during the last few days.

'Most of the money Pa saved for me was . . . lost,' said Jemima, 'but I have a bit from pawning the rest of our things, so I can pay you some rent straight away.'

She was already reaching into her pocket when Mrs Whiting flapped an arm. 'Never mind that now. I'll talk to Pa again and we'll sort something out. The bed's there whether you're paying for it or not, so the best thing is for you to get out today and look for a new job. There must be all sorts of things going for a smart girl like you, even if the school doesn't want you. Shops, that kind of thing. You need to be able to add up money for that, and read. And service is always a good choice for a girl. Although . . .' She couldn't help a glance at the sink in the corner, where Jemima had demonstrated her ineptitude at washing up last night. 'Well. I'm sure you'll find something.'

'Thank you, again,' said Jemima, meaning it from the bottom of her heart. What Mrs Whiting had said about the bed was true, but there was also food to take into account. It had not escaped Jemima's notice that the addition of an extra mouth for last night's meal, the contents of which were no doubt carefully calculated, had resulted in smaller portions for others. She would pay her way, and she would work hard to do so. 'I'll visit schools first, although it's nearly the end of term, so they might not be looking for anyone just now. But I can try.'

'That's what I like to hear,' said Mrs Whiting. 'Why—' She was interrupted by Albert, who flew into the room waving a piece of paper. 'What are you doing home? You get back to school right now!'

'I will,' he panted, out of breath. 'Betty give me this,

and said I just had time to bring it and get back before the bell if I ran fast.' He held out the paper to Jemima, who took it while murmuring 'Betty *gave* me' almost without thinking, then smiling when she realised Henry had said the same thing at the same time.

'Thank you!' she called, after Albert's departing back, but he was already too far away to hear her properly.

She sat down and unfolded the paper, discovering that it was in fact two sheets.

The first was a note from Miss Robinson:

Dear Jemima,

I was deeply grieved to find out what had happened yesterday. I did try to reason with Mrs Silverton, but, I am afraid, to little effect; she would not hear of your coming back, and nor would she take the trouble of writing you a reference. I assume that you will be seeking a similar position elsewhere, which will be difficult without such a document, so please find enclosed a letter from me, which you may show to any prospective employer. This will not be quite to the purpose, as it is not from the headteacher or his wife, but it will, I hope, be better than nothing.

I remain your sincere well-wisher,
Jessie Robinson

Jemima looked at the second page.

Thursday, July 14th, 1864

To Whom It May Concern,
This is to certify that Miss Jemima Jenkins has been employed as an assistant teacher at St. James's School, Liverpool, during the school year 1863–4, and that her work and her conduct during that time have been exemplary.
Signed:
Miss J. Robinson,
Teacher of infants

Jemima shook her head. 'I don't understand.'

'Understand what?' Henry was hovering, though too polite to attempt to read the papers.

She held them out to him. 'Why everyone's being so kind.'

He read them and smiled. 'Don't you?' He gave a brief summary of their contents to Mrs Whiting.

'Well, I'm glad to see someone at that school's got a conscience,' she said. 'You work hard and you're a good friend. Why wouldn't people be kind to you?'

Jemima thought of Mrs Silverton and Mrs Lewis. 'I suppose I'm just not used to it.'

Henry folded the papers neatly and handed them back to her.

* * *

Unfortunately, Jemima was correct in her assumption that schools would not be looking for new assistant teachers in the middle of July. And nor did they take particularly kindly to being approached in person; this was the sort of position which would be properly advertised, and for which one applied in writing. A school was not a shop or business that simply put a card in the window saying 'enquire within'.

Jemima was not deterred. She would find the postal addresses of every school in the city, if she had to, and write letters of application to all of them. If Mrs Whiting didn't want rent money straight away, she could spend a few of her precious coins on paper, ink and a pen, and then she could go to the library and find a directory of Liverpool schools. Such a thing was bound to be available there.

On her way back through town, Jemima paused by a few of the shops. If school positions proved to be in short supply, maybe this was something she could turn her hand to? There was no point in applying to anywhere that was very specialist – she wouldn't have a hope of being able to sell or advise on fashionable clothing or hats, for example – but there might be opportunities in more general places where it was just a case of taking the money. Jemima knew she had a polite manner; she could also add and subtract at a reasonable speed and would be able to serve customers efficiently and give correct change, which would surely be an advantage.

She hovered outside the impressive five-storey frontage of Taylor's department store on Church Street for more than a few moments. Hundreds of people must be employed in a shop this big, and they would surely always have vacancies. But such openings would be for permanent staff, and thus a permanent change of direction for her, and Jemima decided that she didn't want to give up hope of a teaching post so soon. That was what she really wanted.

Her position at St James's hadn't just been a job, something to earn a bit of money until she married; Jemima had seen it as a real career. Partly this was pragmatic, because, as Pa had said more than once, there were good prospects for advancement, and teaching was the only thing that offered a working-class girl the chance of any independence, a possible future that didn't depend on a male breadwinner. But there was also a more personal reason, in that Jemima simply loved teaching the children. It was her calling.

Were there really no other choices, though? Did it truly have to be teaching or nothing? What would she do if there were no school vacancies anywhere? Was there any other way in which she could use her education and aptitude?

Jemima pondered these questions as she made her way along Duke Street, trying not to look too hard at the books and prints she was not likely to be able to afford any time soon. Then a different type of premises caught her eye, one that seemed to be an office rather than a shop, with desks inside. She frowned as she tried to recall whether she'd ever noticed it before, and eventually remembered that the building had been standing empty for a while. A new business must have bought or rented it, and it was quite busy: as she peered in through the window she could see various people sitting down and writing while others moved around, carrying sheaves of paper and speaking excitedly to each other, sometimes jabbing a finger down on to lines of written text as they made a point.

There was a card in the window, and Jemima gasped as she read it.

> **BROWNING NEWS AGENCY**
> **CLERK WANTED**
> *Temporary in the first instance with the possibility of a permanent position.*
> *Must write a clear hand and have excellent orthographic skills.*
> *Some knowledge of literature an advantage.*
> *Apply within.*

This was too good to be true, surely. She easily met the first two qualifications, and even though the third wasn't essential, she could explain that she was familiar with some Shakespeare and poetry and had read books on a wide range of other subjects. It was impossible to tell the exact nature of the work from such a short description, but clearly it would involve writing, which was a much more attractive proposition to Jemima than most other employment that wasn't teaching. And the fact that this notice had caught her eye just when she was looking for work, and just when she was wondering if other fields were available, was some kind of sign, surely? She should be bold and grasp the opportunity.

Jemima went inside.

There was a front desk facing her, on which was a small bell, but she had no need to ring it as a young man bustled forward to greet her. 'Welcome to the new Browning news agency, miss. How may I help you?'

'It's about your card, in the window.'

'Yes, miss.' He launched into a glib and obviously pre-rehearsed script. 'We might be new but we're ambitious and we're expanding. Mr Browning is very fond of literature, says we're living through a great age for it, and he intends a news line about all the latest publications, et cetera, which he will be able to supply to the newspapers. He needs a clerk with a good hand to write out fair copies from his notes and dictations.'

'Ah, this is why the notice says that some knowledge of literature would be an advantage.'

'Correct, miss.' The young man found a sheet of paper and a pencil, which he licked. 'Now, you can take those details home to whoever – whomever – you're asking for, but can you give me his name now, so we'll know who he is when he comes in himself? Your brother, is it?'

'No, I wish to enquire about the position for myself.'

The room froze.

It was as though she'd smashed a window, or screamed an obscenity, or announced that the queen had died. Every conversation stopped, every pen ceased to scratch and every eye turned towards her.

The young man at the desk forced a chuckle. 'Come now, miss, let's be serious. Playing jokes like this won't do him any good in his application, but if you just give me his name and leave, I'll say nothing about it to Mr Browning.'

Jemima's cheeks were becoming hot, but she persevered. 'I'm being perfectly serious. I can write a clear hand, as your advertisement requires, and my spelling and grammar are excellent. My previous employment was—'

'Miss, I'm warning you . . .'

An older man approached. 'Do you need any assistance, Walters?'

There was a snigger from a couple of the desks, probably at the thought of the young man needing any kind of assistance in dealing with a sixteen-year-old girl who was on her own. He made the best of it. 'This young lady is trying to apply for Mr Browning's position as literature clerk, sir. I was just . . .' He flapped his arm ineffectually.

'Well,' said the newcomer, glaring at Jemima, 'I hope you told her we would not be foolish enough to consider any such thing.'

Jemima looked around and recognised the mistake she'd made. She hadn't seen *people* inside the office at work when she looked through the window; she'd seen *men*. She was the only female currently standing in the room. She'd been thinking purely of the work itself, knowing she was the equal of any of these clerks in terms of reading and writing, and it simply hadn't occurred to her that she was in any way different. But these men didn't agree, and the one she now faced was looking at her as though she were a talking dog.

She would persuade them. 'I assure, you, sir—'

He continued as though she hadn't spoken. 'Not only would your presence be *ridiculous*, making Mr Browning a laughing stock, and a distraction for his employees, but—'

'Tell me,' asked Jemima, her anger making her bold enough to interrupt him, 'when you employ men, do you hire the one who is best suited to the job?'

'Of course.'

'So why not ask me about my qualifications and experience?'

'Because,' he replied, in the sort of tone used to explain something very simple to a small child, 'I already know you are unsuited.'

'Why?'

He rolled his eyes. 'Because of your *sex*, my dear. Ask about your education and qualifications, indeed. The very idea!' He gave a patronising laugh, which was dutifully echoed by his juniors at the desks. 'I don't know what sort of ladies' magazines and *novels* you've been reading, but if you knew the slightest thing about science you would be aware that the female brain is totally unsuited to intellectual labour.'

Jemima was so angry she could hardly speak. 'That is absolutely not—'

He continued, his tone lofty. 'The inferiority of the female brain means it is simply not equal to the demands of business or commerce. Indeed, even an *attempt* to engage in such areas can cause a variety of health problems to ladies' delicate nerves and' – his eyes travelled downwards – 'reproductive capabilities.'

Jemima blushed and couldn't get a word out. The sniggers from the desks intensified.

'This is accepted scientific fact, so I believe there is no more to say on the matter. This conversation is at an end.' Both the man's gaze and his tone changed as he revealed the depths of his contempt. 'Run along home to your mother and take up your embroidery, there's a good girl. I have business to attend to. Walters, the door.'

The younger man hastened to open it and hold it wide. His superior was already turning away. Jemima's dismissal could hardly have been more pointed.

There was nothing to do but depart with dignity. 'Good day to you.'

She swept out and managed to make it a hundred yards down the road before the hot tears of shame and humiliation started to run down her cheeks.

Chapter 7

The female brain is totally unsuited to intellectual labour.

The words echoed in Jemima's head as she walked. Now, of course, she could come up with the counter-arguments that she'd been too shocked to think of at the time. She wished she'd been able to say some of them while she was in the news office. She wished she could have come up with something that would have put the odious man in his place. She wished . . . *If wishes were horses, beggars would ride.* It was too late now.

It was still only early afternoon, but she would go back to the Whitings' house. Well, there was no point in trying anywhere else, was there? She was nothing and nobody, and she just didn't *fit* anywhere. As a woman, she would not be employed for any jobs considered to be the preserve of men, even if she had three times the qualifications of any other applicant. But she couldn't really apply for any of the more traditional types of women's work, either, because she could neither cook nor clean, and although she could sew well enough to mend her own and Pa's clothes, she was certainly no dressmaker. And class was an issue, too: with her education she might advertise herself as a governess, working in a private household rather than in a school, but anyone who could afford to employ a governess would want one who was from a more genteel background, not a docker's daughter. An *orphaned* docker's daughter, she reminded herself, harshly, who had lost her respectability along with her beloved father.

The only other option would seem to be the one Jemima had dismissed along with the copy of *Pride and Prejudice*: marriage to a man who would keep her. But that was something she was determined not to do. She would stand on her own two feet, however much the world tried to unbalance her by tipping the scales to make her fall.

Jemima wiped her eyes as she considered for the first time the possibility that her upbringing and education might actually be classed as a disadvantage. What had it done for her? What was she good for?

No. *No*, she wouldn't start thinking like that. She wouldn't swap her old life with Pa for anything, and he'd given her everything she needed to make a success of herself, if only she could find the right path now that he wasn't here to guide and encourage her.

That Jemima's life had been unfair in the short time since she'd lost him was undeniable, but she had to forget that and move on. Her tears dried as anger took over, and her pace became brisker. How dare that man talk to her in such a way? Oh, if only she'd been able to stop him in his tracks at the time. But he'd been so, so . . . what was the word she wanted? *Supercilious*. Which, ironically, she could write and spell perfectly, along with *arrogant*, *pompous* and *condescending*.

By the time Jemima became aware enough of her surroundings to realise where she was, she found that she had been walking in the direction of St Thomas's church and its cemetery, not Back Colquitt Street.

She slowed her pace. On the one hand, she might use this as an opportunity to think quietly, and to talk to and remember Pa. But on the other, was she feeling strong enough? Given the events of the last few days, it was entirely possible that she would throw herself down on the grave and beg to join him in it.

She turned through the gate and followed the path between the tombs in the direction of Pa's plot. When she'd been here the other day she'd been far too distressed and concerned with her own thoughts to notice details of the other graves, but now she idly read some of the stones as she passed them. A few indicated that those interred had led long lives, and she hoped they'd been happy ones; but there were also a good number of younger people's graves, and far too many that held small children.

A plot that was covered in bright, blazing flowers caught her eye, and in curiosity she hesitated and then left the path to look at it. Another child, to be so decorated? No, the size of the grave told her it was that of an adult. When she reached it she could see that some of the flowers were actually growing in the ground, planted just as Jemima meant to do for Pa as soon as she could, but others were freshly cut and had been carefully arranged on top. A glance at the date on the tombstone told Jemima that yesterday had been exactly one year since the occupant had died, which explained why she hadn't noticed the grave before, for such a display would have been noticeable even on the day of Pa's funeral. Someone must have left the flowers in the intervening time, and there were so many of them that the deceased must have been dearly missed.

The rest of the inscription, when Jemima turned her eye to it, took her breath away. Oddly there was no age or date of birth to accompany the date of death, but the entire story of a life was told in a few simple words, carved into the warm, sun-drenched stone:

ABRAHAM DAVIS
BORN A SLAVE
DIED A FREE MAN
MUCH BELOVED

And there Jemima had been, feeling sorry for herself. How pathetic, when Liverpool was full of people who'd had much worse starts in life than she had, and faced worse tribulations, and who'd made something of their lives. She'd lost her job. She'd had some money stolen. A man had been rude to her in an office. What was that, in comparison?

By the time Jemima got to Pa's grave, she was able to kneel beside it without tears and with no desire to bury herself. Instead, she promised him that she would make a new start, and that she would make him proud, one way or another.

* * *

The house was still relatively quiet when Jemima got back to it, neither the school nor the working day having yet finished. There was a gaggle of children in the yard and Jemima longed to ask them whether they'd ever been to school, or if they would like to go if they could, but she didn't disturb them.

The door was standing open. Jemima hesitated, unsure exactly how much of a family footing she was on just yet, and not liking to walk straight in. However, waiting to be admitted seemed a little too formal so she settled for knocking and calling out a greeting before stepping over the threshold.

Henry was at the table, books and papers spread out in front of him, and Mrs Whiting was engaged in a pile of ironing. The laundering of household items, Jemima understood, was almost a constant activity. Wash day itself might be a Monday, with children – girls – absent from school for that reason, but Monday was only for the actual wash, soaping and boiling the clothes and other household items. They still had to be dried, pressed, aired and so on, which took most of the rest of the week until Friday or Saturday, then Sunday might be a day of rest before it all started again. An arduous task, even for a small family, with Mrs Whiting's work so much the greater. Laundry for a household of this size was probably almost a full-time job on its own, so it was no wonder she kept Molly and Maisie at home to help, with her three eldest daughters all at work.

Henry's neat columns of figures, and a volume entitled *Bookkeeping and Accountantship, Elementary and Practical*, were intriguing, but Jemima put them resolutely out of her mind and moved straight to Mrs

Whiting. 'I'd like to help, please, if there's anything I can do which will actually help and not just slow you down or damage anything.'

There were two irons: the one currently in use and the other heating by the fire, over which bubbled a pot of whatever was for tonight's tea. The combination of heat, smoke and steam in the confined space, in such warm weather, made it almost unbearable, but Mrs Whiting was unfazed – if a little red-faced – as she made her way through the pile in the basket. She set her iron down to heat again, showed Jemima how to pick up the warmer one – using a thick rag so she didn't burn her hand – and let her have a try on the corner of a sheet.

This was managed without disaster, so Jemima ironed the rest of it.

'Is this honestly the first time you've done this?' Mrs Whiting was shaking her head.

'Yes. I remember my Ma doing it, but I was only five when she died, so I didn't help her with it in case I burnt myself. And since then, Pa and I lived in lodgings where laundry was included in the rent.'

Mrs Whiting shook her head again. 'It's not right, how a girl can get to your age without knowing anything. I don't mean,' she added, hastily, 'any disrespect to your Pa. Of course he wasn't in a position to teach you. But it's done you no good.'

Jemima kept her attention determinedly on the iron and on a second sheet, so as not to cause a disaster, but she smiled. 'I do know *some* things.'

'Oh yes, but that's only books and handwriting and the capital of France. What good is that, for a girl, when she needs to be learning how to take care of a husband and a house?'

Henry didn't turn round, but he interjected in an amused voice. 'Now, Ma, you know how useful it is to learn to read and write.'

'Well, all right,' she conceded. 'Reading and being able to write your name and reckon with money, so you know you're not getting cheated when you shop, I'll give you that. But as for the rest, a girl would be better off at home or out in service, learning something practical. Put that iron back near the fire, now, and I'll do Pa's shirts with the other one.'

Jemima did so. 'But . . .' she said, not wanting to argue or disagree with Mrs Whiting, who'd been so kind to her, 'may I ask, why does Betty work at the school? I mean, if you think education isn't useful for girls.'

'She wanted to earn a bit of money to help out, and good for her with all these mouths to feed. But she's my eldest girl, so I couldn't have her living out in service, or who would help me here? That job's only down the road, and she's home by five o'clock, which you wouldn't get with factory or shop work.' She folded a pressed shirt with an expertise born of long practice, and flipped the next one out of the basket and on to the board. 'And it's only teaching littl'uns their ABCs and their two-plus-twos, nothing wrong with that. It'll stand her in good stead when she has children of her own.'

Jemima was taken aback. To speak of such a wonderful, fulfilling job as teaching in such terms . . .

'So you see, Jemima,' said Henry, 'what sort of a den of iniquity you've landed in.'

'A what of what?' asked Mrs Whiting. 'You get on with learning how to do accounts, so Pa can get you a job on the site.'

'I will, Ma, for you. But I'd be willing to bet that if Jemima sat down with exactly these same books, she'd pass the examination at the same time I would.'

He meant well, Jemima knew, but all the humiliation of the scene in the news office came flooding back. 'And what use would that be?' she snapped, rather more sharply than she'd intended. 'What would I do with that qualification? I'm better off learning to iron with your mother.' She turned back to the fire, to pick up the second iron and to make sure nobody would see if she began to cry. But she wasn't quick enough to escape seeing the hurt expression on Henry's face.

It wasn't long before the children returned from school, tumbling loudly inside. Jemima was eager to hear about their day, but no sooner had they arrived than Mrs Whiting pushed the boys back outside 'to get out from under my feet' and told Maisie and Molly to fetch another basket of cottons while she fed the baby and saw to the tea.

Jemima continued with her slow, careful ironing until Betty appeared in the doorway. 'Well, there's a sight I never thought to see,' she called out, cheerfully. 'Jemima Jenkins, housewife!'

Jemima looked down without saying anything, and Betty swiftly came to her side. 'Oh my, I'm sorry, I didn't mean— I wasn't thinking. Here, let me do that.' She took the iron, spat on it, made a face, put it back by the fire and picked up the other one. She then went through three small shirts in the time it would have taken Jemima to do one. 'So, how did you get on today?'

In a low tone, Jemima gave her a summary of her lack of success at the schools she'd visited, and her hope that she might be able to make written applications. She didn't mention the news office or the graveyard.

'That's a good plan. We can get paper from somewhere, and Henry's got pen and ink you can use, haven't you?' She paused. 'Henry!'

'Oh, er, yes,' he replied. 'Sorry, in a world of my own.

Anyway, I'd better clear all this up now. You'll be wanting the table soon, Ma.' He began to stack his books and work, dropping several sheets of paper on the floor as he did so. Jemima bent to pick them up for him, and he took them without meeting her eye.

After the return of the workers there was tea and clearing up and bustle, just as there had been the previous evening, but this time Jemima felt a little more at home. She tried to be as domestic as possible, watching Mrs Whiting and Betty so she could learn, but the main thing she noticed was that everything was being done by the females in the family. Mr Whiting, Rob and Matthew had been out at work all day, granted, but once they were home they simply sat to be waited on, while Betty, who had also been at work, and Mrs Whiting, who had been on her feet for longer than any of them, served them, fussed over them and cleared up after them. Similarly, Molly and Maisie were called upon at frequent intervals to wash, or dry, or clean, or fetch, or mind the two little ones, while the boys never were. Jemima now understood Betty's comment of the other day about how 'Ma hasn't got anyone else to help her in the house': with two daughters away in service and a husband, seven sons and a baby all at home, Mrs Whiting was short of the help that only females seemed able to give.

The evening wore on and the family sat, played or drowsed in the crowded little room. The scent of Mr Whiting's pipe tobacco mingled with the more acrid smells of smouldering coals and sweat.

Jemima found that Maisie was sitting on the floor just next to her chair. 'You know what you said about a story...'

'Oh yes,' came several other voices.

'Please?' asked Maisie.

'Not if she doesn't want to,' said Mrs Whiting, still knitting in the semi-darkness.

'Oh, but I do!' said Jemima. 'I did promise, and anyway, I'd love to.'

Half a dozen little faces looked up at her in the dim light, and she was happier than she had been at any time that day.

'Once upon a time...'

* * *

Henry lay on his back, his hands clasped behind his head, and stared up into the darkness. It wasn't his accountancy studies that were keeping him awake, but rather the thought of Jemima, and how he'd managed to spoil everything and upset her *again*.

He didn't quite understand why she'd reacted so

sharply to his comment about the examination. He'd meant it sincerely, because he'd sensed her intelligence from their few conversations since they'd first met, and he'd been hearing Betty singing Jemima's praises nearly every day for years. But she'd obviously thought he was making a joke at her expense, and she'd been hurt. He should watch his mouth more carefully in future and not speak to her unless he had to. That way he wouldn't make an idiot of himself again.

Later in the evening she'd told the most marvellous story to the children, holding them all enthralled, even the older ones, as she made it all up off the top of her head. Heavens, even Rob had been spellbound, and Henry couldn't help noticing the looks Jemima had thrown him. But of course she had. He was a fit, good-looking young man with a steady job, all the things Henry wasn't.

His brother's carefree snores sounded from the other side of the room. *Yes, you sleep easy*, thought Henry, *with your health and your work and your wages and your popularity with the girls*. But he bore Rob no ill will; why shouldn't he enjoy the life he had? It was hardly his fault that Henry was different and also injured. In fact, he suspected that Rob had been seeking more hours and higher-paid work on a different part of the site *because* he wanted to earn more to cover for

Henry's lack of earnings. The family was a team, with everyone pulling different weights according to their abilities at the time. Henry could only hope that his turn would arrive again soon, so the younger ones could stay in school, if they wanted to, and could hold on to their childhoods just a little while longer before they had to join the arduous world of trying to earn a living.

As Henry's eyes began to close, he tried not to think to himself that he had a new and rapidly developing reason for wanting to have stable employment and a decent wage.

* * *

Jemima stood outside the William Brown Library and Museum, on William Brown Street, and reflected that money could buy you more than food and shelter if you had enough of it. But she should be grateful to William Brown, whoever he was, because he'd chosen to spend his fortune on something that benefitted many others who were vastly less well off than himself. She'd been here with Pa on the day that the building was officially opened, her twelve-year-old self excited and a little nervous at being in such a huge crowd, for many thousands had turned out for the event. But Pa had linked his arm in hers, so she knew she was safe, and he'd told her all about the wonders of knowledge that lay behind the huge, pillared frontage. Best of all, access to these wonders was not limited to the rich, and he'd gone on to arrange a library membership for himself as soon as he possibly could. That meant he was entitled not only to enter and read the books but actually to borrow them and bring them home, so the two of them had enjoyed an ever-changing diet of subject matter on top of the content of their own volumes.

Jemima knew that she would be in danger from these fond memories if she didn't get moving and get on with it, so she stopped staring and ascended the stone steps.

The vast entrance hall offered access to the museum on the left and the library on the right, as well as a grand staircase straight ahead, at the top of which she knew lay some lecture rooms. She turned right to enter the main Reading Room, illuminated by the summer sun streaming down through the many skylights, and crossed it to reach the long counter in front of the reference section.

Jemima had a fairly good idea of what she was about to encounter, after yesterday's experience, but today she was ready for it.

'Good morning, miss. How may I help? Are you new here? You might be interested to know that we have a dedicated Ladies' Reading Room, where you can find the latest ladies' magazines and novels. It's over th—'

'Thank you, no. I'm here because I need a list of all the schools in Liverpool. Their size, type of pupil accepted, postal addresses, names of the headmasters, and so on. Do you have such a thing?'

'Yes, miss, that would be included in the current edition of *Gore's Directory for Liverpool*. But—'

'Good. I'll find myself a seat over there while I wait.'

'But that's the Students' Room, miss.'

'And?'

'Well . . .'

'Tell me, what criteria do you use to determine whether someone is a "student" or not? Do they have to prove membership of some academic institution?'

'No, miss, but it's a room for serious study. Ladies generally prefer to—'

'And what, *precisely*, is it about me that makes you think I'm not here for serious study?'

'Er . . .'

'What volume have I just asked you for?'

'A directory with a list of schools in Liverpool.'

'And is that an object of serious study or is it a magazine or novel?'

'Um . . .'

'Just to be clear, is there any law which says that

I may not enter the Students' Room? Or any by-law or official library regulation?'

'No, miss.'

'Good. So, as we could have arranged much more quickly if you'd recognised that to start with, I will take a seat in there, and you will bring me the directory as soon as you've found it.'

'Yes, miss.'

Jemima nodded and swept through into the smaller room, where a number of people – men – were sitting at desks poring over their books in silence. One or two of them looked up and gave a start at her appearance, but most were too engrossed to notice.

She sat down, glaring at her hands until they stopped shaking. Why did this have to be so difficult? Why was anything concerning education or knowledge such a struggle to access? Why did she have to fight like this? If she'd been male, that conversation at the desk would never have happened; it would have been a simple matter of, 'Yes, sir, I'll find that for you, if you'd like to take a seat while you wait.'

But she was here now. She laid down on the desk the paper and envelopes she'd already bought with some of the pawn-shop money, along with a new pen. She hadn't liked to ask Henry to borrow his, as she suspected that he only owned one, so she'd added it to her shopping list first thing that morning. Fortunately ink was provided in this room, as Jemima had correctly recalled from peering in once or twice on previous visits to the library with Pa. A filled and lidded inkwell was sunk into each desk, probably because it was cheaper and easier to provide ink than it was to clear up all the spills that would result from hundreds of students bringing in their own bottles. Whatever the reason, it was a financial saving for which she was grateful, because later she would have to deplete her funds even further by buying penny black stamps. She couldn't really budget more than a shilling for this, so she would have to limit herself to twelve written applications.

It wasn't long until the desk clerk brought the directory – not exactly with a good grace, but he was at least restrained enough not to thump it down and make a noise. Jemima thanked him in a low voice and got straight to work.

There were more schools in Liverpool than she'd thought, but she was able to cut many of them from consideration straight away. She wasn't looking for a position at an industrial school, a reformatory school or anywhere specialist like the institutes for the deaf or blind. Anywhere that accepted only boys as pupils could be crossed off, as could some religious schools, because it was a fair assumption that Catholics or Methodists would want their staff to belong to their own denomination. That made the list more manageable, so Jemima next started to look at where the remaining schools were located, eliminating any too far out of town.

Strict delineations of sex and class were everywhere. A college affiliated to the University of London offered places to 'gentlemen who wish to obtain Degrees in Arts, Science, and Laws', and 'gentlemen not wishing to graduate, but whose only aim is advancement in a particular study, or to qualify for professional life'. Ladies, meanwhile, might attend other establishments, but only for 'finishing' or 'accomplishments'. And the Collegiate Institution was apparently designed to 'supply an education suited to the wants of three classes of society', with an Upper School 'preparatory to the English Universities', a Middle School 'designed to furnish a commercial education' and a Lower School 'providing a Practical Education for the Trading Classes'. No mention was made of whether female students might attend any of these, but Jemima knew the answer to that question without needing to ask it.

Fuming about these injustices, however, would get her nowhere. Applying herself to a search for the sort of place where she thought she would have the best chance of being employed, she found ten that were not too dissimilar from what she was used to: Corporation or

Church of England schools teaching mixed infants and then boys and girls separately up to the age of around ten or twelve. Then she began to write her letters, noting carefully the name of each headmaster and addressing him personally, explaining her previous employment and experience, and saying she could provide a reference on request. There was no need to say that this reference had been written by a young infants' teacher rather than the headmaster or his wife; Jemima would cross that bridge when she came to it. She took her time, knowing that her handwriting and mode of expression would be judged as part of the application, and paying just as much care to the address on each envelope as to the letter inside.

Once those ten were done, Jemima could have stopped, but she still had two sheets and two envelopes left, and had budgeted for twelve stamps. She tapped her pen in indecision for a moment and then came to the conclusion that ambition was no bad thing – after all, what did she have to lose? So she wrote additional letters to the two boarding schools in the directory that admitted only girls, and which were headed by a mistress rather than a master, adding a few extra lines to these ones about her love of reading and enjoyment of literature. A post in either of these establishments would be a dream beyond her wildest expectations, a secure career for life.

Jemima leaned back, flexed her aching fingers, carefully wiped a few ink stains from them with her handkerchief, and then used it to wrap the pen before stowing it in her shoulder bag. She would have to ask Mrs Whiting how one washed ink out of cotton without leaving a lasting mark.

She stacked the letters in a neat pile. The whole course of her future might depend on what she'd written this morning, and she had an irrational urge to kiss the envelopes before she put them away. Fortunately she managed to suppress it, for nothing would tell the men around her that women were flighty creatures suited only to magazines and light novels more than the sight of her doing that.

She returned the directory to the enquiry desk, thanking the clerk politely once again; he would have no excuse to say women should be banned from the reference section because they were difficult to deal with. One fractious man wouldn't result in all men being tarred with the same brush, of course, but if Jemima were to be uncivil she would be taken as representative of her entire sex.

There was one further sad duty to perform before she left to post her letters, and she made her way over to the counter in the main Reading Room to tell them that her father had died, and to ask them to cancel his membership accordingly. This was one situation in which being female did her a positive favour: the paternal-looking clerk there was all sympathy as he dealt with the necessary paperwork. He even asked her, as part of a soothing conversation, whether she was fond of reading herself, and whether having a library membership of her own might help her grief in enabling her to read consoling or moral works. She accepted, with a moment's hesitation at whether he would cease filling in the form when she gave her address as Back Colquitt Street, but he did not. One of the purposes of the library, after all, was the education and improvement of the working classes, so he must be used to dealing with members who lived in all sorts of places.

Jemima left the building with a greater spring in her step than she'd known for some time. Her library membership offered opportunities, and the stamped letters that she pushed into the box at the Post Office represented hope. It was now Friday afternoon, so they would be delivered either this evening or tomorrow morning, and if anyone wrote back straight away she might expect a reply as early as Monday.

She had done Pa and his hopes justice this morning, and she felt that he was smiling on her.

Chapter 8

For the rest of Friday, and through Saturday morning, Jemima occupied herself fully in helping Mrs Whiting with her household chores. She owed it to her hosts, who had still not raised the question of rent with her, and the labour helped to take her mind off what various headmasters and mistresses might be thinking of her letters right at this very moment.

The advent of Saturday afternoon caused a pang, because it was the first Saturday for months that Jemima had missed visiting Hopkins' tea room. Betty chose not to go, either, declaring that she didn't want to be there on her own, and anyway she needed to give every penny of her wages to Ma, because there was only one more week of term and she wouldn't get paid during the school's summer break.

Oddly, the subject of the tea room came up in quite a different context later that evening. Jemima had just told a story to everyone, for the third night in a row, spinning out the tale she'd originally made up on the spot on Thursday into something of a serial. It concerned a boy who'd stowed away on a ship that was docked in Liverpool; initially he was just going to have a short adventure and be returned home to his loving family, but now his voyage was lengthening and he'd already visited one or two exotic places that Jemima and Pa had read about in library books. She felt confident she could keep it going for some while, so when the children were shooed off to bed it was with a promise of continuing the following evening.

A few moments of peace ensued before Betty broke it. 'I forgot to tell you earlier,' she said to Jemima, 'I was talking to Bella from across the yard, and she'd been talking to her friend Kitty, who works in one of those shops round the edge of Saint John's market. Well, *she* heard there's been a to-do up at Hopkins' tea room, which is just near there.'

Jemima had been relaxing, but now she sat upright. 'What sort of a to-do?' She hoped nothing had happened to that nice Mrs Roberts.

'Apparently, Mrs Hopkins's sister ran away last week, and she's been looking everywhere for her.'

'Oh dear.' Jemima paused. 'What, run away from a job, or a husband?'

'No, that's just it. Run away from the tea room itself, so Bella says that Kitty heard. I didn't even know she had a sister.'

Jemima considered the staff in the Hopkins establishment. 'Oh, perhaps it's that girl Hannah – you know, the one who does the serving? There would be quite an age gap between them, twenty years, maybe, but they could be sisters if one was the eldest and the other the youngest.' She glanced at Henry, who was holding baby Tilly while his mother got on with some mending in the last of the firelight.

'Oh yes, I suppose. Funny thing to do, though – they all seemed quite happy every time we were there. Why would she run away?'

'Who knows?' Jemima couldn't work it out, either, though she was very sorry both for Mrs Hopkins and for Mrs Roberts, who would be concerned about her younger daughter.

'Oh, I can't bear to think of it,' said Betty, shivering despite the warmth of the room. 'I can't even imagine what it would be like if one of my sisters went missing. I'd go out of my mind with worry.'

'So would I,' said Mrs Whiting, tying off the end of

her thread. 'Why, I'd turn the whole of Liverpool upside down looking for her.'

Jemima lapsed into silence. It wasn't quite a parallel situation to her own, but it did remind her that she, too, might have sisters out there somewhere, if they were still alive. Her curiosity about them, dormant for the last few days, was piqued again. Did they ever think of her? Had they ever tried to find her again? But no, she told herself. They'd voluntarily given her up, and if they'd wanted to get in touch again all they had to do was to go back to Ma and Pa's house, or, later, to ask for Pa at the docks. They didn't want her, so she wasn't 'lost' in the way Mrs Hopkins's sister was. Hannah must be called Hannah Roberts, which was unfortunate in terms of looking for her, as both her Christian name and surname were common ones, but if Jemima ever got the chance then she would enquire after her. Hopefully Hannah would go back of her own accord once she found out that life in Liverpool as a single girl wasn't easy.

The idea of a common surname started another train of thought, and Jemima wondered what her name would have been if she hadn't been given to Ma and Pa. Smith? Taylor? Robinson? It would be impossible for her to trace her birth family, even if she wanted to, for there were thousands of people in Liverpool with what might be classed as common surnames. The eldest sister, Pa had said, had an unusual name, and then he'd mentioned the Bible, so Jemima spent a few minutes speculating on whether she might have a sister who was called Bathsheba or Hepzibah or something equally outlandish. It certainly wouldn't be Mary or Elizabeth, because those were two of the most popular women's names.

Even discovering that would be no use. Jemima did some quick arithmetic. If this eldest sister had been the one to give her away, as Pa had implied – in which case, what had happened to the other set of parents? – then she must be a good deal older than Jemima herself. In her thirties by now, at the very least, and more likely than not married, which meant she would have a different surname that couldn't possibly be known.

There was no use in going over this. Now that Jemima had been able to reflect on it at greater length, she did believe wholeheartedly that what Pa had said was true. Firstly, because he would never lie to her; secondly, because even though he'd been very ill, he'd said all those things during times when he was lucid, not delirious; and thirdly, because the more she thought about it, the more horribly plausible it seemed. But none of that was the point. The nub of the matter now was that Jemima had no chance whatsoever of being able to find this other family, even if she wanted to, so it was better not to think about it at all.

The problem was that Jemima *had* started thinking about it. She had scratched that little itch in her mind, and all she'd done was to make it worse.

Later, when the whole household was in bed, Betty's voice came out of the darkness. 'I hope Mrs Hopkins finds her sister. Just think how awful that would be if it was Molly or Maisie. And I know Harriet and Anna aren't at home with us, but we do know where they are. Not knowing, that must be the worst thing.'

Jemima's earlier thoughts were so much at the forefront of her mind that she couldn't help voicing them. The younger girls were sound asleep, so it would go no further. 'Betty, can I tell you something?'

* * *

The first two replies to Jemima's letters were delivered on Monday and Tuesday, and both were rejections. Jemima was thanked for her application, but they had no vacancies at present.

By now it was the last week before the summer break, so even if Jemima were to be offered a position by one of the schools she'd written to, it wouldn't start until September. It was therefore imperative that she should find some way of earning a bit of money to contribute to the household, but preferably something of a temporary nature, so she could leave it again in a few weeks' time if one of her applications turned out to be successful. But what? She still fell between two stools, in that – as a woman – she was unlikely to be employed at any of the things she was most qualified for, while she was conversely not good enough at any recognised 'women's work' to make her employable. In one of her more desperate moments she even wondered if it might be possible to disguise herself as a young man in order to apply for a clerking post – in the same way that she'd read once or twice of women going to sea in disguise – but that would be hopeless. She was far too feminine-looking to be convincing, and she'd only end up humiliating herself even more.

Jemima spent much of the rest of the week helping Mrs Whiting, in between sporadic forays out into town to look for work. She was becoming slightly more proficient at some household tasks and already bored and not a little frustrated: there was no variety in anything, and no intellectual challenge. It was just the same hard labour, over and over. Clean clothes were dirtied and must be laundered again and again, along with the endless baby napkins; clean dishes were used and needed to be washed up; coals needed to be fetched; the floor swept and the ironing done; as well as the shopping, the mending... There was no respite. That was not to say that Jemima didn't admire Mrs Whiting; indeed, her appreciation and respect only grew and grew over the course of the week as she watched the older woman toiling non-stop from dawn to dusk, and beyond, at a variety of heavy tasks, none of which would even be classed as 'work' by wider society.

But the most impressive thing to Jemima was the *joy* with which Mrs Whiting laboured. She was genuinely glad to do all this for her family, taking pride in their clean, neatly mended clothes and the scrubbed, dust-free little house.

As they worked together, Jemima came to understand that Mrs Whiting had a vocation, just as she did; it was only that it lay in a different direction. She received plenty of advice as the week went on, not just on practical matters – such as how to get ink stains out of a cotton handkerchief, which was apparently to boil it in milk before a thorough scrubbing with soap and soda – but also on how to approach life. The former she found very useful, but listening politely to the latter just brought it home to her that this existence wasn't for her. 'Once a girl can read and write, and reckon a bit with money, she should leave school and be at home helping out,' was one such opinion, which Jemima didn't seek to contradict, out of respect. Nor did she baulk at, 'A girl can earn a bit of money working while she's young and single, but her main job should be to find a husband,' and she also said nothing to, 'A married woman's place is to stay home and bring up her family.' But when she heard, 'To be honest, if a girl *is* clever and good at all that book learning, she should hide it rather than anything else, or she'll never get a husband,' she had difficulty in holding her tongue.

Jemima knew in her heart that all this was wrong, that girls could and should be allowed an education, and that they might have a life of their own that didn't depend on a husband. But she also knew that the world would tell her that it was *she* who was wrong. Ninety-nine people out of a hundred – and a hundred out of a hundred men – would say exactly the same as Mrs Whiting, and think Jemima was some kind of aberration. What was the matter with her, that she should hold these peculiar opinions? Life would be so much easier if she stayed on the same path as everyone else, and didn't wander off it to get lost with ideas of education and career.

But thoughts of a career never left Jemima, and it was the following Saturday afternoon that two ideas occurred to her, both prompted by workers of the Whiting family returning home after their week of labour.

Betty arrived in the early afternoon, not only with her wages but also with four broken slates from the school. 'Mr and Mrs Silverton told us to have a clear-out for the end of the year, and these were going to get thrown out,' she explained in reply to Jemima's question. 'They don't want the school to get a reputation for being down-at-heel, so they said they'd replace them before September. And I thought it was a shame, as they were still usable, so I asked could I have them.'

'And she said yes?'

'Well, no – she told me to put them out in the rubbish. So I did, and then when I came back out later to come home, I picked them up again. She'll never know, and it's not stealing; it'll actually cost her less to have less rubbish carted away.'

Jemima wasn't entirely sure of the ethics of this, but she certainly veered towards agreeing with Betty. If the Silvertons didn't want the broken slates, and had actually thrown them out, surely it was only right that someone else should get the chance to use them? She and Betty could run some holiday lessons for the Whiting children, so they wouldn't forget everything between now and September.

That would give Jemima something to do, and it might help the household, but it wouldn't earn any money. However, an idea for that arrived only an hour later when Mr Whiting, Rob and Matthew arrived home from the building site. Knowing that Mrs Whiting would hand them back some of their wages to spend on themselves when they gave the coins to her, they had taken an advance and spent some on the way home. Mr Whiting had a screw of tobacco for his pipe, Rob was already halfway through a meat pie, and Matthew was clutching a penny paper.

These were familiar items throughout Liverpool: cheap printed sheets containing stories aimed predominantly at men and boys, sensational in nature and normally in serial form so that a new paper had to be purchased each week. Someone, somewhere, had noted the increase in literacy among the working and lower middle classes, now that more of them went to school, and had found a way to make a profit out of it. Apprentices and shop boys eagerly awaited their next weekly instalment, the publication of which was handily timed to coincide with payday, and tales of Sweeney Todd, Varney the Vampire and Spring-Heeled Jack were all over town. The higher classes looked down on such papers, referring to them condescendingly as 'penny dreadfuls', but this did nothing to halt their popularity. Mr Silverton always confiscated any he found being brought into school, but Jemima, in another of those heretical opinions that most of society would condemn, thought that anything that encouraged the boys to read was a good thing. If they preferred penny-paper tales of Dick Turpin – the current craze, she knew – to their rather dry school primers, then why not?

Matthew, it turned out, was frugal, and he normally paid a friend a farthing to have sight of his copy once it had been read. But that friend had been absent from work today, and Matthew simply couldn't wait, so he'd bought a paper himself. He'd barely shoved his coins at Mrs Whiting before he was outside again, sitting with his back to the wall and his knees up, engrossed in what must surely be about the two-hundredth episode of *Black Bess; Or, The Knight of the Road*.

Mrs Whiting set off immediately to go shopping, declining Jemima's offer of help. 'I'm just going to slip along to the meat market, because early closing on Saturday is when they sell off some cheap cuts that won't keep until Monday morning. We'll have a bit of beef tonight, if I hurry. You can tell Betty to keep an eye on Tilly, if she wakes.'

Jemima watched her head off in a determined manner, basket at the ready to push her way through what was sure to be a crowd of women all bent on the same goal, and turned back to smile down on the absorbed

Matthew. She wished that all children had the opportunity to read for pleasure like that, even if it was only the contents of a 'penny dreadful'.

Albert was trying his best to read over his brother's shoulder, but he was roughly pushed away and he slipped over. 'Don't care, anyway,' he cried, with blatant red-faced falsehood, as he stood up and rubbed his knee. 'I'll find it whenever you put it down. And besides,' he added, stamping off to the other side of the yard, where more children were playing, 'Jemima's story is better.'

And that was what gave Jemima the idea.

* * *

Jemima talked to Betty about it, of course, but the person who was most likely to be able to advise on how to proceed was Henry.

She wanted to approach him, but wasn't quite sure how, given how she'd mismanaged everything in which he was concerned so far. He'd been so kind on the day of Pa's funeral, but then she'd bothered him with questions about his accident and his injury, which hadn't gone down well. Then, while she was still upset about her experiences at the news office that day, she'd managed to insult his accountancy studies, and he'd barely spoken to her since. Henry was also the only member of the family who hadn't really seemed to enjoy her stories in the evening. Although they were meant for the younger children, Matthew and even Rob and Mr Whiting had been enthralled too, and Jemima had been both amused and gratified at seeing two hulking builders hanging on her every ridiculous word as the continuing tale of Tom the Stowaway got wilder and wilder. So Jemima was, by now, feeling self-conscious around Henry, a little awed by his intellect – for he was almost at the end of that accountancy book now – and sensing that he disapproved of her in some way she couldn't quite define.

But there was nothing else for it, so she went inside, where he was alone except for the sleeping baby in the corner, and rather diffidently took a chair at the table where he was working. He was just in the middle of adding up a column of numbers, so she waited until he had written several neat figures at the bottom of the page before she spoke.

'May I ask you something?'

He put his pen down. 'Of course.'

'It's about penny papers.'

He frowned. 'Well, I wasn't expecting that, but carry on.'

'There are lots of different ones, aren't there?'

'Oh yes. But if you want to know more about the stories, Matthew would probably be—'

'That's not it.' Jemima was excited enough by her idea to interrupt him. 'Or, at least, not quite. What I was wondering is, who publishes these papers, and how do they get hold of these stories? They must have people who write them.'

'Yes, they must.' He rubbed his face, not realising that he was smudging ink on his chin.

Jemima almost reached for her handkerchief to wipe it off, and then remembered that he was a grown man, not one of her pupils. 'Do you know anything about the process? Or do you know anyone who might?'

'I don't know offhand, but I would imagine that if we look in the bottom corner of one of the sheets – if we can prise it off Matthew when he's read it – that the name of the publisher would be given. Then it would be a case of contacting them to ask if they employ specific men to write for them, or if they accepted submissions from anyone.'

Jemima did not fail to catch the word *men*, but this was balanced out by her pleasure at hearing the word *we*. Betty was enthusiastic about Jemima's idea, but she wasn't sure what Mrs Whiting's reaction would be, and Henry's support would be invaluable.

'Why are you—' Henry was continuing, and then he tutted at himself. 'Of course: your stories.'

'And what . . .' Jemima hesitated, not sure whether

she wanted to hear the answer. 'What do you think of the idea? That I could write some of my stories down and try to sell them to the papers?'

She braced herself. It wouldn't be as bad as what had happened in the news office the other day – he wouldn't actually laugh, surely – but she didn't think she could bear to see hesitation, uncertainty, scepticism, anything that indicated his disapproval or his conviction that she couldn't do it.

'I think it's a wonderful idea.'

'Really?'

'Of course. That is to say . . .' he added.

Here it comes.

But Jemima was pleasantly surprised as he continued. 'What I mean is, you easily have the talent to be able to produce these stories: I've only had to watch the children these last few nights to know that. But I have no idea how difficult or how easy it might be to get them accepted by the publications. It's something I have no knowledge of, and I wouldn't want to raise your hopes only for you to see them dashed.'

'Oh, that's such a relief! I thought you were going to say . . .'

'Say what?'

'It doesn't matter.' Jemima was still too distressed by the news-office incident to tell anyone about it. Even

Betty didn't know. If she told Henry about it now, his attitude might change. His support and enthusiasm would wane as he saw her in the same light as those other men had done: not as a person who was qualified for the task in hand, but as a woman who was trying to step out of the role that society had prescribed for her.

Henry's face fell. 'I'll go and ask about the paper, shall I?' He got up and made his way to the door. 'Matthew! Bring that in as soon as you've read it!'

Matthew made a reply that Jemima didn't catch.

'Oh, you have? Good, give it here, then. Yes, of course you can have it back after. We only want to look at it for half an hour, then you can see if any of your friends will give you a farthing to read it.'

Henry returned with the paper in his hand. His limp was less noticeable than it had been a week ago, but Jemima decided not to mention it.

'Now, let's see.' He sat down and smoothed the paper out flat on the table.

'There!' said Jemima. She pointed at the small words *Robert H. Grundy, Printseller and Publisher. 26, Church Street, Liverpool.*

'Good. Here, let me write that down before we have to give the paper back – we'll probably never see it again once Matthew passes it round his friends.' He took the paper on which he'd been entering the numbers, which

Jemima now saw were sums of money, and turned it over so he could write the name and address. 'So, what next?'

'Well, I don't suppose there's any point in contacting him until I actually have a written story in hand.'

'Yes, of course. I should have thought of that. So you'll write something – Tom the Stowaway, perhaps? – and then take it to him?'

Jemima's cheeks flushed again at the thought of what had happened the other day. 'No, I won't take it to him personally. He probably won't even read a story if he knows it's written by a girl, and then it won't matter how good it is. I'll send it by post, and I'll just sign my letter "J. Jenkins", not "Jemima".'

'That all seems a bit . . . sceptical of you? Surely what he would be interested in is the quality of the story. I mean, if you were trying to get a job on a building site or something, I suppose they would turn you down for being a wo—a gi—I mean, a young lady, but not for something like this.'

'That's easy for you to say.'

And perhaps it was because he'd been so encouraging up until now, and they were alone with nobody else to hear about her shame, or perhaps it was because she just wanted to get it off her chest, but the entire history of the incident came pouring out, even though it was only a few minutes since she'd been determined to say nothing about it.

Henry sat in stupefied silence for a few moments. Then he made a move forward with his hand before checking himself. 'I'm so sorry to hear that,' he said. 'It was unforgivable behaviour on his part.'

'You think so? You're not going to come up with an excuse about how he was just surprised, or something like that?'

'No.' He spoke decisively and with warmth. 'It was absolutely inexcusable, and there can't be any mitigating factors. What's the point of advertising for a clerk if you don't want the best applicant?'

'That's exactly what I thought, but I was beginning to think I was the only one and I must be mad.'

'Well, you're not.'

'Your mother thinks that if a girl has intelligence and education, she should hide it.'

'I love my Ma dearly, but on this point I would have to disagree with her.'

There was a pause as their eyes met, and then he cleared his throat and tapped the paper. 'We've only got this for half an hour, so why don't you read what's here, get a feel for the style?'

Jemima nodded and bent her head over the story, which spared her from having to say anything. He went back to his books, and for a while there was a companionable silence.

It was broken by Matthew bursting in. 'Have you finished with my paper yet? Jack and Tom have both said they'll give me a farthing to read it.'

'And how much of your original outlay will that repay you?' asked Jemima, smiling as she pushed the paper across the table.

'Half, of course.' He made a face. 'You can tell you're a teacher!'

Jemima and Henry both laughed as he clumped out. The loud interruption had woken Tilly, and Betty came in from where she'd been chatting and sunning herself outside. Then it wasn't long until Mrs Whiting was back and the house was full of activity again.

Jemima heard none of it. Henry had cleared away his books and left her with his ink and some paper, and she was so deep in thought that the noise and the beginnings of tonight's meal washed over her. The penny papers didn't publish anything that started with 'Once upon a time'; they wanted action and thrills. On the plus side, she could allow her imagination free rein, as it wouldn't matter if she strayed a little way from strict realism.

Jemima picked up her pen and dipped it in the ink.

Chapter 9

By the following Friday, Jemima knew that she had reached a crossroads in her life.

She'd received another seven rejection letters in reply to her applications, which only left the two girls' boarding schools – from whom she didn't really expect a response at all, given that they'd probably treated her application as a joke – and the Corporation school on Park Lane. So it seemed that teaching was not for her, or at least not at present, so everything depended on whether or not she could get her stories accepted for publication.

Jemima had written out two episodes of *The Adventures of Stowaway Tom,* to show the publisher that she intended to make it into a serial, and she had now also completed a covering letter to go with them. Everything was in the envelope, upon which she had written the address and affixed a stamp, but now she hesitated. What if she was just setting herself up for more failure and humiliation?

'Is that it?' Betty paused in the act of sweeping last night's cold ashes from the fire.

'Yes.'

'Well? Aren't you going to go out and post it?'

'I . . .'

Betty looked at her more closely. She stood up, wiped her hands and came over to the table. 'What?'

'It's just . . . is this all a nonsensical idea? I mean, telling stories to the girls at school, or round the fire in the evening, is one thing. Trying to get them in print is another. Maybe I'm getting above myself.'

'You're not,' said Betty, confidently. 'And I can try to persuade you all I like, but instead I'm going to ask you one question: what would your Pa say, if he was standing here now?'

Jemima sighed. 'He'd say I should post it, that I should at least try, and that he believed in me.'

'Well, then.'

Jemima remained hesitant, still haunted by the horror and embarrassment of what had happened in the news office, and the concept of women being *totally unsuited to intellectual labour* – an idea that had only been drummed into her more thoroughly by Mrs Whiting's well-meaning but constant commentary on what sort of life was appropriate for girls.

Betty snatched the letter out of Jemima's hand. 'If you won't post it, I will.'

'But—'

'No buts! Are you coming with me, or not?'

Jemima reminded herself of Pa, and she followed Betty out of the house and round to Duke Street, where there was a green Post Office pillar box. 'Wait!' she said, as Betty was about to post the letter. 'I'll do it.'

She heard it fall inside the box, and they turned away. 'You never know,' said Betty, 'this might be the start of something big.'

Jemima thought that chance would be a fine thing, but she made no reply.

When they returned to the yard, several children were already loitering while they waited for her, and the sight cheered her up. 'One moment! I'll get the slates and chalks.'

She fetched them from inside the house and made her way over to the sunny corner where they were congregating. Maisie had brought out a chair for her, and she sat with the children cross-legged on the ground facing her. There were six, shortly made up to eight as two more ran out of one of Back Colquitt Street's other houses and threw themselves down behind the others.

Jemima's original plan had been to work with the five children from the Whiting family who attended school, so that they continued their studies in an informal – and, she hoped, enjoyable – way over the summer. But she had been clear that only children who *wanted* to attend should join her, as she had no intention of forcing anyone or imposing traditional school discipline. And this had resulted in two and a half attendees: Maisie and Ralph, who were keen, and little Sid, who wandered in and out as the mood took him. Albert had completely refused, saying he wasn't about to waste his time when he could already read, and that he might be able to earn a few pennies over the summer running errands. And, much to Jemima's regret, Molly had also declined the offer. She and Maisie, although twins, were completely different both in looks and in character, and Molly very much took after her mother. She was robust and practical, saw little use for school learning, and was much happier helping around the house.

Jemima had started her little 'school' at the family table, but after a couple of days they had moved it outside: partly to get out of the way, and partly because it was a fun novelty for the children to be doing lessons out of doors, and Jemima didn't see why they shouldn't enjoy the experience. This had resulted in another very welcome development, in that several of the neighbouring children had sidled over to watch and then eventually plucked up the courage to ask if they could join in. Jemima had been delighted, even though it meant dividing the little group into two classes, for only one of the others had ever been to school before, and the rest needed teaching from scratch. This morning, therefore, she set Ralph and Eddie to share a slate and write out some whole sentences, while she and Maisie worked with the others at the basic recognition and formation of letters.

Maisie, at the age of eight and having been to school for three years already, was far in advance of any of the others. She enjoyed helping, but Jemima also ensured that she made time for more advanced exercises so Maisie could learn as well as teach. It wasn't fair for bright children to lose their own opportunities. Jemima wished that she might be able to go back and redeem a few of Pa's books, at least the Shakespeare and the volume of modern poetry, so that she and Maisie could read and talk about them together. But that was impossible for now: Jemima hadn't earned one penny in the time she'd been with the Whitings, and her stock of money had been depleted by the contribution towards food that she had insisted on making, as they still hadn't charged her any rent. Fortunately a few sticks of chalk were cheap, and the slates themselves hadn't cost anything at all, although if any more children wanted to join in she might have to consider sourcing more.

As she oversaw the writing, and then later some simple arithmetic, Jemima wondered about the progress of her letter to the publisher. Would it have been collected from the pillar box yet? How soon would it be delivered to Church Street? Would it be read by the publisher himself, or by someone who worked for him? At least she could be fairly sure that whoever opened the envelope wouldn't dismiss it immediately because it had been written by a woman; Jemima had, as she'd intended, signed her letter merely 'J. Jenkins'. But would they like the story, would they publish it, would they pay her, and would they commission more? These were all questions to which she had no answers.

School was over at dinnertime, as Jemima didn't want to prevent the children from having plenty of opportunity for play as well as learning. They scampered off and she collected the slates and chalks, noting that the latter were almost worn down to stubs already. She would have to see if she could afford to buy any more.

When Jemima had first left the lodgings at Pitt Street, she had been sure that she would never let her money out of her sight again. But after a couple of days in the Whiting household she'd extracted the coins from her pocket, wrapped them in a handkerchief and stowed them in her carpet bag. She'd later managed to find a piece of scrap material from Mrs Whiting's rag basket, and had sewn it into a decent drawstring purse, which is what she was looking for now as she knelt by the bed in the attic. It was, of course, exactly where she had left it, but in moving a spare shift to one side she also uncovered the flower book.

Jemima had never yet summoned the will or the courage to take it out and open it, so it remained exactly as it was when she'd stowed it on that dreadful day of Pa's funeral, the spine cracked and some loose pages sticking out past the cover. Her hand hovered again now, but once more she withdrew it. What use was there in reading the book, when she would never be able to find her other family even if she wanted to? And they wouldn't want her, anyway – as she kept reminding herself, they had given her up freely and made no attempt to find her since. Plus, as she had added to her list over the last week, even if they did want to find her, they would be shocked or horrified or possibly even amused when they met Jemima. She was neither one thing nor the other, the girl who didn't fit in anywhere. The idea of finding a long-lost family and then being ridiculed by them was simply too much to bear.

She opened the purse. Five shillings and eightpence was all that remained to her in this world, until she could earn some more. She had been standing at this crossroads long enough now, and it was time to travel one way or the other. She would give this publisher a week, and if she had no reply then she would give up on writing and on teaching, and look for a job in a shop.

'Jemima!' Betty's voice floated up the two flights of stairs.

'Coming!' Jemima decided that she could afford twopence, which would buy a box of chalk sticks. Teaching the children in the yard was not just useful to them – she enjoyed it immensely, and she would keep going right up until the last possible moment, the moment when she had to stop because she'd found a position that would take up most of her waking hours.

She came downstairs to find that Betty was holding out a letter. 'Just came, in the afternoon post.'

Jemima's immediate thought was of her story, and the publisher, but that couldn't possibly be right – she'd only sent the letter a matter of hours ago. So it was probably another rejection from one of the three remaining schools. She sighed and took it. Best open it, in any case, for the sake of completeness.

She slit the envelope with the pocket knife that Henry held out to her, for he was present too, working with his accountancy book.

The letter was a single sheet, and Jemima's eyes widened as she scanned its contents.

'What is it?' asked Betty, impatiently. 'Is it from a school?'

'It is,' said Jemima, slowly. 'It's from the Corporation school on Park Lane.'

'And?'

'And they thank me for applying for the vacant position as an assistant in their girls' section, which will be available in September. That's lucky – they must have thought I was writing to them in reply to an advertisement, but I wasn't really. I didn't know. They've had a number of applications, which they've considered, and now they wish to invite three of us to a trial day on Tuesday the sixth of September.'

Betty gave a squeal of joy. 'They're bound to choose you! How could they not?'

'It's certainly a chance.' Jemima looked up to find that Henry was smiling widely at her. 'Isn't it?'

'Of course it is,' he said. 'You've got at least a one-in-three chance, and probably better, given your experience. Does it say what you'll have to do?'

Jemima looked down at the letter again. 'Just to take part in all the activities of a normal school day. The girls' mistress will be watching us, and the headmaster from time to time, and then they'll make a decision at the end of the day.'

'Congratulations,' he said. He held out his hand to shake hers, as though she had been a male work colleague. 'And good luck.'

'And to you, too.' Jemima looked at the books and papers on the table. 'I'm sure you'll pass your examination this week and get a wonderful position.'

'And then it'll be beef and pudding for dinner every day!' crowed Albert, who had wandered in from outside to see what was going on, making them all laugh.

This new prospect took a weight off Jemima's shoulders; a weight she hadn't comprehended was quite so heavy until it was gone. She would be appointed to this post, she was sure. And it meant she could either stay living with the Whitings, if they would let her – paying them proper rent now she was earning – or, if she secured new lodgings, she would still be very close to them, as Park Lane was less than half a mile away. She would still be able to see Betty and H—to see Betty and her family very often. They could resume having chocolate and buns at Hopkins' tea room on Saturday afternoons.

The only slight downside that Jemima could see was that she would have to walk along Pitt Street to get to the school, passing by Mrs Lewis's boarding house twice a day, which would bring back many memories, some of them unwelcome. But if she was secure in a new job, and growing in the confidence this would give, then Jemima thought she would be able to bear it. Besides, she might be able to see Sarah for a quick word every now and then, if she could do it without Mrs Lewis seeing her. Leaving the maid with no friends at all in the household had made Jemima feel guilty, although it was hardly her fault she'd had to go.

This new optimism also brightened Jemima's thoughts about sending off the letter and story to the publisher. If they said no, they said no, and she hadn't lost anything apart from the cost of the stationery and the stamp. They wouldn't laugh at her, and she wouldn't be destitute, because she would be earning a wage. And, in fact, if they accepted her story and wanted more, there was even a possibility that she could do that as well as teaching, if she was efficient with her time in the evenings and on Sundays.

In the meantime, she would be able to continue with her little school in the yard, as there wasn't quite so much pressure to go out and find an immediate job. Indeed, there was no point in looking for anything else unless it was just for a few weeks, because she would have to be free in September, and that prospect was an unlikely one. So a few contented weeks beckoned, during the course of which she could teach, help in the house, make up more stories for the children in the hope of also eventually writing them, and perhaps also use her new library membership.

Jemima took some time that afternoon to visit the graveyard and tell Pa all about it.

* * *

On the Tuesday of the following week there was a treat for the Whitings, and Jemima was able to meet the two family members she'd never seen, because both Harriet and Anna came home for a visit during their fortnightly afternoon out. It was a fine affair, because they brought cake with them, and the whole family, except for Mr Whiting, Rob and Matthew, who were at work, squashed into the downstairs room of the house to eat, drink tea and catch up with loud jollity.

Jemima stayed a little way back from the table, standing at the edge of the room so as to allow the girls to sit with their family, and she observed them as she bit into her slice of seed cake. They were both instantly recognisable as Whitings, though in different ways: Anna, who was thirteen, very much resembled Betty and Rob in being robust and no-nonsense, while the slighter fifteen-year-old Harriet was the image of Henry. It was Anna who was speaking now, telling her mother all about the larks she and her fellow maid got up to, and what the gossip was among the other servants on the street, and how the cook looked after them both and the mistress was kind. 'She even said to pass on her best wishes to you, Ma – fancy that!' She bounced up and down on her chair, and Jemima thought that here was a girl who would take after her mother in cheerfully making the best of whatever life brought her.

Harriet also had her share of the conversation, though her contributions were quieter and more measured. She'd been in service for longer than Anna, and she was able to relate with pride how she'd recently been promoted from being the 'tweenie' – which Betty explained to Jemima was a lowly rank of servant who helped out both upstairs and in the kitchen – to second housemaid. 'And,' added Harriet, her face shining, 'it might not even end there. The housekeeper is pleased that I can read and write and add up, because some of the others can't, and she's going to show me how she keeps the linen records and the budget for the shopping!'

There was a general congratulation, and she blushed and smiled. Henry flashed a quick, conspiratorial glance at Jemima and then said, 'So you see, Ma, that education came in useful, for all she's a girl.'

'Oh, get away with you,' was Mrs Whiting's only reply, busy as she was with Anna and Harriet on either side of her, offering them more tea and beaming with pride.

Jemima wondered for the first time whether this was what a gathering of her own family, her other family, would be like. Were they as numerous as this? What did they all do for work? But it was difficult to imagine when she didn't know their names, or ages, or anything about them or even how many there were. All she could visualise was a room full of faceless figures.

And then, all of a sudden, she was struck with a recollection that was so vivid that she could almost see it playing out in front of her. She was very little, playing in the street, and then she picked a flower from a crack in the pavement and skipped into the house. She'd tried unsuccessfully to stick the flower on Ma's dress, and there had been someone else in the room. Not one of the neighbours; a stranger. A woman, of whom Jemima could only recall her gowned lower legs and knees, because that was what had been at her eye height. She couldn't picture a face.

The words *Your Ma wasn't so lucky*, spoken by Jemima's own Ma, echoed in her head, though she couldn't hear or recall anything else. *Your Ma*. Had that woman been one of Jemima's sisters? But she hadn't picked Jemima up, or cuddled her, or even spoken to her directly – or, at least, not as far as Jemima could remember – so perhaps not. But *why* could she now picture the flower in her hand so clearly, and what did it have to do with anything?

She came back to herself to find that the conversation in the room had moved on to education and school in general. Albert was making a case that he shouldn't have to go back in September, that he should be allowed to leave and get a job with his Pa and older brothers.

'Never mind that,' Betty was saying. 'You're only ten, and you should stay at school until you're twelve.'

'But I can already read and write, and all what Mr Silverton does with the older boys is just things I don't need to know, like history and geography and mathematics.' He appealed to his mother. 'Ma!'

Mrs Whiting looked dubious. 'I don't know, Bert. You're a bit young to be going out to work just yet, especially on a building site.'

'But Ma . . .'

'Wait until Pa gets home, and I'll talk to him about it.'

This was evidently meant to be the final word, and Albert was satisfied for now, but Molly spoke up. 'Well, if Bert's leaving then I want to go too. I don't like school.'

There was a more general disagreement this time,

with both Betty and Harriet telling her she was far too young to leave yet.

'But I don't need to get a job,' she countered. 'I can stay home and help Ma. Can't I, Ma?'

Mrs Whiting hesitated and opened her mouth to reply, but was forestalled by Maisie bursting into tears. 'I don't want to leave school!' she wailed. 'I like it, and I want to stay. And when I'm older I want to be a teacher like Betty and Jemima!' She looked at her mother and sister as she said it, but it was towards Jemima that she flung herself, winding her arms about Jemima's waist and crying into the front of her dress.

Jemima was embarrassed. Had she caused this? Had she upset a happy family by bringing in her outlandish opinions? If so, she was sorry, but at the same time she sympathised with Maisie, who was, after all, only eight and could stay at school for a good while yet even if she didn't go on to be a pupil teacher or assistant later.

Mrs Whiting sighed. 'Now then. Maisie, my love, nobody is going to make you leave school just yet.'

Maisie raised her head. 'Really?'

'Really.'

'Not even if Molly does?'

'Not even then. Although I don't think she'll be leaving just yet, either, if Pa has anything to say about it.'

That started Molly off again, and Mrs Whiting was hard put to regain order.

'Come on,' said Anna, holding out her hand to Molly. 'Let's go outside and I'll tell you more about what I've been doing, so you're ready for it when you do leave school and look for a place.'

Harriet held her hand out likewise to Maisie, and the room was soon at peace.

'I'm truly sorry,' began Jemima, as soon as she could command Mrs Whiting's attention. 'I know she's been enjoying helping me and doing some schoolwork during the holidays, but I never meant . . .'

'Oh, don't you fret yourself. She's said before how much she likes school – it isn't you coming here that's put the idea in her head.'

Jemima was relieved. The last thing she wanted was to upset lovely Mrs Whiting or to cause strife in her family.

Harriet and Anna were able to stay just long enough for the men to come home, and Harriet ran to hug her father while Rob caught Anna up and threw her in the air, joking that he wouldn't be able to do it much longer, and what were they feeding her at that place?

Before long the girls had to set off back to their respective places of work, Rob volunteering to go with them, which Betty loudly put down to the fact that the kitchenmaid in Harriet's house was a very pretty girl indeed. He only grinned in reply as he swaggered out.

After Mr Whiting had downed the tea and the slice of cake that had been left for him, he was told of what Albert, Molly and Maisie had said.

He considered for a few moments. 'The girls? No, they're far too young to leave. They've been at school – what, three years? They've a mite more to learn, and let's leave them to be children a little while longer.' He paused. 'Bert, though.'

Henry made as if to interrupt, but Mrs Whiting threw him a look and he subsided.

'He could stay in school a while longer, I know, but if he really doesn't like it, and he wants to get out and earn himself a bit of money, that's worth considering.' He looked at his wife. 'What do you think?'

Mrs Whiting nodded. 'If it's what he wants. But it would have to be something suited to his age, you hear? I'm not having him crippled by carrying heavy loads of bricks, nothing like that.'

'I agree. But I can always ask the foreman if he needs a boy for running messages, that sort of thing. So Bert could make himself useful while seeing what's going on. That way he'd be in a better position when a proper job comes up later on.'

'Errands is all right. Like I said, though, nothing heavy. Not until he's bigger.'

'That's decided, then. I'll ask tomorrow.'

Jemima, who was wiping the cake plates over by the sink, had heard all this. She must have made an involuntary movement, because Mr Whiting now addressed her. 'What is it, lass?'

She coloured. 'I'm so sorry. It's not my place to interrupt.'

'Are you going to say something about school, or education? I know you value it, and I wouldn't argue, but it might not be what's best for Bert.'

'I wouldn't dream of interfering,' said Jemima. 'It's just . . . sorry, may I ask a question?'

'Ask away.'

'Is it completely safe for everyone in the family to be working in the same place? If anything goes wrong there, it might be . . . bad.'

Jemima held her breath, worrying that she'd said something foolish, or, worse, insulting to Mr Whiting as a working man. But he only rubbed his chin and nodded as he reached for his pipe. 'Bless you, that's not a bad question. But we've plenty of work. Once this terrace of houses is finished that we're working on, there's plans for many more. Builders aren't often out of work in Liverpool these days.'

'I'm glad. I'm sorry, I hadn't meant to be impertinent – I was just worried about you all.'

He reached out and patted her hand in a paternal manner. 'Don't you worry. You're a good lass, and all those littl'uns think the world of you.'

'Not just the littl'uns, neither,' called out Betty.

Jemima turned away and began washing the teacups. She'd been silly to think of such a thing. There was building work going on in virtually every corner of Liverpool, and of course Mr Whiting knew his own business much better than she did. There would always be work for builders.

She turned her mind back to the sudden memory that had assailed her earlier, trying and trying to see it more fully and more clearly, but to no avail.

Chapter 10

Jemima stared at the letter in disbelief.

It had arrived the morning after Anna and Harriet's visit, and, as it was addressed to 'Mr. J. Jenkins', there was only one possible sender.

Her hands had been shaking as she took it, and for a few moments she simply gaped.

'Aren't you going to open it?' Betty was hopping from foot to foot, with Henry looking on anxiously from behind her.

'I'm not sure I can.'

After another few moments of inaction, Henry put out a hand. 'Shall I do it for you?'

Jemima passed it over, then watched in agony as he slit the envelope and removed a sheet of paper. There was a thick silence in the room as he scanned the contents.

And then a slow smile spread over his face.

'Is it . . .?' Jemima couldn't even bear to ask.

'It's a yes,' said Henry, glowing with happiness. 'And even more than that.' He passed the letter back to Jemima.

Tuesday, August 2nd, 1864

Dear Mr. Jenkins,

Thank you for your letter of the 29th ult. enclosing two instalments of a proposed new serial for our line of penny papers. We are pleased to accept them for publication and should like to commission a series of 20 weekly episodes of "The Adventures of Stowaway Tom" in the first instance, on the stipulation that each shall be of a similar length and style to those already submitted.

Individual instalments, written in a fair hand, must reach our office by Tuesday of each week (beginning on August 23rd, given that we have the first two already in hand), to enable editing and typesetting ahead of publication the ensuing Saturday.

We are able to offer payment of 7s 6d per episode, this payment to be made by Money Order redeemable for cash at any Post Office, posted to your address on a weekly basis after the perusal and acceptance of each story instalment.

If this arrangement should prove satisfactory to both of us, there exists the possibility of us commissioning further instalments of the same story, or of a new one, in due course.

If all of the above is acceptable to you, please reply by return of post, confirming in particular your willingness and ability to have instalments with us every Tuesday.

Yours sincerely,
Robert H. Grundy
Printseller and Publisher

Jemima found herself absolutely speechless, other than a tiny squeak at the pay offer. Seven and six! He was offering *seven and six*, a whole week's wages for many women, for a story that would not take anything like an entire week to write. Yes, there would be the pressure of having to produce the episodes of the story on time, which she knew would be different from simply making them up whenever she felt like it, but still.

Betty had been reading over Jemima's shoulder and she now exclaimed at the offer as well. 'That's nearly as much as I get for a whole week at work!' Jemima felt an elbow in her ribs. 'And if you get that school job as well, you'll be a woman of means and no mistake!'

'I'll be a woman who can start paying her way in the

world,' replied Jemima, more composedly, but inside she was shaking with excitement and anticipation at the future prospects now open to her.

She looked again at the salutation. *Dear Mr. Jenkins* . . . 'He's probably only offering that much because he thinks I'm a man.'

Henry was still smiling broadly. 'Possibly. But what this also means is that Mr Grundy judged your story on its own merits, without any prejudice. And he judged it to be worthy of publication. So please, allow yourself some pride in your achievement.' He paused. 'With an accountant's eye, I can tell you that he will be making a great deal more money than you will be.'

'That's fine by me. After all, he's the one taking the risk – I'm only writing the story.'

'Each individual paper contains one instalment of one story,' he continued, musingly. 'If we assume he pays the writer seven and six, then add on the costs of printing and the paper itself . . . buying in bulk is always cheaper, and of course they only need to set the press up once, which is much more cost-efficient . . . Anyway,' he concluded, 'he sells *thousands* of copies at one penny each. He's probably making between ten and twenty pounds profit on every issue.'

'I don't care about all that,' said Betty. 'All I know is I'm made up for Jemima, 'cos she deserves it.' She engulfed Jemima in a hug. 'Beauty, brains *and* money, eh? You won't want to know us.'

'Oh, stop it.' Jemima was embarrassed. 'It's just a bit of luck and I'll need to work hard to keep it all going. And we don't know – he might decide not to renew at the end of twenty episodes.'

'Yes, but you'll still have . . . I don't know how much you'll have, but twenty lots of seven and six. If you put some of it by then you'll still be in credit.'

Jemima looked at Henry, but he'd turned away and was beginning to shuffle papers on the table. 'Oh, of course,' she said. 'Your examination is next Monday, isn't it? You'll need to work and I'm getting in your way, sorry.'

'No, it's not—'

'I'll go outside. It's time for school, in any case.'

There were ten children waiting outside for Jemima this morning, two of whom weren't even from houses in the same yard but had been invited by their friends. She was pleased to welcome them, but worried about having to share only four broken slates between them all before realising, still in a state approaching disbelief, that it would soon not be a problem to buy some more. She intended to offer Mrs Whiting four shillings a week, which she knew was above the odds for a shared bed in a shared room, but she hoped that Mrs Whiting wouldn't be aware of that and would take it anyway. That would still leave Jemima three and six, which would give her more personal money than she'd ever had, even after allowing sixpence for paper, ink and postage each week.

It was just possible, she admitted to herself, that she wasn't concentrating as fully as she normally would during the morning's lessons. But she was so happy that it spread through the little group, which laughed and giggled as it learned before breaking up at dinnertime. One of the new children, a girl who looked about six or seven, even ran up and hugged Jemima before she went, exclaiming, 'I never knew school was like this!'

Jemima collected the slates and found herself the object of attention among the yard's women, who were taking advantage of the fine weather to air their laundry. They all smiled at her, making comments about how they never thought to see the day when their children would go to school or even want to have lessons. 'Katie showed me how she can write her name,' called one, appearing from behind a row of shirts. 'Well I never!'

A second woman, whom Jemima recognised as Eddie's mother, sidled over. 'He's doing so well,' Jemima told her. 'Not just with his writing, but his arithmetic too.'

'That's what I wanted to talk to you about,' said the woman, in a low voice. 'Can I ask, are you going to keep doing this once real school starts again, or is it only in the break?'

Her demeanour and tone told Jemima straight away that the question was being posed from a financial point of view. Why pay the pennies to send Eddie to school when he could learn the same for free in his own back yard? The extra money would no doubt be wanted in the household soon, judging by the size of the woman's swelling belly.

Jemima tried to let her down gently. 'I'm hoping to have a new position at a school myself in September, so I'll be there every day, which means I won't be able to do this as well. I'm sorry for it, really, because I enjoy it so much, and it's lovely to teach children who want to learn, but it's a wage, and . . .'

The woman nodded in understanding. 'You have to earn your living as well as anyone else,' she sighed. After a pause, she added, 'You're an orphan yourself, I understand?'

'Yes.' To her surprise, Jemima found she could answer the question without tears springing immediately to her eyes.

'Well, you're in the best place with Betsy and Harry. Crowded there, I know, but kinder neighbours you couldn't wish to have.'

Jemima knew these were the first names of Mr and

Mrs Whiting, and she nodded in fervent agreement. 'I'm so lucky.' And, despite everything that had happened to her recently – not only with Pa but with Mrs Lewis and Mrs Silverton – she realised that she truly meant what she said.

* * *

On Monday afternoon Jemima found herself walking to the library with Henry. She'd offered to help with wash day, but Mrs Whiting had very tactfully made it plain that she would merely be in the way, so she'd proceeded with school in the morning and felt it better to make herself scarce after that.

Henry was on his way to the examination, which was to take place in one of the lecture rooms at the library, and Jemima had decided to start on the next few instalments of *Stowaway Tom* in the Students' Room there. With so many episodes to write she would need to send her hero to more exotic and far-flung places than he'd been to before, and, although most of the readership probably wasn't all that well informed about such locations, she wanted to get at least a few basic facts right. The reference section of the library would have atlases and so on, plus she could make a small saving by using their ink.

They went their separate ways once they were inside the main building, Henry to go upstairs and Jemima to turn towards the library.

As luck would have it, once she reached the reference desk she was confronted by the same clerk she'd seen previously. She wasn't about to waste even a single minute in arguing this time, so she merely skewered him with a look while asking for an atlas and any other works he could find on deepest Africa, noting that she'd be waiting at her desk for them. Then she swept off into the Students' Room before he could reply.

The books arrived and were placed on the table with a less offended air than they had been last time, and Jemima got to work.

She was still engrossed in sketching out new adventures when she was disturbed by the sound of a throat clearing just behind her, and she turned to find Henry.

'What's happened?' she asked, confused. 'Was the examination not today?'

'Um, yes? It's over, so I came down to see if you were still here.'

Jemima looked at the clock on the wall and was startled to find that she'd been sitting at the desk for two and a half hours.

'Tom has been to many places this afternoon, I gather,'

said Henry, in a voice low enough not to be overheard by anyone studying nearby.

'Yes, he has, and I've learned a great deal,' replied Jemima, starting to gather up her papers.

'May I carry those back to the desk for you?' Henry stacked the weighty reference volumes.

After dropping the books at the counter they made their way out into the late-afternoon sunshine and set off.

'So, how was it?' asked Jemima. 'The examination, I mean.'

'I think it was all right. That is to say, I didn't show any company making a loss when the question asked me to determine profit, and I believe my calculations were mostly correct, but we'll have to see.'

'How long must you wait?'

'I can come back on Friday morning for my result. And then, hopefully, set out on Saturday or next Monday to find a job. Having the certificate, assuming I get one, will be a real help. In fact, one of the other candidates said he'd heard that some businesses actually send representatives to the results day, to make offers to the best performers.'

'Well, I'm sure you'll be one of them. And your parents will be proud of you, I know.' Jemima surprised herself by only just avoiding the addition of *And so will I.*

She had certainly been less awkward and more comfortable in Henry's company recently – was this what it was like having a brother?

They walked on, Henry now with only the slightest trace of a hobble. Jemima had previously heard him saying to his father that he thought the residual limp might be permanent, but Mr Whiting's reply was that somebody would only notice if they were looking for it, and anyway, if he were to get a collar-and-tie job he'd spend much of his time sitting down, so it wouldn't signify.

When they reached Duke Street they both paused to look in the shop windows. The new instalment of the Dickens serial was available, and Jemima thought to herself that she would soon be able to count herself as a writer of serial literature, albeit at a much humbler level. Oh, and anonymously, of course, because unlike Dickens or any other man, her fledgling career would be over if anyone ever found out who she was.

She sighed loudly enough for Henry to hear. 'Sorry, I'm dawdling,' he said. 'Were you in a hurry to get back?'

'Oh, nothing like that. I was just thinking about . . . all sorts of things.'

'About how clever you are, I hope, and how you're going to get your just reward.'

'Clever? Goodness, I'm not—'

'Careful, now.'

'Careful what? I mean – why should I be careful?'

'Because you're starting to sound like Ma. "If a girl is clever, she should try to hide it." Be modest and retiring, and so on.'

'No, it's just . . .' Jemima recognised that this was exactly what she was doing. 'I suppose I was,' she admitted.

'And, while we're on the subject of intelligence, I'm sorry I upset you with what I said about the accountancy book the other day.'

'What do you mean, you upset me?'

'Didn't I?'

Jemima tried to recall the scene. 'Oh, of course, that was it. You said I could learn all about accountancy, and I said there was no point because nobody would employ me.'

'Yes. And I can only apologise again if you thought I was making a joke at your expense, because I most certainly was not.'

She remembered his hurt expression as she'd spoken. 'No, it's I who should be sorry. I was just upset because it was only just after what had happened in the news office – you know, what I told you about, and . . .'

Enlightenment dawned on Henry's face.

'Anyway,' said Jemima, 'I won't be training as an accounts clerk, but I *do* know a lot more about darkest Africa than I did yesterday.'

'Good for you. Learning is never wasted.'

'That's just what my Pa used to say.'

'Oh, sor—'

'Please don't apologise,' Jemima said, in a rush. 'You're not upsetting me, and it's nice to be reminded of him.'

'Perhaps . . . would you like to talk about him? Tell me about him?'

'I would, actually,' said Jemima, truthfully. 'Now I'm coming more to terms with the idea that he's really gone, I'd like to – I want to – I *need* – to talk about him, so he stays alive in my mind.'

'In that case, I'd like to listen.'

They resumed walking.

* * *

The following morning, Henry presented himself in the yard just before school was due to start. 'I wondered if I might be allowed to join you,' he said to Jemima. 'I can't look for work until I know whether I've got the certificate or not, so I'm more or less at leisure until Friday, except for helping Ma out in the house now and then.'

Jemima bit back a light-hearted retort about the commotion that would be caused in the yard by the sight of a man helping with laundry or cleaning. She'd very much enjoyed talking to Henry yesterday, and felt they understood each other a little better after several misunderstandings, so the last thing she wanted was to jeopardise that by being flippant. She also recalled what he'd said to her on the day of Pa's funeral, about wanting to be a teacher and never having had the opportunity. 'Of course you can. But do bear in mind that they're all only little, so nothing too advanced for them, please. I want them to *enjoy* being here, not get sad and upset because they think they can't keep up.'

In the event Jemima was quite glad that Henry had offered to help, because today fourteen children turned up. Two of the newcomers, a girl of about nine or ten and a younger boy, were very ragged indeed. They hung back until Jemima caught their eye, at which point the girl said, 'We heard we could come and learn letters.' Her tone was both belligerent and defensive, as though she was expecting to be sent away with boxed ears.

Jemima smiled. 'That's right.'

'And it doesn't cost nothing?' The child was sceptical beyond her years, probably with good cause.

'That's right, it doesn't cost anything,' said Jemima, gently. 'All you have to do is want to learn.'

'We do. And my brother Joey,' she prodded the boy so he took half a pace forward, 'he's clever, he is, but nobody's ever taught him anything.'

'I'm very glad to hear it. And I'm sure you'll do well, too. You're both very welcome.'

The two children still seemed hardly to believe what they were hearing, but they sat themselves cross-legged, bare feet tucked under them, on the very outer edge of the group.

Jemima now found that she had to divide her school into three classes: one for the new absolute beginners, one for those who had been with her a couple of weeks already, and the more advanced set of Maisie, Ralph and Eddie. She entrusted the latter to Henry and turned to the others, wondering how in the world she was supposed to manage with only four slates.

Fortunately it turned out that chalk could be used to write on the paving stones of the yard, as well as on the slates, so they got along quite easily. Little Joey did indeed pick up the idea of letters and numbers very quickly, holding the chalk in his left hand as he scratched his marks. Back at St James's that had been forbidden, with children coerced into using their right hands, but Jemima saw no reason why he shouldn't just work in whatever way suited him best.

Joey's sister, Mary, also proved to be a keen pupil.

Initially she was more concerned with pushing him to learn and trying to help him, but she soon became engrossed herself, her tongue sticking out as she copied the strange symbols that were now starting to mean something. By the end of the lesson she could produce a creditable upper-case *M*.

She remained staring at it, chalked on the ground, long after the school was dismissed. '*M* for Mary,' she said, in a wondering tone. 'And you've done *J* for Joey, and what's that other one?'

'It's for Alfie,' he explained, pointing to a more or less recognisable *A*.

Jemima looked up from wiping the slates. 'Is that another brother?'

Joey nodded without speaking.

'Well, he's welcome too, if he wants to come.'

'We buried him yesterday,' said Mary.

'And he was only four,' added Joey, 'so he'd be too little to come anyway.' He gazed down at the letter *A* and sighed.

Jemima felt tears coming to her eyes and wanted to sweep them both up into her arms to comfort them. But she wasn't sure how they might react to such a gesture from a stranger, so instead she crouched down so she could speak to them on their level. 'I'm truly sorry to hear that,' she said, gently. 'I'm sure that you loved him, and you'll miss him very much. And I'm also sure that you were the best brother and sister he could have had.'

Mary put her arms protectively round Joey. 'I used to help look after him,' she said. Then panic came into her eyes. 'But it weren't my fault he died, honest – Ma said so when I was crying.'

'Of course it wasn't!' Jemima tried to soothe her. 'It can't have been your fault at all.'

'He had a fever,' said Joey, firstly to Jemima and then twisting to look at his sister. 'Anyone can get them, and you know his ear was bad for a long time, and that wasn't nobody's fault, specially not yours.'

Mary clutched him more tightly. 'Anyway, we'd better get back. You say thank you to the lady, now.'

'Thank you, miss,' said Joey, politely.

His words were echoed by Mary, who hesitated before adding, 'And . . . we can come back tomorrow?'

'Of course you can. I'll look forward to seeing you.'

Jemima watched them run out of the yard.

'Are you all right?' Henry had been standing quietly throughout.

'I . . . I'm not sure, actually. Those poor children.'

'What a loss for them.' He glanced at the house, the door of which was open to show Mrs Whiting bustling about inside. 'Sometimes I can't get over how lucky we are.'

'You've never . . .'

'Lost anyone? No. Not even with two sets of twins in the family. We're blessed and I don't know why, but I'm thankful for it.' He looked fondly at his mother. 'It was bad enough when Harriet went into service, and then Anna did too, even though they're both less than a mile away. The idea of us all being split up, or even of losing someone, is just . . . I don't know how Ma would cope. I don't know how any of us would.'

Jemima said nothing. Henry was still looking at her in concern, probably assuming that she had Pa in her mind. And so she did, but she was also thinking of her other family. She wondered whether the rest of them had stayed together after they moved away, or whether they were scattered. Perhaps there were separated brothers and sisters all over Liverpool or even beyond, each wondering what had happened to the others and destined never to find out.

'This morning went well,' Jemima said, to change the subject. 'You're a natural teacher, from what I could see.'

'Really?'

'Yes. And it was very nice to have you here. But I don't know what we're going to do if any more children want to come. Except,' she said, recalling the situation with a flush of joy, and still hardly able to credit it, 'Mr Grundy is going to send the money order for the first two instalments, so as soon as I've cashed that, I can buy some more slates.'

'And as soon as I've earned my first money, I'll do the same.'

'Oh, you don't have to do that . . .'

'I don't have to, but I want to. This is such a wonderful enterprise of yours, and I want to support it.' He looked around the yard. 'But you've been lucky with the weather so far – what will you do when it rains? If it was just our Maisie and Ralph, and maybe Eddie, Ma wouldn't mind you coming inside and sitting round the table, but she's not going to want dozens of children she doesn't know piling in.'

'I know.' Jemima sighed. 'But I think we'll have to cross that bridge when we come to it. Your Pa thinks the weather will hold at least a week.'

'Well, I can join you each morning up until Friday, if you'll have me, and we'll hope for sunshine and roses at least until then.'

It was Mr Whiting who solved one of the school's problems that evening, when he came home from work with a sizeable piece of broken board. 'From an old place being torn down,' he explained. 'No good for using again, as it's had woodworm, so it was going on the fire. I asked if I could have it, all above board, so to speak' – he paused to chuckle at his own joke – 'and

I thought you could write the whole alphabet on it, for your littl'uns to copy.'

'Oh, how wonderful!' Jemima was effusive in her thanks, and Maisie ran over to kiss her father on the cheek.

Unfortunately, not everyone was as enthusiastic or as supportive as Mr Whiting when it came to the school's expansion. The yard's mothers, who had thought it a fine thing to occupy their own offspring, were markedly less keen on the arrival of more and more children they didn't know, especially the dirty, ragged ones. Jemima heard murmurings about how this was a respectable place – that word again – not one of those terrible courts, and they didn't hold with grubby urchins coming in, when they had places of their own, and no doubt spreading lice while they were at it.

Jemima and Henry were able to ignore this for a couple of days, and Jemima's excitement when she received her money order and took it to the Post Office was more for the prospect of slates for the children than for herself. She was delighted with their progress, and was even starting to wonder if lessons might be continued in some way even once she had a new job as well as her writing commitments. She hummed to herself as she returned with the precious coins on Thursday afternoon, looking at the part of the yard that was now called 'school corner' by almost everyone, and stepping carefully around the chalked *A* that she hadn't had the heart to erase.

* * *

Friday was the day Henry was to receive his examination results, which would be available as of nine o'clock in the morning. He set off in good time and Jemima thought of him throughout most of the morning's lessons, which she undertook with Maisie's help and with a few unfriendly eyes cast towards the now twenty-strong group.

Jemima was calculating in her head how long it would take Henry to walk to the library, get his result and come back. If they were ready exactly on time and he really hurried on his way home, he might be expected any time from *now*, but of course he wouldn't be that quick; he would stop and chat to some of the other students. Even then he should probably be back round about *now*, but then again, if he'd also stopped to take out a book from the library while he was there, or dawdled on his way through town . . .

Henry did not arrive.

Jemima wasn't the only one who was worried by dinnertime. She dismissed the children and took her things back inside to find Mrs Whiting and Betty looking glum as they sewed. She joined them at the table, taking up a needle herself; Mrs Whiting had recently bought a length of calico and there was plenty of work to be done in making new shirts for Mr Whiting, Henry and Rob, while also salvaging pieces of their old garments that still had some wear in them in order to turn them into smaller ones for everyone else down the line.

'What can possibly be keeping him?' fretted Mrs Whiting. 'Surely he knows that he doesn't need to be afraid to come back and say so, even if he's failed.'

Betty bit off the end of a piece of thread. 'I can't understand it. If it was Rob or any of his friends, I'd say they'd gone to the pub and hadn't come out of it yet, but not Henry.'

Jemima looked over at the corner shelf, where *Book-keeping and Accountantship* was lying. She'd had a look through it herself, just out of interest, and she was absolutely sure that someone as clever and diligent as Henry must have learned enough from it to pass any examination on the subject. But if that was the case, where was he?

That question was answered at half past four in the afternoon, when he burst in with more energy than she'd ever seen him display and a broad smile on his face.

Mrs Whiting turned from stirring a pot on the fire. 'Henry?'

He threw his arms about her. 'I passed, Ma.'

She exclaimed in delight, and so did Betty and Jemima. 'But why didn't you come back to tell us straight away?' asked Betty, clouting him on the shoulder. 'We've been that worried about you!'

'Ah,' he said. 'That's because I have even better news.' He stepped back. 'I think I might have mentioned that some businesses send representatives to results day. It turns out that I had the highest marks, so some of them wanted to talk to me.'

'And? Oh, Henry, don't leave us in suspense or I swear I'll wallop you,' said Betty.

'Well, two of them invited me to come to their premises on Monday for an interview, because they have positions available. And a third had a short job that he was looking for someone to do straight away, just to check through one book of accounts. So I sat down and did it for him, and he paid immediately.' He reached into his pocket and pulled out some coins. 'I'm sorry I've had no money to give you for a while, Ma, but this is for you now, and the first of many more, I hope.' He put five shilling pieces down on the table.

'Now, you know I've told you not to feel bad about that,' said his mother, hugging him again before she made any move towards the money. 'It wasn't your fault you had that accident, and you've worked hard at what you could do in the meantime.' Now she looked at the coins. 'My, my, though – five shillings, for work that took you half a day?'

'And all for you, with my love.'

'No,' she said, decisively. 'Rules is rules, and you get some of it back to spend on yourself.' Mrs Whiting pushed two of the shillings back at him.

Henry pushed one of those back at her. 'All right. I can think of a few things to spend a shilling on' – he glanced at Jemima – 'but we'll wait to see what I can bring in regularly before we decide anything else.'

There was great celebration in the house that evening, with the whole family – regardless of each individual's views on education – congratulating Henry. Jemima was so pleased for him.

There was just one brief moment of tension, when Mr Whiting said that he'd ask at the building site tomorrow morning about a job for Henry there.

'But, Pa, I don't want—' began Henry, before checking himself. 'All right. But don't make any firm arrangements, because I've already agreed to go to those interviews on Monday, and it would be rude not to.'

'Best try them all,' said Rob, making a rare entry to the family conversation, 'and see which will pay the best. I know Pa wants to keep us all together, but if someone else will pay more then it makes sense to take that.'

Jemima saw Henry throw his brother a grateful look.

'All right,' said Mr Whiting, lighting his pipe and evidently not wanting to argue about it. 'I'll try to find the foreman tomorrow. I need to ask him about Bert, anyway, 'cos I haven't had the chance to speak to him since I said I'd do that. He hasn't been around on the site much for a while – too busy having meetings with the bosses about money and costs and plans.'

* * *

After the workers had left on Saturday morning, Henry turned to Jemima. 'School this morning?'

She looked out at the sunshine. 'Yes! It looks like our luck is still holding.'

'Good. I'll help, if I may, and then afterwards I'll get out to the shops before they close.'

'You really don't have to spend your money on slates.'

'But I want to.' He lowered his voice. 'I thought I might also buy something for Ma, if I can. She deserves a treat.'

Jemima replied in an undertone, though Mrs Whiting was busy on the other side of the room washing children's faces, and probably wouldn't have heard anything less than a bellow. 'What a lovely idea.'

'I wondered,' he said, with deliberate nonchalance, 'whether you might like to come with me?'

'I would, thank you.'
'Well, then.'
'Well.'
The sounds of children protesting against the scratchy facecloth continued, all the louder when set against the sudden silence surrounding Jemima and Henry.

* * *

'The thing is,' said Jemima, as they peered in the window of the stationer's, 'that I'd really like to find a way to carry on with the school, but I just don't see how.'

'I agree,' said Henry, 'on both counts. Look, those new slates are threepence each, but there's a sign saying they're selling off some scratched and damaged ones at a penny apiece. They'll do, won't they? If I buy six, I'll still have sixpence to find something for Ma.'

'Yes, I think quantity is more important than quality. I've got sixpence too, so I'll buy another two and put the rest towards your mother's present. Which reminds me, I haven't spoken to her and your Pa about rent yet. I must do that this evening.'

'That's kind, but will it leave you enough for paper and stamps? And how is Stowaway Tom getting on?'

'He's on his way to Africa,' said Jemima, the shop bell ringing as they stepped inside. She laughed. 'That would sound very odd if you didn't know that I was talking about a story! But in practical terms, I have the third instalment already finished and ready to send, the fourth drafted and good ideas for the next three after that.'

They paid for the damaged slates, the shopkeeper glad to get them off his hands, and left.

'What do you think your mother would like?'

Henry blew out a breath. 'I don't know. Diamonds? Jewels? A carriage and horses?'

'You'd be hard put getting that for tenpence.'

'True, true.'

'What would she say, if you asked her?'

'She'd say,' said Henry, drily, 'that she didn't need anything and I should save my money. Either that or she'd ask me for something for someone else, like wool to knit Ralph's socks, or cotton to make caps for Tilly, or something really extravagant like new dishcloths. Pa's much easier, because you can always get him tobacco for his pipe, but Ma?'

Jemima thought for a few moments. 'Has she got a shawl? I haven't seen her wearing one, but she wouldn't need it in this weather. And that would be something that was useful *and* just for herself.'

'That's a good idea. She has, yes, but it's very old and threadbare. But I have no idea how much one would cost – are we likely to find something for tenpence?'

'Not a new one, no, and not in any of the shops round here. But if we set our sights a little lower, and look carefully, we might find something.'

They headed in the direction of St John's market; not into the great building itself, but to the rather more informal marketplace that existed outside it, where various vendors displayed their wares in baskets or on blankets laid on the ground. There were a number of women selling clothes, and Jemima rummaged through until she found a nice woollen shawl that was certainly not new, but still had plenty of wear in it. 'It's got one fraying edge,' she pointed out to Henry, 'but if we can smuggle it in to the house without her noticing, I can sew it up before you give it to her.'

'You don't mind?'

'Of course not! I just hope she likes it.'

Their luck was in, because when they got back Mrs Whiting was taking a few brief moments to chat to one of the other women in the yard, and they were able to slip past.

Jemima took the shawl up to the attic. She wasn't often up here during the day, and of course there was no table to work at, but she couldn't do the mending downstairs as Mrs Whiting was bound to come back in. She reached under the bed to pull out her bag and the little roll of needles and thread, then positioned herself to make best use of the bright sun streaming through the skylight and set to work.

Sewing was the sort of task that occupied the hands but left the mind free, and Jemima's now wandered over all sorts of subjects as she inserted neat stitches. The little school, obviously, and how it might be continued . . . schools generally, and her forthcoming trial day . . . possibility of a new job . . . would have to walk past Mrs Lewis's boarding house . . . that terrible day . . . money . . . pawn shop . . . books . . .

Books.

The flower book was still in Jemima's bag. She couldn't see it from where she was sitting, but she knew it was there. Her absolute unwillingness to look at it had faded as the days and weeks had gone by, and now she wondered if she might be curious enough, and brave enough, to pick it up. It was something that had been very special to Pa and Ma, so did she have the strength to look through it without crying as she thought of them? Or might it even give her courage, to be reading something in the knowledge that they had read it too?

As she finished the hem and knotted the thread, Jemima's resolve became more steadfast. She would look at the flower book. She would do it now, while there was plenty of light and she was alone in the room.

She'd just folded the shawl on her lap, and was actually

in the act of reaching for the volume, when the sound of a scream came from downstairs.

It was quickly stifled, but it was enough for Jemima to forget everything else and rush down to the main room, where she found Mr and Mrs Whiting, Henry and Rob. Betty was just shooing several of the smaller children outside, after which she took the unusual step of shutting the door on them.

Mrs Whiting was sitting down in pale shock, having presumably been the origin of the scream. Mr Whiting looked hardly better as he wrung his hands, while Henry and Rob wore grim expressions.

'What is it?' cried Jemima, her first thought being that there had been some kind of accident, that one of the family was hurt, lost . . .

She had addressed the question mainly at Betty, but also to the room as a whole, and it was Mr Whiting who answered. 'It's work, lass.' He stared at her, his eyes a little wild. 'And it was you who spotted the danger, an' all. I should've listened to you.'

Jemima was perplexed, not being able to recall having spotted any danger at his workplace, which she had never even seen.

'I was just telling Ma,' he continued, 'and you might as well know too, for there's no hiding it. I said, didn't I, that the foreman was in lots of meetings recently.

I finally found him today, and I asked about jobs for our Henry and our Bert, and he just laughed.'

'Laughed?' Jemima was recovering slightly. Nobody was injured, lost or dead, and if there were no more positions at the site then surely—

'Aye, a bitter laugh, like. He said not only was there no new jobs, but they had to lay off some who were already there. The money's run out, see, or someone's made a bad investment, or I don't know exactly what he said, but they're stopping and they're not going to do any more terraces for the time being. So the long and the short of it is that I've lost my job, and so have Rob and Matthew. We've been paid today, but now me and my four eldest sons haven't got one job or the prospect of one further shilling between us.'

Chapter 11

No wonder Mrs Whiting had screamed. This was a disaster of truly epic proportions, and at first Jemima could hardly take it in. The main breadwinner losing his job was always terrible, but to lose the supplementary earnings from his sons – and with Rob no doubt almost on full men's wages by now – was almost unthinkable. And with Henry not earning after his accident and Betty on the school summer break, too.

It was all happening again, misfortune and catastrophe falling on the Whitings just as it had struck Pa down. It wasn't *fair*. What would . . . ? How could they . . . ?

It was Mrs Whiting who recovered herself first. 'We've today's wages,' she said, firmly. 'And there's a bit put by in the tin. We can manage a week, maybe two, and you'll surely have found something else by then.'

Jemima was still frozen in shock, but this gave her a reminder. Money. She had some money. She would get it now.

As she tried to force her feet to move, she realised she was holding the shawl, which she must have grabbed to stop it falling off her lap when she jumped up.

Mrs Whiting noticed her. 'You look like you'd best sit down too, pet. I'm sorry you had to hear all that – it's not for you to fret about.'

Not quite sure what she was doing, Jemima held out the shawl. 'We just bought you this. Henry did. At the market. A present for you, as a treat.'

Now Mrs Whiting looked as though she wanted to cry. 'Well now, that was kind of you both. I'll put it by, and if we need to then we can . . .' She had to stop.

Jemima turned and ran upstairs. Her hands were shaking as she found her purse and hurried down again. She pushed it at Mrs Whiting. 'There's eighteen shillings and tenpence in there. I got fifteen shillings for those first two stories, though I had to keep back sixpence for paper and stamps, sorry, and then I had four shillings and fourpence left from the pawn-shop money after I'd bought those . . .' She tailed off, but she couldn't regret buying the slates for the children. And there would be no point in attempting to sell them back, damaged as they were.

At the sound of the words *pawn shop*, Mrs Whiting's mouth set in a line and she began to push the proffered purse away.

'Please,' Jemima almost begged, 'please take it. You've been so kind, taking me in when I had nothing and nobody, and you've never even charged me any rent. It's only right I should pay my way now I'm earning, just like everyone else.'

'A bit of rent, maybe,' said Mr Whiting, putting his arm round his wife. 'But eighteen, nearly nineteen shillings? No.'

'Please,' said Jemima, again. And then, pulling herself together as she had done that first day in the library, she was bold enough to add, 'I really must insist. And there'll be more in two weeks' time.'

That seemed to break the spell. 'You'll have found something else by then, Pa,' said Henry. 'And don't forget I've got those interviews on Monday.'

'In the meantime,' added Rob, 'if you can look for both of us, Pa, I can take myself down the docks and try to find some daily-paid work. One or two of the other lads who've been let go said they'd be doing the same.'

'Yes,' said Mr Whiting. 'Yes. It's not as black as it first seemed, love. I'm sorry, I shouldn't have come home and shocked you like that. I'll get out right now and see if there's anything doing anywhere. And even if there isn't, at this time on a Saturday, I'll be out at daybreak on Monday. There's bound to be work somewhere for a skilled builder.'

Mrs Whiting and Jemima both still had their hands on the purse, each trying to give it to the other. 'There, you see . . .' began Mrs Whiting.

'No, please take it,' said Jemima, equally now the mistress of herself. 'I want you to have it, and I'd be much happier if you did.'

The older woman was unsure, but perhaps some thought of hungry children came into her mind. 'I tell you what. I'll take it now, seeing as you're set on it. But I'm not taking the money out of it. This whole purse is going right at the bottom of the tin, and I'm only touching it if we *really* get desperate.'

Jemima agreed and watched as Mrs Whiting deposited it, adding to the tin the money her husband and sons had brought home. 'There. We'll be all right,' she said, sounding as though she was trying to convince herself as much as anyone else. 'Now, let's get that door open so the children and the neighbours don't fret that something dreadful's happened.'

Something dreadful has *happened*, thought Jemima. But in the world of the Whitings, lost jobs and lost income were much less important than family. They had not lost parents or children, and they could work through their troubles together.

All of a sudden, Jemima missed Pa more than ever.

* * *

The following morning Jemima put on her Sunday best and went to visit the churchyard. There were a few other people doing the same, she noticed, leaving flowers, praying or simply standing in contemplation.

As she reached the far side of the church, she was taken aback to see the figure of a young woman standing by Pa's grave. Jemima checked herself, thinking she might inadvertently have taken the wrong direction, but no – she was on the correct path and there really was someone there.

There was gravel underfoot, so she deliberately made as much noise as she could as she approached. The girl turned in alarm and began to flee, and Jemima could see that it was Sarah. The maid's face bore an expression of panic and fear, but it subsided as Jemima called her back. 'Thank goodness it's only you, miss.'

'Sarah. I didn't expect to see you here. How are you?' Jemima glanced past her at the grave, to see that on it lay a few wildflowers, the same type that grew around the edges of the churchyard.

'I'm sorry, miss.'

'Sorry? Why?'

'To be here in your way. But Mrs Lewis is out this morning, and I missed my half-day last week so I just slipped out for a bit of air.'

'And this is where you came?'

'There isn't time to go far, and . . . I did like your Pa, miss. Like I said, he was ever so kind to me, all the time I've been with Mrs Lewis, and I just thought it wouldn't do no harm if . . .' She tailed off, plainly expecting to be scolded, or worse.

'I think it's lovely of you to come,' said Jemima, warmly. 'I suppose you know that Pa didn't have any other family except me, and I can't get here all that often, so I'm glad you decided to visit.'

A rising hope, almost disbelieving, began to show on Sarah's face. 'Really?'

'Really. And I see you've even picked some flowers. I didn't bring any, but perhaps I can do the same if I can get away with it. When I can afford it, I'm going to buy some to plant in the ground, so they'll grow all year round.'

'Oh, that would be lovely, miss.'

'And please, there's no need to call me "miss". I know you were supposed to when we were Mrs Lewis's tenants, but that's not the case any more, and we've known each other such a long time. It's Jemima.'

Sarah seemed unsure at the thought of such a bold step. 'I know you had to leave, mi—Jemima, and I was sorry.' She looked down at the grave.

Jemima wondered if Sarah knew anything about Mrs Lewis and the stolen money, or whether she simply assumed that Jemima had left because Pa had died.

'Anyway, I'd better get back,' said Sarah. 'She won't be gone long and I'll get what for if I'm not there when she gets back. She'd probably hand me my notice.'

Jemima looked at the girl's pale face and tired eyes. 'Would that be such a bad thing?'

Sarah stared at her in horror. 'Lose my place? I'd never get another – Mrs Lewis keeps telling me how useless I am – and I'd have to go back to the workhouse. Even working for her is better than that, and there is some nice people at the house, sometimes.'

Sarah was on her way even as she spoke these last words, and Jemima watched her hurry off. There were so many people worse off than herself, and she shouldn't forget it.

Jemima spent an hour or so sitting on the grass next to the grave, as the early-morning dew dissolved into warmth. She didn't speak out loud, but in her head she related to Pa all the things that had been happening to her, the good and the bad. She told him about her little school, how much she loved it, and how she hoped it would help the children who had no other opportunities of learning. She asked him if he could come up with any ideas as to how they could keep the school going when they had no money, no time, no books and no classroom, and she herself had to concentrate on earning. She told him of how kind the Whitings had been, and how calamity had struck these good people through no fault of their own, and that she was sorry he wouldn't have a cross for his grave as soon as she'd like, because she had to use her money to help them.

What would Pa say to all this, if he could reply? Jemima had no doubts about that. He'd say that she shouldn't let her friends down. She must stay with the Whitings while they were going through this time of trouble, so she could pass over to them the entirety of the very generous pay she was getting. It wasn't merely fair, because they had taken her in; it was *right*, and she would have done it anyway, regardless of what she owed them. Her pay wasn't the same as a male breadwinner's wage, of course, but it all helped, and if she could get the teaching position in September as well, then that would be even better. The Whitings were her friends, and that's what friends were for: to help each other when they needed it. The thought of the family having to split up because they couldn't afford their home was just too awful to contemplate.

Family. Everything came back to family, didn't it, and Jemima's sense that she didn't really belong anywhere. She loved the Whitings, but she was still somehow apart from them, drifting and lost.

'What did you mean, Pa,' she whispered, breaking her silence, 'about my other family? Why did you leave it so long, until it was too late for you to tell me the whole story? All you've left me with is a trail of breadcrumbs that have been eaten before I can follow them.'

He had no reply to that, or none that Jemima could discern, so she got to her feet and brushed off her gown. Pa had left her one trail that she hadn't explored yet, and it was past time that she did. She was going to go back to the house, right this minute, and read the flower book.

* * *

It lay there, at the bottom of her bag, clearly visible now she'd moved everything else. Jemima took a deep breath, mustered as much courage as she could, and picked it up. *Flora Domestica; Or, The Portable Flower-garden.*

She was so nervous that the first thing she did was to drop the book on the floor, and some of the loose pages fell out. In consternation she got down on her hands and knees to gather them, looking to see if they were numbered so she could fit them back in correctly.

But the three sheets of paper on the floor were not pages from the book.

All this time, Jemima had assumed that the volume had been damaged when it had been thrown from the bookcase at the boarding house. The spine certainly was, but she'd been wrong about the pages; they were intact, and the papers she'd thought were loose pages were actually a handwritten letter, a long one, tucked away and hidden.

Was this what Pa had meant, when he'd urged her to find the volume? Was she about to get some answers, some clues as to her origins? Oh, *why* hadn't she looked at the book before? She was her own worst enemy.

But now Jemima wasn't sure if she wanted to. Nerves were overcoming her; her breathing was fast and shallow, and her hands were cold and clumsy. But this was it. This was what Pa had wanted her to do, his last wish before he died. For his sake, even if not for her own, she had to go on.

Jemima held the letter in her shaking hands and began to read.

Chapter 12

Sunday, July 6th, 1851

My dear Ellen,
You know I can't write very well, so I'm telling this to William and he's writing it down, so it will all be neat and spelled properly. If you have trouble with it, you can ask James to help. I know he can read because he lent me that book on flowers that time and he looks at newspapers.

I'm sending this in a letter because I know I won't be able to say it all properly if I come to see you, and anyway what I need to say is that I'm going to stop coming to see you altogether. This isn't because I've stopped loving dearest Jemima, in fact quite the opposite, but I need to do what's best for <u>her</u>, regardless of what I want.

It was the worst night of my life when Ma died having Jemima. You know that: you were there. You were at her side just like you'd been through all her other labours, looking after her. Then you came downstairs to tell me that she'd gone, and you put little Jemima in my arms. I held her for all the rest of that night, but we had nothing to feed her. I thought she was going to die, and I couldn't stand it, not losing her as well as Ma.

When you said that you and James would take her in, and find someone to nurse her, you saved her life. I thought it would just be for a while. I thought we would come and get her back as soon as we could. But things got worse for us, not better, as you know, and she stayed with you a long time.

It's taken us so long to get back on our feet that when I came to see you a few weeks ago, I could hardly believe how much Jemima had grown – a proper little girl now, three years old! And she ran in and called you 'Mama', and I could see how much she loved you, and how much you loved her.

I know that you already know all this part, but bear with me, please, because I have to say it. William says he'll write down my exact words even if it doesn't sound like a proper letter.

By then things were looking up a bit, but I knew I couldn't take Jemima away from you, no matter how much we wanted her back. It was too late. She had lived with you her whole life, and she truly believed that you and James were her Ma and Pa. We loved her too, but if we'd tried to take her back, she would have thought we were taking her <u>away</u> from her parents, and she would have been terribly upset. So we agreed that she would stay with you forever.

I cried a lot over this, afterwards, but we had to do what was best for Jemima even though it was such a sacrifice for us. Besides, you had been Ma's best friend all your lives, and losing her must have been just as terrible for you as it was for us. Having Jemima as a reminder of her, having a daughter you could share with her, if you know what I mean, might help you.

And now we're coming to the part you don't know. When you brought Jemima to my wedding, it made me so happy. I could get married with <u>all</u> my family around me, and you more than anyone know what I mean by that. And I wanted to see you and her again, see you all the time, and keep up with how Jemima was getting on, but I realised that I couldn't. It was just another thing *that would end up making her unhappy. At some point one of us would have let slip something about her having two families, or other brothers and sisters, or something, which would have confused her. The last thing any of us would want is for her to feel that she didn't fit properly, or that she wasn't really yours and James's daughter.*

So what I'm saying now, and what I wouldn't have the strength to say if I was standing in front of you, is that I will stop visiting you. It breaks my heart, but the best thing for Jemima is for her not to know anything about me or the rest of us here. To me she will always be Jemima Shaw, my beautiful sister, but to everyone else – to you, to the world and even to herself – she will be Jemima Jenkins. She will be much happier that way.

I'll leave it up to you whether you ever tell her any of this when she's older, but if you find it better not to, I'll understand. We all need to do what's best for her. If you ever do want to tell her, and she wants to find out more, you know where we'll be.

It's a good thing William is writing this. I'm crying so much while I talk that the paper would look terrible.

Although you can't say this to Jemima now, and she wouldn't understand if you did, we all love her with all our hearts. She'll have that love always, whether she knows about it or not.

I have to stop now. I hope you understand from all of this why you won't see me again. I wish you and James and dearest Jemima all imaginable happiness. Next time you kiss her, give her an extra one from me.

Love,
Delilah

Jemima sat with tears pouring down her cheeks.

She remained there for so long that her absence was noted and Betty came up to find her. 'Jemima? Are you up here? You've been – oh my word, what's the matter?'

Jemima choked on a sob and waved the letter.

Betty came to sit next to her and gently took the sheets out of her hand. 'Eighteen-fifty-one? What—?' Comprehension dawned. 'Is it something about your family? Your other family, I mean?'

Jemima nodded. 'They loved me,' she gulped. 'They didn't want to give me up, but they had to, because my mother died having me. Read it.'

'Oh, I can't . . .'

'Please. I need to talk to someone about it.'

Betty hesitated. 'If you're sure.'

She began to read in silence, and Jemima sat shivering

and trying to control herself. She pulled out a handkerchief to wipe her eyes and noticed that it was Pa's old one, with the 'JJ' in the corner. *Oh, Pa! This is what you meant when you told me to find the flower book. If only I'd realised sooner.*

It was some minutes before Betty finished and looked up. Her face was pale. 'Well. No wonder you were shocked.'

'But what shall I do?'

Betty hesitated. 'Jemima, I know I'm the only person you've told about this, but can I fetch Henry? Two heads are better than one – or three are better than two – and he might be able to help.'

Jemima considered for a moment and then nodded, so Betty went down to the next landing to call down to the main room. Henry was there, and Jemima heard him ascending the first flight of stairs. Then there was a whispered conversation.

'But I can't come up to your bedroom!' Jemima heard that clearly, as Henry had raised his voice a little in concern.

'Oh, don't be an idiot. You're our brother, and we're not undressed or anything.'

He murmured something else and they both came up. Jemima scrubbed her face with the handkerchief again.

Betty appeared first and resumed her position sitting next to Jemima, putting an arm around her. Henry perched tentatively on the very edge of the other bed.

Betty looked expectantly at Jemima.

'No, you tell, him, please. Tell him from the beginning.' Jemima couldn't face going through the whole story.

She listened as Betty explained to an increasingly stunned Henry about how Jemima's Pa had told her on his deathbed that she was adopted, but that he hadn't been able to give her enough information to trace the family she'd been born into.

Jemima was glad that Betty hadn't said 'real family'.

Betty touched on the fact that Jemima had been upset at finding out, and at the idea of being abandoned by her birth family. But today – just now, in fact – she'd found a letter that explained it all.

Henry's sympathy increased along with his astonishment. His eyes, as they met Jemima's, were . . . well. She dropped her gaze.

'So I suppose,' he began, in a soft tone, 'the question is, what are you going to do next?'

Jemima nodded.

'What have you found out? Enough to start a search?'

She held out the letter, pushing it into his hand when he didn't take it. 'Please.'

He echoed Betty's words. 'Are you sure?' At her nod, he looked down and then up again almost straight away. 'Ellen?'

'My Ma. My *real* Ma, I mean, the one who brought me up.'

Henry got through the letter more quickly than Betty had done, making only the occasional pause to expel a breath or to murmur. When he'd finished, he shook his head as he passed it back. 'That's an awful lot for you to take in all at once.'

'What do you think?' That was Betty.

He paused for a moment. 'I think you should let it all sink in a bit more before you make any kind of decision.'

Jemima nodded. 'That makes sense. It's all . . .' She didn't know what to say. There weren't really any words.

Henry looked at her earnestly. 'I tell you what – why don't we go out for a walk, just the three of us? We can go up to the paths at Saint James's. Plenty of other people will be doing the same, on a Sunday.'

Some air would be a very good idea, Jemima thought, and she stood up. Then she swayed.

Betty regarded her. 'You look better than you did a quarter of an hour ago, but you can still tell you've been crying, and Ma's bound to notice and ask about it.

Henry, you go down first and distract her, so we can slip past, and then you can come out as well.'

'Good idea.'

Their plan was successful and Jemima soon found herself outside with both of them, and headed for St James's. Not to the school, of course, but to the small park on the other side of the church, a rare green space within Liverpool, with pleasant serpentine paths winding around it. It was a popular location for leisurely strolls on a Sunday, so they didn't look at all out of place when they got there.

Jemima was still in something of a daze, and she tripped over her feet as they entered the first walk. Betty took her arm on one side and instructed Henry to take the other, which, after some hesitation, he did. Jemima felt herself to be supported both physically and emotionally, and she was thankful for having such good friends. She breathed in some of the flower-scented air.

They walked in silence for some while, the others obviously waiting until Jemima felt strong enough to speak.

Eventually, she did. 'Shaw. My name is Jemima Shaw, or at least it was when I was born.' Then she sighed. 'Pa did say it was something very common. There must be hundreds of Shaws in Liverpool.'

'Ah,' said Betty, in an encouraging tone. 'But now

you know your sister's Christian name, and there can't be many *Delilah* Shaws.'

Jemima shook her head. 'But Shaw would have been her name before she got married, and in the letter she mentions her wedding. So she'll have changed her name.'

'All right, then, let's think about the William who was writing the letter for her. William Shaw?'

Jemima saw the problem with that, and so did Henry, who replied. 'It doesn't actually say in the letter who he is. If he was Delilah's brother then yes, he'd be called Shaw. But it might be her husband, or even someone completely unrelated. And even if it is her brother, I would imagine that "William Shaw" is quite a common combination of names.'

'I suppose.' Betty was thoughtful for a few moments.

'I don't think there was a mention of a father, was there?' Henry added.

Jemima thought back. 'No.'

'Perhaps he was already dead by then?'

Jemima considered the idea. 'I suppose it makes sense. If they'd lost their breadwinner, that would explain why they got so poor and why they had to move out of their house. That wasn't in the letter, but Pa told me before he died that they'd been evicted from their house that was next door to ours in Brick Street.'

Henry sighed. 'You're probably right. So it's brothers

and sisters you're looking for, not parents. Some of whom might or might not still be called Shaw.'

They all fell into silence again. *Shaw*, Jemima kept thinking. *Shaw. I've seen that name somewhere, and quite recently, too. But where?*

Betty spoke again. 'There was a Shaw in all the news-sheets a couple of years ago, wasn't there? That soldier who was wrongly accused of something, and then it turned out he was actually really brave. Wasn't he called Shaw?'

He might well have been, but that wasn't it. Jemima was thinking of something much more recent, though she still couldn't put her finger on what. 'Besides,' she said out loud, 'I can't remember his Christian name, but I don't think it was William.'

'No,' said Betty. 'I think you're right. I'm sure it was something that began with an S, like his surname, 'cos I remember wondering why we didn't have a William or a Walter Whiting, or anything like that.'

They walked on. Jemima tried to admire the scenery.

She considered Delilah's words in the letter again, and the pain and anguish they so clearly represented. *This isn't because I've stopped loving dearest Jemima, in fact quite the opposite. We all love her with all our hearts. She'll have that love always, whether she knows about it or not.* And, heart-wrenchingly, *The last thing any of us would want is for her to feel that she didn't fit properly,* the very sentiment that had occupied Jemima's own mind for so long. Perhaps she and this sister might sometimes think alike; perhaps Delilah might still love Jemima now, if they could find each other. What if—

'But this is all irrelevant,' said Henry, 'until we have the answer to the most important question. Which is: do you *want* to try to find them?'

The daze returned, and Jemima's head was so full that she couldn't think straight.

'There's no need for you to decide now,' said Henry. 'This new information isn't going anywhere, so let's just walk for now. If you decide you want to look for them, a really close examination of that letter might give us more clues.'

'Us?' The word cut through Jemima's stupor. 'You'd help me?'

'Of course we would!' That was Betty, squeezing Jemima's arm. 'Friends are friends through thick and thin, and we'll do everything that we can. Even if it might end up in you leaving us once you find your family.'

Henry said nothing, but Jemima felt his arm tense.

'Let's just walk for now,' she said, 'and enjoy the sunshine.'

Jemima's thoughts were still jumbled when they got back to the house, but they came into much sharper focus when Mrs Whiting served up tea, which consisted of boiled potatoes only. Although the family workers had brought home wages only yesterday, there was no way of predicting when they might have any more, so she was already beginning to practise a stricter economy, dousing the fire as soon as the pot was boiled and managing to salvage a few half-burnt coals to push to one side for tomorrow's use.

As Jemima ate, and as she watched both parents trying to deflect the questions and complaints of their children at this unusually frugal Sunday meal, she knew she could not leave them. *Friends are friends through thick and thin*, Betty had said, along with *Your problems are my problems*, the latter on the very day Jemima had been made homeless and then welcomed with such generosity into the Whiting household. She couldn't leave them, because they would need her money until they got back on their feet, and who knew when that would be? And she couldn't really even start her search, because that would take her time and attention away from the Whitings when they needed her efforts most. She could *never* be responsible, even in part, for forcing them to split up through lack of means, not when she could help. It would be the most appalling, most selfish act imaginable, and Pa would be bitterly disappointed in her.

In a month of momentous upheaval, it was the greatest irony and sadness of all that Jemima had finally found a means of searching for her long-lost family at exactly the time when it was impossible for her to do so.

Chapter 13

Jemima didn't mention the subject again that evening, and neither Betty nor Henry brought it up, for which she was grateful. Trying to explain to their faces her reasons for deciding against beginning a search would be very difficult, because she knew that they would both immediately make light of their family's needs and tell her that she should concentrate on her own.

She roused herself enough to try out a new episode of *Stowaway Tom* on the children, which went down well.

Maisie was sitting on the floor with her head resting on Jemima's knee. She yawned comfortably, and then asked, 'Why are stories always about boys?'

Matthew's response was immediate and scornful. 'Because nobody wants to hear stories about *girls*.'

'I do. I'd like to hear one.'

'But what would they do? A story about cooking and

washing – that'd make a fine exciting adventure, wouldn't it?'

'That's not all that girls do!' Maisie was sitting up straight now.

'Ha—' began Matthew, until Henry and Betty both waded in to try to keep the peace, the former by starting on a rational explanation, and the latter by the simple expedient of telling her younger brother to keep his mouth shut, or else.

'It's not, is it?' asked Maisie, addressing Jemima. 'Girls can do things that aren't just cooking and cleaning.'

'That's right,' said Jemima, soothingly. Then, with a glance over at the indefatigable Mrs Whiting, knitting in almost complete darkness, she added, 'Although that's not to say that cooking and cleaning aren't important. Where do you think your family would be, if your Ma didn't work so hard all day?'

Matthew looked as though he might be on the verge of interrupting this with a retort; but, happily for his own health, he decided against it. Maisie stuck her tongue out at him.

'Bed, now, all of you,' said Mr Whiting, placidly, from behind the toddler on his knee. 'Here, Matthew, take Benjy up with you, and let your elders and betters get some peace and quiet.'

Peace and quiet were available in abundance after the

children had gone up, for none of the others felt like talking, and each sat silent in their own way. Jemima tried to take her mind off family matters by wondering how she would go about telling or writing stories about girls, and what they might feasibly get up to in terms of adventures without straining the bounds of credulity too much.

Her attempt at distraction was moderately successful until she went to bed, because she was then assailed by a vivid dream – or was it a memory, surfacing because she was half-asleep and her mind was open to it?

She was with Ma, and they were in a church. Jemima had a flower in her hair that she could not help playing with. It was a wedding, she now understood: Ma pointed out the pretty lady walking up the aisle on the arm of a man in a suit. As with Jemima's earlier recollection of the scene at home, what she could mainly see of everyone was their legs, because she was so small and they were big. All except one: a little girl of around five years old, who was also walking up the aisle, and who was carrying a whole bunch of flowers. *Flowers*. Why were there always flowers, and why was this so important?

There was some talking from the front of the church, to which little Jemima paid scant attention. Then people started to leave, and Ma picked Jemima up and carried her out. She knew that her arms were wound around

Ma's neck, and the touch of her face and her hair, the smell of her clean skin, almost made the older Jemima cry, half-asleep in bed as she was.

Outside, Ma paused to talk to someone. A woman with black hair. Was she the bride? In her dream, Jemima couldn't picture the face, but she had the impression of smiles and happiness. The woman gave Jemima a kiss, and then a flower from her bouquet. Jemima clutched it in her hand all the way home, by which time it was hot and wilted, but she continued to treasure it for the rest of the day, and put it under her pillow that night.

Jemima awoke, her hand beneath the pillow as she searched for a flower that wasn't there.

* * *

It was a very sober and different kind of Monday morning.

Mrs Whiting was up early, as usual, and had already boiled several kettlefuls of water for the washtub before anyone else stirred. But then, instead of setting off together for work, Mr Whiting, Rob and Matthew went their separate ways. The boys were off to the docks, to queue up for any daily-paid labour that might be available whenever ships arrived and needed to be unloaded, while their father visited some of the city's many building sites to explain his and his family's experience, and to ask if they had any vacancies.

And then it was Henry's turn to leave. He was wearing a shirt that had been laundered to a pristine whiteness, and so ferociously starched that it could probably have stood up by itself, and to this he fastened an even stiffer collar. There was a little shaving mirror over by the sink, and he tied a tie with careful precision before turning to the rest of the household. 'How do I look?'

'Just lovely, my dear,' said Mrs Whiting, giving his jacket a final unnecessary brush before passing it to him.

'Do I look like the sort of fellow you'd want to employ as an accounting clerk or a bursar's assistant, though? That's the question.'

'I'd employ you,' said Betty, loyally.

Henry turned to Jemima. 'Wish me luck.'

'I do,' she replied. 'Though I'm sure you don't need luck. And . . .' she lowered her voice, 'I hope you get the one you want.'

Everyone knew that Henry had two job interviews that day, but he had confided only to Jemima, as they were tidying up the yard after lessons, that he had a decided preference for one of them, the position of bursar's assistant in a private boys' school. It wasn't teaching, of course, but it was at least in a school, and who knew what opportunities might come up in due course? The other was to work as an accounting clerk, one of many, in the office of one of Liverpool's largest grain merchants. It was certainly a decent job and one he was qualified for, but his heart lay in teaching, and the nearer he could get to it, the better. However, given the unemployment of his father and brothers, the most important thing was that he should be offered one or the other, and this was uppermost in his mind.

Henry kissed his mother. 'Nobody at the interviews will look smarter than me, that's for sure.'

'Will you have time to come back in between, for your dinner?'

'I shouldn't think so. May I take some bread?'

Mrs Whiting paused with the knife in her hand. 'I don't know whether it's the done thing, in these fancy offices and schools, to bring your dinner with you. What if they think it's common? I don't want you having to feel ashamed.'

'Ma, I would *never* be ashamed—'

'Best to make sure. Here.' She put down the knife, went to the money tin and dug out a sixpence, which she held out to him.

'Ma . . .'

'You take it, and don't argue. It's an investment,' she

added. 'What if they think you're qualified but then they take on someone else, 'cos he's got better manners, or says he's going out to a chop house for his dinner?'

Henry still hesitated, but she opened his hand, slapped the coin into it and closed his fingers around it. 'Now, you do as you're told, and get going before you make yourself late.'

He did so, and Mrs Whiting shooed all the other boys out into the yard. 'Stay out from under my feet while it's wash day. Molly, pour that last kettle into the tub outside. Maisie, fetch the soap for Betty and me to get started on that first load.'

Jemima's offer of help was once again diplomatically declined, and she began to set up the morning's school, wondering how she was going to manage without either Maisie or Henry. She did, however, thanks to the good behaviour and enthusiasm of the pupils. As she packed up at dinnertime, Jemima reflected on how children's behaviour was not regulated according to class, whatever Mrs Silverton and the educational system in general might think. There were several youngsters in Jemima's little school who wouldn't have been let within half a mile of St James's, and yet their willingness to learn could be compared very favourably with that of some of the sons and daughters of respectable shopkeepers and clerks.

After they'd all shared a few thin slices of bread, with

a minuscule scraping of jam for the children, Jemima offered her help once more. Mrs Whiting told her to take what time she needed for her writing, as that was her real money-earning work now, but Jemima couldn't see them all at their hard labour while she sat apparently idling with pen and paper. She insisted on turning the handle of the wringer for an hour – a job even she couldn't get wrong – to give the smaller girls a break, as they looked almost fit to drop by the middle of the afternoon.

Then she sat down at the table to concentrate on *Stowaway Tom* and to plan his next set of rollicking adventures. For a while Jemima considered the conversation of the previous evening, and wondered whether she might be able to introduce a female character, but reluctantly she decided against it. These stories were aimed at Matthew, not Maisie, and most of the men and boys who read them would agree wholeheartedly with his sentiments. It was too early in her career as a serial writer for Jemima to consider alienating either her audience or Mr Grundy. However, in a small act of rebellion on a different note, she managed to slip in a few very slight allusions to the benefits of education for the poor. Tom would be saved from danger at some point by the fact that he could read and add up.

It was while Jemima was thus engrossed, and the

others wearily and gratefully reaching the final load of washing, that a smiling Henry appeared.

Mrs Whiting paused her vigorous dollying for a moment. 'Well?'

'Ma, I'd like to introduce you to Henry Whiting, esquire, the newest accounting clerk in the firm of Bingham and Company, corn merchants of Brunswick Street.'

His mother gave a squawk of joy, rushed forward to embrace him, and then stopped when she remembered she was soaking wet. But she took his face between her hands and kissed him, while Betty gave him a congratulatory thump on the back and the girls did a little dance of joy.

'Starting tomorrow at nine a.m. sharp, and at a salary of seventy-five pounds per annum, since you ask,' he added, when he'd extricated himself.

Mrs Whiting stood back. 'A salary! My, my. But how much is that a week?'

'Twenty-eight shillings and tenpence each week, except the week of Christmas, when twenty-nine and six will be payable, to make up the round number for the year, even though Christmas Day is a holiday.'

Mrs Whiting was amazed. 'Twenty-eight shillings a week! Why, that's more than Pa earns . . . earned.'

'Yes, Ma. And I'm grateful that you all put up with

me bringing in so little for so long, because it's paid off in the end.' He grimaced a little. 'I'm afraid it's not enough to support the whole family, but it'll certainly help until the others find something. The rent will be paid, at least.'

He didn't say it, but what this meant in practice was that the family were safe from eviction, a fate which would almost certainly mean them having to be split up. The relief Jemima felt was almost as overwhelming as that of Mrs Whiting, which occurred a few moments later when she reached the same conclusion. Of course, there was still the question of food, clothes, shoes, coals and so on, but she, Jemima, was going to contribute to that, and surely a builder as experienced as Mr Whiting wouldn't be out of work for long. And once the family were back on their feet, Jemima would be able to turn her mind to other matters . . .

'Oh, I nearly forgot,' said Henry. 'I have something for you.'

He was addressing Jemima. 'Me?'

He took some coins and a folded paper from his pocket. 'Ma, I didn't buy any dinner because I was in a rush to go from one interview to the other and I wasn't hungry, but I'm afraid I did lay out a penny on this.' He passed five pennies to his mother and presented the paper to Jemima.

Puzzled, she looked down at the picture of a ship in a storm and the words emblazoned above and below it.

THE AMAZING ADVENTURES OF STOWAWAY TOM
FOLLOW HIS LIFE–AND–DEATH STRUGGLES AT
SEA AND IN FOREIGN PARTS
A LIVERPOOL LAD TAKES ON THE WORLD
NEW SERIAL STARTING TODAY!

Jemima gasped. 'I'd been so concerned with writing the new episodes that I forgot the first one would be in print!'

'The day before yesterday. The boy I bought it from said it wasn't going quite as well as Dick Turpin – which I suppose is only to be expected, as that's so established – but he'd sold most of his stock of this one on Saturday and was down to his last few copies today.'

Jemima looked at the paper again. Of course, it didn't have her name on it, because the serials in penny papers didn't, but there were her own words, printed in black and white.

'Well, now, I'm made up for the both of you,' said Mrs Whiting, who had gone back to her dollying. 'Jemima, pet, we're nearly done here, so why don't you light the fire and put the kettle on, so we can all have tea when the others get home.'

Jemima went inside.

Henry followed. 'Here, let me fetch the coals for you, while you set the kindling.'

They knelt to set and light the fire, coaxing the first tiny flames into a modest blaze that wouldn't use too much fuel but would allow the kettle to boil.

Jemima sat back on her heels. 'I'm very glad for you, getting that job, but I'm also sorry the school didn't offer you theirs. I know you would have preferred that.'

He looked at the door to check that nobody else had yet entered. 'They did.'

'What? But—'

'Shhh,' he whispered, urgently. 'They did, but they were only offering nineteen shillings a week, plus dinner at the school every day, and the work was only in the term time, which I hadn't realised when I agreed to the interview. You mustn't tell Ma or Pa, or Betty.'

'Oh, Henry.'

'It was a wonderful school,' he continued, wistfully, as they stood up and brushed the coal dust off their knees. 'Classrooms with such fine furniture, and even one with real scientific equipment. Pens, ink, books, maps, dictionaries . . . everything a young gentleman needs for his education.'

Jemima could see that he was thinking the same as

she was. 'Good for them. But such a shame that not every child has those opportunities.'

'Yes,' he sighed. 'But such is the way of the world. You've taken steps to change that – in a small way for now, and with just a few children, but every journey starts with a single step. And who knows whether some of your pupils might not end up bettering themselves in future, because of you.'

'I *wish* we could find some way of continuing it. But with you at your new job, and hopefully me at mine . . .'

'I know. And the children are going to be disappointed when it all ends. But they won't forget what you've done for them.'

They were interrupted by the arrival of Rob and Matthew, who stamped in and flung themselves in chairs.

'Nothing doing?' asked Henry.

'No,' said Rob. 'The overseer has regular men that he knows, and he always picks them first. But he did say I looked a likely lad, and to keep coming, and if he had a day with more work he'd try to find something for me.'

'That's not a bad start.' Henry tried to sound encouraging. 'And what about you?'

'Nothing at all,' said Matthew, gloomily. 'They all said I was too young and too small, and I'd be better off going somewhere else. Might get some oakum picking, one of 'em said, but there's a lot of competition for that from older fellas that used to labour at the docks and need lighter work.'

'Hard luck,' said Henry. 'But maybe Pa will have found something.'

'He hasn't.' Mr Whiting entered with a face as long as Matthew's and sat down in a dispirited manner.

'Oh, Pa, I'm sorry.'

Mr Whiting sighed and then squared his shoulders. 'Plenty more places to ask at tomorrow.' He took out his pipe, started to reach in his pocket for tobacco, and then changed his mind and put it away again. 'But Ma says you've got a job, and a good one, too.' He reached forward to shake Henry's hand, while Rob perked up and slapped his brother on the back.

'What's this?' Matthew picked up the penny paper.

'Ah, that's proof we have a writer in the family,' said Henry.

'Stowaway Tom!' exclaimed Matthew. 'You wait till I tell the lads that I know the writer.'

'You mustn't!' The urgency in Jemima's voice was such that they all looked at her. 'I mean, sorry, Matthew, it's not up to me to tell you what to do. But if anyone finds out this story was written by a woman, word might get back to the publisher, and he'll cancel it.'

'But . . .' Matthew spluttered at the idea of not being able to boast of his superiority.

'Please, Matthew,' said Jemima.

'But why—'

'I'm sure you know why,' cut in Henry. 'Wasn't it you, only last night, who said women were only good for cooking and cleaning? If Mr Grundy finds out about his author and then suspects that further instalments will all be about domestic duties, he'll cancel the serial in a heartbeat.'

'But I didn't mean Jemima,' Matthew managed. 'She's different.'

Jemima wasn't quite sure whether to take that as a compliment or an insult, but she was grateful for Henry's support.

Mr Whiting gave Matthew a half-hearted clip round the ear. 'You'll do as you're told. If Jemima says not to say, you don't say anything. And the money she gets for those stories is paying for your tea until the rest of us get work, so don't you forget it.'

'Sorry, Jemima,' said Matthew, in a contrite tone.

'It's all right,' she replied. 'And don't forget, the better you can keep quiet, the longer the story will go on.'

He brightened.

'If it goes on as long as Dick Turpin, you'll be fair set as an author of serials,' Henry pointed out, poking the fire. 'Matthew, run and tell Ma the kettle will be boiling in five minutes.' He turned to Jemima again. 'A rival to Mr Dickens.'

'Dickens! That's it!'

Her response was so unexpected that he stared.

'I mean,' she added, 'of course I'll never be like Mr Dickens. Sorry, your comparing me to him surprised me, that's all. Shall I fetch the teapot and the cups?'

Jemima kept her face away from the others as she busied herself collecting the tea things from the shelf. Her exclamation had not been about her writing prowess being compared to that of Mr Dickens, however flattering that was. It was because the mention of the name had reminded her where she'd recently seen the name *Shaw*.

* * *

HUGHES AND SHAW, BOOKBINDERS AND PRINTERS.

So read the sign above the door of the premises in Duke Street. It was a shop in front, with what looked like a workshop, offices and a yard behind. The shop window featured a display of *Our Mutual Friend*, by Charles Dickens, Fourth Instalment, Price One Shilling, but that was not why Jemima was here.

If anyone else on the busy street had been watching

her, they might well have thought that the girl outside the shop was fascinated with the new publication, as she'd been standing motionless and staring at it for a good five minutes already, even though it was starting to rain. Or, rather, she was staring *through* it. Jemima was trying to make up her mind. She was breaking her promise to herself not to try to trace her family while the Whitings needed her, but would it really do any harm just to check this one place? Because, as she had told herself multiple times already, it was really just to cross it off any list of possibilities.

Jemima rehearsed to herself all the reasons why this Shaw would turn out *not* to be related to her. There were many hundreds of people with the same name in Liverpool. The chances of this one being the right one were a fraction of one per cent. A member of a family of manual workers who'd had to give away a sibling, and then been evicted from a modest house near the docks, would hardly be the part-owner of a prosperous business like this one. And she didn't know how long the business had been here: the Shaw of the title might be ninety years old, or long dead. He might be a stout, red-faced, middle-aged man who wouldn't appreciate having a strange girl in his shop asking questions. He almost certainly wouldn't be Jemima's brother. Of course he wouldn't.

But.

What if he was, and she didn't take the trouble to find out? She walked along here every time she went from Back Colquitt Street to the library and back again, and the sign above the door would taunt her more with each passing day. She had already caused herself untold harm by failing to read the flower book in good time – what if this was a similar situation? The best thing to do would be to go in, discover that Mr Shaw was nothing to do with her, and then lay the matter to rest. She would then be able to pass the door without the agony of not knowing, and she could go back to concentrating her energies on assisting the Whiting family in their time of trouble.

If Jemima did go in – which she was still not convinced of, as she might well decide to turn round and walk away – then how would she approach the situation? If this man was her long-lost brother, surely just dropping her own name into the conversation would be enough. But that was no good: she wanted to find out about *him*, not to have him find out about her. She would have to think of some other plausible way to elicit information. Of course, just seeing him would give a clue: if he looked older than about thirty, maybe thirty-five at the outside, then he wasn't her brother. If that turned out to be the case, she would just say she'd come in about the Dickens serial, and then pretend she'd accidentally left her purse at home, because she certainly didn't have a shilling to spare to buy a copy. If he was in his twenties, she would engage him in conversation, to try to find some way to discover his first name. That would be much more difficult for her than it would be for a man, and she would have to be careful not to give off the impression of being a young woman of loose morals.

She shouldn't really, should she? But even as Jemima's mind was thinking this, her hand was pushing open the door of the shop.

The bell rang and a smart young man appeared at the counter. 'Good day to you, miss. How can I help?'

'I—' Jemima cleared her throat. 'I was wondering if Mr Shaw was available?'

She waited to be laughed at, to be told that Mr Shaw had died in 1825 or had never existed at all.

'I'm afraid he's not on the premises just now, miss.' He picked up a pad of paper in ink-stained fingers, then took a pencil from behind his ear. 'Would you like to leave a message, and I'll give it to him as soon as he gets back?'

What in the world was she supposed to say to that? *Could you ask him if he's ever lost a baby sister?* And asking this young man how old Mr Shaw was would be the height of impertinence, not to mention making her look like a mad woman. She looked at him standing with his pencil poised, and memories of the day at the news office started to flood back to her.

This had all been a mistake.

'Er, no. No message, thank you. I'll call back another time.'

Jemima ran out of the shop into the pouring rain.

Chapter 14

'. . . And we'll find out tomorrow what happened to Tom when his ship sailed again.'

It was the evening of Monday 5 September, which meant that it had been the first day of the new school term. But Betty had made her way to St James's alone. There was no money for five sets of school fees a week because, much to Jemima's surprise and everyone's consternation, Mr Whiting had not yet secured a new job. There were streets of new terraces going up all over the place, as Liverpool expanded, but there were also many men looking for work, and all the employers seemed to be looking for cheap manual labour rather than skilled builders with years of experience. The terraces were all the same and quite simple to erect, and besides, in some circles *experienced* was just another word for *old*, so a man in his mid-forties couldn't compete with those twenty years his junior when all that was required was to carry heavy loads of bricks all day.

Rob had got some occasional work at the docks, a day or half-day here and there, which had contributed a few shillings to the household, but it was no substitute for the both of them having steady employment, and the money in the tin was dwindling rapidly.

One bright spot was that Henry had been doing well in his new position so far, and he'd even managed to find a job for Matthew. The corn merchants' office was at the top end of Brunswick Street, but it needed to be in frequent contact with the docks about the shipments coming in; they'd been on the point of advertising for a boy to run back and forth with messages when Henry had mentioned that he knew a likely lad. That had saved them effort and expense, so Matthew was taken on. It was only five shillings a week, but it all helped. Henry himself was beginning to look pale and drawn with the responsibility of being the primary breadwinner for such a large family, a heavy charge for someone who had only just turned nineteen.

Jemima also felt listless this evening, and Stowaway Tom had been a little less spirited than usual. Today had been the very last day of her little school – which was not so little these days – and it had been so hard to tell the children that it couldn't continue. They'd had some disruption over the past few weeks anyway, with rain and more overt complaints from neighbours about the number of ragged children appearing in their yard every day. But Jemima had weathered it all, right up until she had to give the fateful news this morning. Mary and Joey had both cried their eyes out, and so had Maisie, deprived not only of her lessons with Jemima, but also of her wish to return to proper school. Unless the situation changed, and changed quickly, her education would end and her working life of cooking, cleaning and washing would begin at the age of eight. She'd been at the laundry all day, tears falling into the tub as she took her turn, knowing that term had started and she was missing out, and she was now sitting exhausted with her head on Jemima's knee.

This was one issue that Jemima hoped she might be able to solve, as she stroked Maisie's hair in the evening gloom, because she had wrung from Mr and Mrs Whiting the agreement that if she succeeded in getting the job at the school in Park Lane, she would use some of her wages to pay the school tuppences, at least for Maisie and Ralph, who were the two who were keenest and most affected, but also for Albert, Molly and Sid if they wanted. Her trial day tomorrow was of the greatest importance in so many ways.

She had not been back to Hughes and Shaw, too

embarrassed to call there again, and nor had she made any further attempt to trace her family. As her mind wandered now, Jemima recalled another lost sister, and hoped that the Hopkins family were safely reunited. She wouldn't be going to the tea room to spend precious sixpences any time soon, so she wouldn't find out herself, but perhaps she could ask Betty to ask her other friend. Jemima still felt a warmth towards Mrs Roberts, even though their interaction had been so brief, and she hated to think of such a nice old lady racked with anxiety.

There were plenty of yawns around the room that evening, and the adults went to bed not long after the children did.

* * *

Jemima awoke the next morning with a combination of nerves and anticipation. Today was the day she was going back to a real schoolroom, returning to the role of assistant teacher. And surely, *surely* they would give her the job and she would be able to fix the broken ends of her career and tie them into a smooth thread that led off into the future. It would mean that once again she had prospects – and the possibility of planning Pa's grave marker and plants, and of redeeming his books – and it would also provide more money for the Whitings and the opportunity for their own children to return to school. Jemima couldn't let them down.

She dressed in the outfit she had used to wear at St James's, the gown brushed and the clean white apron having been subject to Mrs Whiting's very best efforts. If soap and starch were the main criteria for employment, Jemima would be taken on immediately.

Amid everyone's good luck wishes, Jemima set off in good time. She tried not to look at Mrs Lewis's boarding house on the way past, concentrating instead on all that she had learned in her previous employment, and also from her experiences with yard school over the summer. Children who wanted to learn made the best pupils. Encouragement was better than threats. Each child was an individual who learned in a different way.

Jemima wondered how many girls there would be. At St James's there had been forty in her section, a nice number for Mrs Silverton and an assistant, and manageable even for Jemima alone if the mistress was otherwise engaged. She hoped it would be similar here, and of course they would be about the same age to her previous pupils, because all the Corporation and church schools were organised along similar lines, with mixed infants and then separate girls and boys aged from seven upwards.

These were the thoughts that occupied Jemima's mind as the school came into view. It was significantly bigger than she had expected, but she was undeterred as she made her way to the entrance that had GIRLS AND INFANTS carved in the stone lintel above it.

Her knock was answered promptly by an older woman. 'Yes?'

Jemima curtseyed. 'Jemima Jenkins, ma'am, here for a trial day for the post of assistant teacher.'

The woman looked her up and down. 'Mrs Greenaway, headmaster's wife and teacher of the older girls. You're a little younger than I was expecting, but you're smartly turned out, and you're punctual to your time, I'll give you that. The others aren't here yet.'

Pleased to have made a good first impression, Jemima followed Mrs Greenaway inside and then stopped in shock. The schoolroom was *huge*, with rows and rows of desks banked in tiers, so that those at the back were some ten or fifteen feet higher than the floor. Jemima tried to imagine what it would be like when they were all populated, with so many eyes looking at her. Almost like being on the stage of a theatre or music hall.

'We have three hundred and fifty boys and two hundred and fifty girls enrolled,' Mrs Greenaway was explaining, oblivious to Jemima's stupefaction. 'Some of those are in the infants, of course, so we have one hundred and seventy in our section.'

Jemima almost choked, then tried to recover herself and say something intelligent. 'That's rather larger than my old school, ma'am,' she managed, 'though I'm sure I'll get used to it.'

'I'll explain the rest when the others are here,' said Mrs Greenaway, looking up at the clock on the wall, which stood at twenty-five minutes to nine. 'That way I won't need to repeat myself.'

'Yes, ma'am. Is there anything I can be getting on with in the meantime, to prepare for the day?'

'I think— ah, here they are.'

Jemima followed the other woman's gaze, expecting to see her two rivals for the position, but in fact the newcomers entering were a dozen girls who all looked to be about eleven or twelve. The top class, perhaps?

'The monitors,' said Mrs Greenaway. 'You are aware of the monitor system, I take it?'

'I've not worked with it myself, ma'am, but I know of it, yes.' Monitors were older pupils who helped younger ones, especially when a class was large: the teacher would instruct the monitors, who would in turn go and instruct groups of pupils. There had been no call for such a thing at St James's, but it would certainly be needed here.

Jemima doubted if a hundred and seventy girls would even be able to hear a general lesson, let alone gain much from it or receive any personal attention.

Mrs Greenaway was ordering the girls to fill inkwells and distribute a sheet of ruled paper to every desk, and by the time she'd done that, there was another knock at the door. Consulting the clock again and clicking her tongue, she moved to admit two more young women.

Jemima eyed them while trying not to be too obvious about it. One, who introduced herself as Emma, was a couple of years older than Jemima, smartly turned out like herself and with neat manners and a pleasant expression, although she was perhaps a little hesitant. The other, Lucy, was older again – in her early to mid-twenties – and was a square, robust woman with a decidedly no-nonsense expression that was enough to intimidate Jemima, never mind the little girls who would soon be pouring in. Jemima shook hands with them both, wondering which would turn out to be her main rival.

Mrs Greenaway repeated the size of the class, for the benefit of the others, and then went on to explain the rules and the course of the school day. Lessons were from nine until twelve and two until half past four from Monday to Friday, and from nine to twelve only on Saturdays. Children were to assemble outside punctually at quarter to nine and quarter to two, because it took fifteen minutes to get them all in and seated. There was no morning recess, and the children went home for their dinner in the middle of the day. Fees were payable on Monday mornings, at which time new enrolments were also accepted. It was a very busy time at the start of term, which was why this trial of candidates was taking place today rather than yesterday.

Jemima listened carefully, thinking that there was an awful lot about organisation and timetables in Mrs Greenaway's explanation, and very little about the actual teaching. No doubt she would come to that in a moment.

She did, but it was rather disappointing. 'There is no need for these children to learn anything exceptional – we concentrate on the three Rs, plus scripture, of course, and some useful needlework for the girls. Discipline is our main concern, and this must be *strictly* upheld at all times. Lateness is not tolerated, and nor is chattering, inattention, fidgeting and sloppiness in any aspect of the children's work.'

'Are you ready, Mrs Greenaway?' called a voice from the other side of the room. Jemima looked around to see a smallish, neat man with a very impressive moustache putting his head through a door in the partition wall that separated the girls from the boys while school was in session.

'Yes, Mr Greenaway.'

He disappeared back to his own domain, and she went to the girls' entrance, being joined by another severe-looking woman – the infants' teacher, Jemima guessed. They stood looking at the clock until the minute hand moved precisely to quarter to nine, then opened the outer door, and Jemima heard some barked instructions about standing to attention and making lines straighter.

The infants and older girls entered in two very long lines, the former marching along the edge of this classroom and through a partition into another. Jemima looked at the many, many girls as they walked past her, smiling encouragingly, but none of them met her eye as they stared straight ahead. When each was at her place on a bench, and they were told to sit, they did so in rigid silence.

It was a long morning, and a loud one. The vast building was divided into three by the partitions, but they only blocked sight, not sound, and with hundreds of children simultaneously reading aloud, reciting Bible verses and chanting multiplication tables, there was an almost continuous cacophony, punctuated by the regular swish and *thwack* of the cane from the boys' section. Thankfully there was no cane for the girls, but Mrs Greenaway made liberal use of a wooden ruler across the knuckles of any malefactors.

It was all very different from what Jemima was used to, at either her old job or her yard school, but she tried to fit into this new system as well as she could, as the girls of different ages worked on different exercises. She, Emma, Lucy and Mrs Greenaway patrolled the room to oversee the teaching of the monitors and to check that each pupil was following her instructions to the letter. 'You have to be sharp-eyed,' Mrs Greenaway had warned them. 'In a class this size, there will always be some lazy little girl who is doing nothing and hoping not to be noticed.'

Jemima spotted one girl now, right up in the back tier, whose pen was not moving. She climbed up and squeezed between rows until she reached her. 'Is something the matter?'

'Please, miss,' said the girl, in a desperate whisper. 'We're supposed to be copying down what it says on the blackboard, but I can't see it properly. It's all just blurry and I can't see the writing. I'm trying, I really am.' She had tears in her eyes.

Some people did have poor eyesight, Jemima knew, even when they were young. 'Perhaps you could be moved to a different seat, one nearer the front. Shall I ask?'

The girl opened her eyes wide at the audacity of such an idea.

'I'll see what I can do. In the meantime, as you're only copying anyway, I wonder if your neighbour would let you look at what she's already written.' She smiled at the girl in the next seat, who had already completed the exercise, in a beautiful copperplate hand that rivalled the one on the board, and who was sitting with her arms folded. This child looked cautiously about the room, saw that Mrs Greenaway was some way off, and then nudged her paper to angle it so her neighbour could see.

Nobody else around them was more than halfway through the text. 'Do you get given anything else to do, if you finish early?' whispered Jemima.

The girl shook her head.

'You be careful,' warned another voice.

Jemima looked up to see one of the monitors. 'Why do you say that?'

This girl also checked Mrs Greenaway's whereabouts before replying, which she did in a low voice. 'Be careful not to look too clever. If you do, you end up like me – just showing everyone else the basic things and never getting to learn any more yourself.'

'But isn't it an honour to be monitor? I mean, a reward?'

The sound of the girl's derision was almost audible above the noise of the nearby infants bawling out their twice-twos and twice-threes. 'Reward? My Pa pays tuppence a week for me to come here, and I don't get to learn anything myself, only work at going over lessons I knew years ago.' She looked with sympathy at the girl who had finished the exercise. 'You take my advice, and just do whatever you need to finish properly and not stand out. Anyone starts saying you're clever, or how well you're doing, you just hide it, or you'll end up like me.' With a glance around, the monitor nodded and made her way further down the row.

Mrs Greenaway had, by now, noticed the little knot, so Jemima descended to the teaching floor to speak with her. She said nothing about the girl who had finished her copying, but explained about the one who couldn't see properly. 'So I wondered if she might exchange places with someone else? She'll be able to learn much better if she's nearer the blackboard.'

Mrs Greenaway stared. 'Exchange places? Dear me, no – that would be far too much trouble and disruption, and to rearrange my classroom for the sake of one girl? The very idea. She can stay where she is, and she'll just have to make the best of it.'

'But, ma'am, if she can't see . . .' Jemima belatedly remembered that she was at a job interview. 'Yes, ma'am.'

The older woman looked again at the clock. She

clapped her hands. 'Pens down, now, girls. Papers will be collected, and there will be a ticket for anyone who has not completed the exercise. Standards Four, Five and Six will now move on to silent arithmetic, performing the calculations I have written on the board, while Standards One, Two and Three will say their multiplication tables aloud.'

A few minutes later Jemima was helping a couple of girls with their sums when she was startled almost out of her skin by Mrs Greenaway's ruler smacking down hard on one of their hands. The pupil in question gave a little shriek, soon stifled, and clutched at her reddened skin.

'What have I told you?'

The girl stood as she was addressed. 'Always to hold the pen in the correct hand, Mrs Greenaway.'

'And what were you doing?'

'Holding my pen in the wrong hand, Mrs Greenaway.'

Jemima hadn't noticed that the girl was using her left hand, and she wondered again why this was such an issue in schools, and why children couldn't just hold pens however they thought best.

'That's another ticket for you. How many have you got now?'

'Five, Mrs Greenaway,' said the girl, miserably.

'And with the term less than two days old. Off you go, then.' She pointed.

Jemima watched the girl, who was about Maisie and Molly's age, trudge over to the teacher's desk and pick up the dunce's cap. Then she moved over to a stool in the corner, sat down, put the cap on her head and tried hard not to cry.

There was an outbreak of whispering and giggles, quickly stifled when Mrs Greenaway slapped her ruler down on the desk.

Jemima was quite glad when it was dinnertime and the children were released. They held their rigid discipline and silent straight lines exactly as long as it took them to leave the school premises, and then they were whooping and running.

'Normally,' said Mrs Greenaway, 'assistant teachers also leave the premises for their dinner, but for today only, Mr Greenaway and I would like to invite you to eat with us in the schoolhouse.'

This was going to be part of the selection process, Jemima knew, as she, Lucy and Emma followed the mistress across the yard. The dining-room table was already set, and a simple but tasty meal of soup and bread was served.

As they ate, the four women were treated to a lecture

from Mr Greenaway on his views of modern education. 'There is simply no need,' he opined between mouthfuls, 'for children of the sort we teach to have an extensive education. We are preparing them for a life involving shop work, perhaps some low-level clerking, or' – with a nod to his wife – 'as housewives, perhaps with an interlude as a shop girl or something first. Reading, writing, arithmetic and a few practical skills is all that is required, alongside a good moral grounding, of course. Besides, we get paid by results.'

Jemima saw from the bemused faces that Lucy and Emma were as clueless about this as she was, so she ventured to ask for an explanation.

He was glad of the opportunity to expound at greater length. 'The fees paid by pupils form only one part of the school's income. The rest comes from the government, and the amount depends not on the number of pupils but on the results they obtain in annual examinations. So all that is required is rote learning to enable as many as possible to pass.' He wiped his moustache.

Jemima wanted to ask *But what about the children, and the benefit to them of education?*, but she reminded herself again that it was she who was on trial, not Mr Greenaway or the education system in general. She needed to put her own ideas and principles to one side.

'Did you have a question, Miss...?' He'd noticed that she was about to say something.

Jemima took a moment to dab at her mouth with the corner of her napkin, while she thought of something acceptable. 'May I ask your opinion, sir, on the new ideas about extending school education to the poor?' It was another subject close to her own heart, but she hoped that the way she'd phrased it wouldn't make her sound too unconventional.

Fortunately, as Jemima had already noted, Mr Greenaway was a man who was very fond of the sound of his own voice. 'Ah, you keep up with educational news, I see. So no doubt you see how ludicrous the idea is. Why would dock labourers and scullery maids need to read, or write, or – Heaven forfend – recite poetry? And what possible purpose would be served by attempting such a thing?'

Jemima thought of dear Pa, denied a proper education as a boy, and doing everything he could to make up for it in later life, learning and enjoying it for its own sake. *Learning is never wasted*, that's what he used to say.

Again she was forced to swallow her real feelings, but she was saved the trouble of answering by Emma and Lucy, who, seeing which way the wind was blowing, agreed vocally with Mr Greenaway. Then there was time for a few approving comments on the value of discipline in schools, and on disciplining children more generally, before it was time to return to the schoolroom and prepare for the afternoon.

Jemima spent most of the next two hours wrestling with a dilemma. After the experiences of the day so far, she had no desire to work in this school – a place where children's ambitions and personalities were ruthlessly crushed rather than encouraged and supported. Where there could be no possibility of getting to know the pupils personally, as she had enjoyed so much over the summer, and as had even been the case under Mrs Silverton. But she desperately needed the job, both for the wages she would earn and because it meant she could stay working in education.

She knew very well what sort of behaviour would be expected of her in the afternoon, if she were still to remain in contention, but she couldn't help herself: she smiled at the girls, she encouraged them, she helped them. Emma, meanwhile, had changed her earlier pleasant expression to one of greater determination, while Lucy had gone so far as to equip herself with a ruler the same as Mrs Greenaway's. She marched up and down, ensuring strict silence and conformity and raising it in her hand once or twice, though Jemima didn't actually see her hit anyone. Mrs Greenaway watched them all, and her husband came in once or twice to survey the scene.

At the end of the day, after the children had been dismissed, the three candidates were told to wait while Mr and Mrs Greenaway conferred, over in the boys' section where they could not be seen.

Jemima was called through first. She would have liked to think that they were starting by summoning the successful candidate, but she knew in her heart that they were in fact dismissing the failures so they could speak at greater length to the new assistant at the end.

'We thank you for your application, Miss Jenkins,' said Mr Greenaway, brusquely, 'but I'm afraid we don't find you suitable for the position.' He looked at his wife.

She continued. 'There is no problem with your knowledge of the curriculum, and I would be happy to attest to that, if asked. However, your discipline is sadly lacking, you smile far too much, and you appear to want to make *friends* with the girls instead of acting as their superior and instructor.' Mrs Greenaway made it sound like the worst sin imaginable.

Jemima was not going to bother arguing or attempting to point out that she disagreed with their ethos. She only wished she were both rich enough and successful enough to have had the opportunity of turning them down before they could reject her. But, as it was, there was nothing to do but retire with dignity. So, thanking them for their time and attention, she left the schoolroom, hearing Mrs Greenaway call Emma in next.

As she paused outside to take in what had happened, Jemima wondered if she would ever be a teacher again.

Chapter 15

She had let the Whitings down. That was the most important point, and Jemima knew that it was, at least in part, her own fault. She should have appreciated more quickly the qualities that would have secured her the job and played to those, however much they contradicted her own principles. But, had she been offered the position, she would have been expected to demonstrate a sternness and discipline that she didn't feel, alienating the girls and probably even being forced to hit some of them. So, other than her guilt on the Whitings' account, she couldn't be sorry that she'd not been offered the job. She wouldn't say any of that to the Whitings, of course, except perhaps in confidence to Betty or Henry.

A sigh escaped Jemima as she stood irresolute on the pavement. It was not long after half past four, and it would be light for a good while yet, so there was no harm in walking to the nearby churchyard and telling Pa all about it.

She did so, and then tried to give herself strength by reading some of the gravestones, veritable essays, some of them, about lives well lived and virtues amply demonstrated. But none of them, however verbose, struck her with the force of the one she'd seen on her first visit after the funeral, so she went in search of *Born a slave, died a free man, much beloved*. There was a woman by that plot, a shawl over her head as she cleared away some dead flowers and placed new ones, so Jemima turned away and pretended to be engrossed in the story of a woman who had *exhibited the moſt Chriſtian values throughout her blameleſs life*, and who sounded like she must have been either a saint or a doormat.

Once she was sure the other visitor had departed, Jemima moved to the grave in question and read the carving several times. Oh, to be 'much beloved'! But she had been, hadn't she, for many years, and that was better than never having a Pa or a family, like poor Sarah and all the other maids around the city who had come straight from the workhouse.

Jemima thought of Sarah as she left the churchyard, and of maids in general. They were invisible to most of the city's population, spending all but half a day each fortnight shut away in the houses in which they served, but they were real people with real feelings and lives of their own.

Why are stories always about boys? Maisie had asked, and the words came back to Jemima now. Maids earned money, and so did shop girls. They might send some of it to their families, but they would also keep a little something back to spend on themselves. They probably didn't buy penny papers because the stories of male derring-do weren't interesting to them. But what if . . .?

These musings were brought to a halt as Jemima reached the boarding house on Pitt Street, and her anger at Mrs Lewis's double-dealing and theft came surging back. If she'd had access to the money Pa had saved up and left to her, Jemima wouldn't be in the position of having to apply for jobs she knew she'd hate. She would have been able to buy a bit of a breathing space to look about her. But there was no possibility of being able to get any kind of justice, so she'd better just—

These thoughts were in turn interrupted by the sight of Sarah herself, going down to the basement entrance of the house. *Invisible, spending all but half a day each fortnight shut away.*

Jemima waved and managed to attract Sarah's attention so that she paused on the steps. 'I just wanted to say good day and see how you were.'

Sarah shrugged. 'Fine, mi—Jemima, thank you. Just the same as usual.'

'This is going to sound like an odd question, but may I ask what you do on your afternoons out?'

'Mostly I walk round town and look at the shops, just to see some different faces from the ones in the house. It's nice to look, even if you've no money to spend. And,' she added, unexpectedly, 'I like looking at all the big new buildings, and the ones they're still putting up. It's like magic, how they build them so high without them falling over. I passed that giant place at the Exchange Buildings last time I was out, and there was builders halfway up to the sky!'

Jemima was about to comment on this when she was struck by something else. 'Why don't you have any money to spend? Mrs Lewis pays you, and you don't have a family to send it back to.'

Sarah made a face. 'She's supposed to pay me. But every week there's some reason why she has to take money away – I've been lazy, or not cleaned properly, or broken something. I'm lucky if I get sixpence a week most of the time, and I have to save that, 'cos I have to buy my own aprons.'

Jemima's antipathy to Mrs Lewis, and her frustration at her own inability to do anything about the landlady's misdeeds, swelled even further.

But there was one tiny thing she could do. 'Next time you have your afternoon out, could I come with you? I probably won't have much money to spend, either, but at least we could look round town together.'

'Really?' Sarah looked as though someone had just given her a gold sovereign, and Jemima was full of remorse that she hadn't thought of the idea sooner.

'Yes, really. Is it this week, or next?'

'This week, the day after tomorrow.'

'Well, then. I'll meet you – hmm, perhaps I'd better not call at the house, or Mrs Lewis will find an excuse not to let you out. Shall I wait for you at the far end of the road? On the corner near the Customs House?'

'That's another one of my favourites,' said Sarah. 'Yes, at one o'clock.' A sound from inside the house made her jump. 'But now I'd better get back, or I'll be in trouble.'

'Yes. I'll see you on Thursday, then.'

Sarah descended and disappeared, and Jemima continued on her way. *Maids.* They all had something in common, in that they were girls who were unnoticed by their betters most of the time, but other than that, their experiences might vary wildly. Jemima thought back to what Harriet and Anna Whiting had said during their visits home.

The thing was, if stories were going to be interesting

to girls, and bought by girls, then they really ought to be *about* girls. And that was a challenge for a serial writer. A runaway girl was a much less suitable subject for a story than a runaway boy, for obvious reasons – the sort of 'adventures' she might fall into were very different and not fit to print. But what about a group of maids who all lived on the same street, and who got up to a few acceptable capers and perhaps outwitted some ne'er-do-wells intent on causing trouble for them and their employers? Jemima would certainly have time to write a second serial alongside *Stowaway Tom* now that she wasn't going to start a new school job.

As soon as she got back to the house she was assailed with enquiries about how her day had been, and commiserations that she hadn't been offered the position. Mrs Whiting, despite her views on education and suitable work for girls, and her worries about money, was genuinely sorry for Jemima personally, because she would be so disappointed, and Jemima's heart went out to her again.

'It's all right, it really is,' she said, from inside the enveloping embrace. 'And as to earning more money, I've already got another idea.'

* * *

By nine o'clock the following morning, Jemima's letter was ready to take to the Post Office.

'Another story?' asked Mr Whiting, as he got up from his bread and cold tea, ready to head out to continue his increasingly disheartening search.

'Not quite. I already sent this week's, as it was due yesterday. This is an idea for a new one.'

'Well, good luck with it, after your disappointment yesterday. One of us could do with some luck, that's for sure.' He reached for his cap.

Jemima recalled something Sarah had said. 'Mr Whiting,' she began.

He paused. 'Yes?'

She wasn't quite sure how to continue. 'Have you thought . . . I mean, I wonder if . . . I know you don't need advice from me . . .'

He came back to the table. 'I'm not so proud that I can't listen to a woman, especially a clever one like you. Spit it out.'

'I know you've been mainly looking at the sites where terraced houses are being built. But have you thought about some of the places in the centre of town? Where they're putting up huge, grand buildings? Yesterday I was near the Exchange Buildings' – a tiny white lie, but it would be too awkward to explain – 'and there were lots of builders there. And with such a big, complicated project, surely they'd need men with experience, not just labourers?'

He paused for a moment and then nodded. 'I'll ask there tomorrow, if none of today's places are any good. I'm not overly hopeful, but it's worth a try. Besides, you were right about the other site, so who's to say you're not right about this, too?'

He left, and Jemima went to the Post Office for a stamp. Once the letter was on its way she returned to help with the household chores, attempting to cheer Maisie up as she did so by asking her questions of mental arithmetic and attempting to remember some poetry quotes. But at the same time, the tale of *The Maids of Maddox Place* was already forming in her head.

* * *

'Ma, this girl is our lucky charm!' Mr Whiting swept into the house at dinnertime on Thursday and kissed his wife roundly on the cheek.

'You mean . . .?'

'Work! For me and for Rob. At the Exchange Buildings.' He turned to Jemima. 'It was just like you said. Some difficult work going on, so they need good men who know what they're doing.'

Mrs Whiting threw up her hands and exclaimed in joy.

So did Maisie. 'Does this mean I can go back to school?'

'Yes, love, it does,' said her father, and she squealed and ran over to kiss him.

Mrs Whiting spoke to Maisie while embracing Jemima. 'And do you know what? If you end up like this one here, I'll be proud of you.'

Jemima was buoyant with happiness as she walked to meet Sarah. And not only that, but she had a sixpence in her pocket to spend on them both. The purse she'd given to Mrs Whiting had been raided, out of necessity, a couple of times, but there was still some money left, and on hearing of her husband and son's new jobs Mrs Whiting had immediately pressed her to take it back. Jemima had pointed out that they wouldn't be paid until Saturday, and then only for a day and a half, so it would be safer to save it for now, but on being pressed she had accepted the sixpence, and was glad for Sarah's sake. There wouldn't be time for them to make it all the way up to Hopkins' tea room – and besides, Sarah would probably feel intimidated and therefore not enjoy it – but they would be able to find something at a baker's.

It was a very agreeable afternoon, and Jemima rejoiced in Sarah's pleasure. They sauntered through the centre of the city, admired some of Liverpool's finest buildings, looked in shop windows and decided what they would buy if they were fine ladies with lots of money, and finally they found a corner bakery that sold reasonably priced currant buns. It also stocked a range of confectionery in large glass jars, so Jemima recklessly laid out for a quarter of barley sugar for Sarah to take home and a quarter of toffee to bring back for the children. It was a day of celebration, after all.

They slowed their pace as they reached the end of Pitt Street. 'It's not that I don't want to walk all the way home with you . . .' began Jemima, awkwardly.

'Oh no! Don't worry about it. It's much better Mrs Lewis doesn't see you, anyway. She can't get at you any more, but she'll find a way to take it out on me.'

'Speaking of Mrs Lewis . . .'

'Yes?'

'I'm not suggesting in any way that you cheek her, or answer back if she scolds you. But try to remember, on your inside, if you know what I mean, that you're not lazy and you're not useless. You're a hard-working, honest girl.'

'Your Pa once said to me that he could see I worked hard, back when he was helping out around the place.'

'Well, then. He was right, and I'm saying the same.'

It might have been Jemima's imagination, but she thought that Sarah stood a little taller as she said goodbye and walked off up Pitt Street, prepared to disappear for another two weeks in the long wait for half a day of freedom.

* * *

Thursday, September 8th, 1864

Dear Mr. Jenkins,
Thank you for your letter of 7th inst., in which you propose a new serial featuring female protagonists, to be aimed at a female audience.
This would be a new departure for us, and unusual — indeed unique, as far as I am aware — among Liverpool's publishers of penny papers. However, you make a persuasive case about the increase of literacy among the younger female population, and the disposable income available to those who work as maids, shop girls, &c.
We are therefore willing to undertake a modest trial, and should like to commission six instalments of "The Maids of Maddox Place" in the first instance. Terms would be as per your current agreement with us, viz. instalments of suitable content and length to reach us on a Tuesday.

However, you will no doubt understand that a serial aimed at girls and young women is likely to be less popular than our usual lines – or, at the very least, to take time to establish itself – so our initial monetary offer is 4s per instalment. This amount can be added to your existing money order, making 11s 6d per week in total.

The possibility of renewal will depend upon reception and sales of the first tranche of episodes.

If these terms are acceptable, please reply by return of post.

Yours sincerely,
Robert H. Grundy
Printseller and Publisher

Postscript:
I am pleased to say that initial sales of "The Adventures of Stowaway Tom" are encouraging.

Jemima realised she'd been holding her breath while she read all this, and now she let it out. It was a shame she wasn't doubling her money, given that she was expected to produce double her previous output, but eleven and six was a very decent wage for a woman. And the most important point was that she'd managed to push a previously closed door a little way open. *Who wants to hear stories about girls?* Lots and lots of other girls, Jemima hoped.

* * *

On Friday morning she set off for the library. During her first visit, the clerk had mentioned that there was a dedicated room for ladies, and this was her destination. She would read as many existing publications aimed at women as possible, to get an idea of style and so on. Jemima allowed herself a little smile at the thought that she'd finally be doing something at the library that would meet with no raised eyebrows or looks of disapproval. She, a young woman, would be going into an area set aside for women and their inferior intellects, and society – or such of it as was in the library, at least – would smile benevolently upon her. They wouldn't know that she was doing something as subversive as earning money by writing for publication, not to mention daring to write an adventure story for and about girls.

Nobody batted an eyelid as Jemima followed the sign marked 'Ladies' Reading Room', walking as demurely as possible and revelling in what she thought of as a disguise. She might even use that in one of her stories.

She found a place – just tables in here, no desks with

ink provided, but luckily she'd expected this and brought a pencil – and then began to peruse the shelves. Her hopes were soon dashed, as the results were extremely disappointing. The magazine section was her first port of call, but there was nothing remotely adventurous here. Most had titles such as *The Ladies' Gazette of Fashion* or *The Ladies' Fashionable Repository*, which she didn't even bother to pick up. *The Englishwoman's Domestic Magazine* was almost entirely exactly what it sounded like, with recipes, sewing patterns and advice on dress all listed in the contents, but just as she was about to put it down, Jemima's eye was caught by mention of an essay on the subject of 'Female Education'. This was more promising. However, when she turned to the correct page, the first two sentences that caught her eye were, 'It is to the subject of domestic duties, however, that the utilitarian part of female education should be chiefly directed,' and 'These are things of which she must acquire a knowledge before she can duly perform the duties of a wife and mother.' Jemima only narrowly avoided throwing the magazine at the wall.

Novels, then. They were by definition fictional stories, and Jemima saw with some hope that there was even a section labelled as being 'For Our Younger Readers'. But they were either fairy tales or they were called things like *Minor Morals for Young People* or *Good Little Girls*. She would get nothing there. In fact, it looked as though she was about to embark on an entirely new genre of literature: exciting stories aimed at a female readership of the middle and lower classes. She would be a pioneer. Men would sneer at the idea of female-led stories, and the literary establishment would scoff at the presumption, but why shouldn't hard-working women and girls have something all to themselves?

Jemima's trip to the library was saved from being a complete waste of time by a fortuitous discovery. A copy of *Pride and Prejudice* caught her eye, and she was reaching out to pick it up, intending to leaf through it for old times' sake, when she saw that the author had written a number of other books as well. Jemima hadn't read anything new for quite some time, so she treated herself by choosing one at random and taking it back to her table.

She began to read. Ostensibly it was the tale of a young girl who was taken to Bath by some friends, in the same sort of strange, distant, privileged world as the other work. But there was more. *Pride and Prejudice* had slipped in some covert criticism of women's social position, but *Northanger Abbey* was a more obvious and biting satire on women's education and reading habits. Men, she read with amusement, might be praised for something as simple as being 'the nine-hundredth abridger of the History of England', or for collecting and publishing extracts of someone else's poetry, while conversely there was 'a general wish of decrying the capacity and undervaluing the labour' of female novelists. When Jemima got to, 'A woman especially, if she have the misfortune of knowing anything, should conceal it as well as she can,' and 'imbecility in females is a great enhancement of their personal charms,' written with a savage sarcasm that echoed through the fifty years since the book was published, she almost laughed out loud. She wondered what Mrs Whiting would say if she could see her own words reproduced in print in this way.

None of this was exactly of use in terms of content for Jemima's new story, but it cheered her and she picked up her pencil with renewed enthusiasm.

A couple of hours later she had the skeleton of her ideas in place. When would Harriet and Anna next have their afternoons out? Would she be able to try some of these plots on them, before the finished instalments had to be delivered? If not, Jemima was sure that Betty would sit and listen to them, and even though she wasn't a maid herself she knew more about it than Jemima did, from having talked to her sisters.

AN ORPHAN'S DREAM

As Jemima was passing out of the library into the grand hall, she was thinking so much about her stories that she almost failed to notice a board that was advertising forthcoming lectures that were free to attend. She paused to read it properly, thinking fondly of Pa and how he'd loved such chances to learn, whatever the subject might be. Most of it was of little interest to her, but then one poster, for a lecture to take place on 15 October, jumped out at her. She gasped, fumbled for paper and found her pencil to write down the details. Henry wouldn't be home until this evening, so she would have to spend the whole afternoon bursting with the news.

She finally got her chance to speak after tea that evening, and Henry was just as surprised and pleased as Jemima had been.

'So, wait, you're telling me that the sort of school we'd like to set up has been done before, in other places, and there's actually an established network of them?'

'According to the poster in the library, yes. The speaker who's coming to Liverpool is from something called the London Ragged School Union, and he's going to talk about how they're trying to extend the movement further across the country.'

'Well, well.'

'So I think you should go.' Jemima still had painful

memories of the way she'd been forced to stop attending lectures with Pa, as she grew up, and she didn't want a repeat of the humiliation, especially after the news-office incident, which still made her cheeks flame with mortification every time she thought about it.

'Surely you mean that *we* should.'

Jemima shook her head.

'Of course,' he added hastily, 'we could always ask Betty to come with us.'

She shook her head again. 'It's not that. It's . . . it doesn't say so in so many words on the poster, but when things like this say "open to the public", they mean men.'

'I'm sure that in this case . . .'

'Anyway,' Jemima briskly changed the subject. 'I should help your mother with the washing up.'

He took the hint, and they went their separate ways.

* * *

The rest of September passed in something of a blur, as everyone settled into their new jobs, tasks and routines. Jemima continued to write both her serials, though she was now about to start on her final commissioned instalment of *The Maids of Maddox Place*, and with no information either way from Mr Grundy as to whether he'd like to continue. This was frustrating, because

Jemima also had no idea about how the story was being received. Sales were important, of course, but what she really wanted to know was whether any girls or young women of her own class had come across this new type of literature written specifically for them, and whether they were enjoying it.

Anna Whiting, on her most recent visit home, had enthused about how she and her fellow local maids had been overjoyed to read such a thing, and how they were taking it in turns to buy a copy each week and then circulate it eagerly among themselves. But this was not the sort of disinterested opinion Jemima was looking for. Anna knew who the author was, and she was under the same strict instructions as Matthew not to reveal anything. The effort of keeping quiet about something that would instantly have enhanced her status among her peers was obviously killing her, so her enthusiasm about the serial when she came home might just have been her letting off some steam while she could.

Both Anna and Harriet had been of great help in talking Jemima through the minutiae of maids' lives in different types of household. She was hugely grateful for this, considering the realism of the background to be just as important here as it was for Stowaway Tom in Africa, and had offered to share some of her fee with them. They had both been horrified at the thought, as had Mrs Whiting, so Jemima had instead bought them each some new hair ribbons as a gift.

It was a windy afternoon, with autumn very much in evidence, when Jemima took another walk out with Sarah during her fortnightly half-day. It was chilly but not raining, so with their shawls wrapped round them and keeping up a brisk pace, they were fine. Once again they made their way along some of Liverpool's finest shopping streets, on the basis that they might not be able to afford to walk through the door but nobody could stop them looking in the windows.

'Ah, I love being outside,' said Sarah, as they turned away from a sparkling display of jewels, the shop's doorman eyeing them suspiciously until they were well on their way. 'Let's get a bun and find somewhere to eat it out of doors. And this time I'm paying – Mrs Lewis paid me in full this week.'

'Really? That's a good sign.'

'She was in a good mood, for some reason, though I don't know why, 'cos she'd just had to throw out some tenants for keeping bad company.'

Jemima paused mid-stride. 'May I ask who? Anyone I know? I mean – anyone who was there when I lived with you?'

'No, you wouldn't know 'em, 'cos they were the ones who moved into the rooms that you and your Pa moved out of. A widow lady, it was, with a daughter. Very quiet they were, too, and I thought they were as respectable as anyone, which just goes to show that you never can tell.'

Jemima knew at once what had happened, and her anger began to seethe anew that Mrs Lewis could cheat defenceless women this way and get away with it. She was desperate to try to find out whether Sarah knew anything about it, or whether she suspected, or even whether she might be able to find out, but how could Jemima ask such a thing of her? A maid-of-all-work with nothing to fall back on except the workhouse? It would only take one wrong word or look towards Mrs Lewis, and Sarah would be out on the street.

Jemima managed to disguise her feelings for the rest of the afternoon, so as not to spoil Sarah's rare treat, but after they parted her pace quickened significantly as she hurried back to the house.

Once she was inside, Jemima took pen and paper and began to write at a furious speed. She ignored the plan she'd already worked up for the sixth and possibly final episode of *The Maids of Maddox Place*, and started afresh. Up until now, the maids had outwitted scoundrels from the outside – burglars and swindling tradesmen – but this time it would be different. And if this was to be the last instalment of the story, then why not?

One of the maids in the street worked for an employer who was a landlady. This landlady had not been a major character up until now, but she had been mentioned a few times, so this gave Jemima the scope she needed. Olive, the maid, became suspicious about the way in which some tenants, always women or girls with no male protector, were suddenly accused of keeping bad company and then evicted without a right of reply. Olive investigated her mistress and found that she was stealing from these defenceless women before using the 'bad company' excuse to throw them out.

Jemima paused to dip her pen and to expel her pent-up breath. Then she continued, letting her fury and frustration pour out on to the page.

Olive took advice from the other maids in the street, and between them they set a watch on the landlady. She was seen selling a necklace that was recognised as having belonged to a former tenant, and then, through the ingenuity and bravery of the maids, she was caught red-handed by a policeman as she stole from one of the house's rooms. The landlady was arrested, the ex-tenants got their goods back, and Olive was lavishly praised by everyone for her courage and exemplary moral behaviour.

Mrs Hooke was sent to prison in disgrace, Jemima concluded, *and the brave and honest Olive was able to find a much better position*. That left the door open for further adventures, if Mr Grundy wanted to commission them, but if not then it was as good a place as any to stop.

It wasn't as neatly written as her normal work, admittedly, but she didn't want to copy it out again in her best hand in case she was tempted to water it down. So Jemima folded her sheets of paper, put them in the envelope with the latest adventure of *Stowaway Tom*, which she had finished yesterday, and ran out to post the letter before she could change her mind.

Chapter 16

'Jemima. Are you awake?'

It was the second week in October, and the temperature in the attic bedroom had changed from stiflingly hot to distinctly chilly. Rain was pattering noisily on the roof, and Jemima wondered what it would be like in December and January when the rain turned to sleet and snow.

She turned over so she could face Betty. 'Yes. Is something wrong?'

'No, not "wrong", exactly. It's just that you've never said another word about your family, or whether or not you wanted to look for them, since that day we went out for a walk with Henry. And that was weeks ago now.'

Jemima was silent.

'Sorry. I didn't mean to upset you, or say the wrong thing.'

'You didn't, don't worry.' Jemima sighed in the

darkness. She didn't want to explain to Betty why she'd initially postponed any kind of search, and in fact she was now wondering to herself why she'd never picked up the threads again, even though she could have done so. It was probably because of the seeming impossibility of it, with the number of Shaws there must be in Liverpool. She'd never been back to Hughes and Shaw, realising in hindsight how absolutely ridiculous she would have looked if the conversation had continued any longer. But she owed it to herself to have another try, she knew. And, thinking of the letter, she owed it to them, as well, didn't she? Especially the sister called Delilah who had poured out her heart to Ma. She might at least be glad to know that Jemima was still living, even if she'd forgotten her over the years and now wanted nothing further to do with her.

'I'll get the letter out again tomorrow,' she whispered. 'There might be some clues we missed the first time round.'

'Good. And we'll help you, whatever you need, even if it takes you away from us. You deserve to know about them, and it's what your Pa wanted.' Betty yawned. 'Sorry.'

'You've had a busy day at school. Best get some sleep while you can.'

'Ooh,' said Betty, drowsily. 'I can't tell you how keen

I am to give that Mrs Silverton my notice, and thumb my nose at her while I'm at it. But until I have another job to go to, or a husband, I can't.' She gave a little sleepy giggle as she settled further into the pillow. 'Maybe we'll find you've got lots of handsome, rich, unmarried brothers.'

Her breathing soon deepened.

Jemima wouldn't need to take the letter out of the book tomorrow, because she already knew every word of it by heart. The evident love for her that it contained – *to me she will always be Jemima Shaw, my beautiful sister; we all love her with all our hearts; she'll have that love always, whether she knows about it or not* – was the most important thing, even if she never found her family again, but she needed to put that to one side for a while and think practically. In terms of tracing them it was the names that were most important: the family name of Shaw, plus the Christian names of Delilah and William – although she certainly, and he possibly, wouldn't be called Shaw at all. But it was a start.

What else might be gleaned from the letter? *One of us would have let slip something about her having two families, or other brothers and sisters.* So, brothers and sisters, plural, indicating more than one of each, so someone out there was still called Shaw.

If only Delilah had put an address, or even mentioned an area of Liverpool. But of course she hadn't needed to, because she was writing to Ma, not to Jemima. *If you ever do want to tell her, and she wants to find out more, you know where we'll be.* That was the line that ran most frequently through Jemima's head, as it taunted her with its partial information. *Oh, where are you, Delilah, my sister? Are you still nearby?* Jemima could only hope and believe that the family were still in Liverpool, because otherwise her situation would be genuinely hopeless.

There must be something else. Unable to sleep, Jemima ran through the letter again in her head. There must be something she'd missed. *Things got worse for us, not better* – that was in the immediate aftermath of Jemima being given away, and tied in with what Pa had said about them being evicted. But they hadn't sunk without trace, because by the time Delilah wrote to Ma three years later, *things were looking up a bit*. Enough for them to be able to take her back, although they hadn't done that, for the reasons Delilah spelled out. *I need to do what's best for her, regardless of what I want.* But it gave Jemima a tiny clue as to the sort of area and class of people she should look for, and reassured her that they hadn't all ended up in the workhouse.

Thinking of what Pa had said about them being evicted brought Jemima's mind back to his deathbed murmurings, when he'd tried so hard to communicate with her. But she'd exhausted those already. A common surname; an eldest sister with an unusual biblical name; their Ma was her best friend. All of this had been confirmed by the letter, and the letter itself had been found in the flower book, which explained Pa's emphasis on the idea of flowers.

And was that shadowy bride, who had more than once appeared in Jemima's dreams to give her a pretty bloom, her sister?

The thoughts were starting to confuse themselves in Jemima's head now, so she let herself drift off. She would ... tomorrow ...

Next time you kiss her, give her an extra one from me.

* * *

Two letters were delivered to Jemima the following morning.

Tuesday, October 11th, 1864

Dear Mr. Jenkins,

Thank you for the sixth instalment of "The Maids of Maddox Place," received today along with the latest "Adventures of Stowaway Tom".

I trust that you received our letter of 4th inst., in which I proposed commissioning a further twelve episodes of "The Maids". I received no reply, and as you do not mention the subject in today's missive, I conclude that our communication must have gone astray.

The pertinent details are that we request further episodes of the same length and style, and that we propose increasing our fee to 6s per weekly instalment. Please reply immediately by return of post, or call in person to our office at 26, Church Street, to confirm whether you would like to continue with the serial.

I commend you, sir, on observing a gap in the reading market, of which we have been able to take full advantage ahead of any rival, and I also congratulate you on somehow being able to understand exactly what girls of that class enjoy reading. Sales, and the general public response to the serial, are very encouraging, and your insight is as remarkable as it is unexpected.

I have the honour to remain, &c,
Robert H. Grundy
Printseller and Publisher

So he did want to continue! And girls liked her stories! Jemima turned eagerly to the second letter, which turned out to be the earlier one that he referred to, which had somehow been misdirected at first to Back College Street rather than Back Colquitt Street. If only she'd seen that one a week ago, she wouldn't have spent the intervening time worrying that her serial was of no interest. And, possibly, she might not have written that angry 'final' episode about the thieving landlady, but it was too late to worry about that now.

There was no time to lose; Jemima needed to reply to Mr Grundy straight away. Given that turning up at his office in person would be the surest way to see the serial cancelled, that meant writing a letter, so she dashed one off, apologising for the lack of previous reply and explaining that she had received both his letters together this morning.

On her way out to the Post Office, in the rain, Jemima had the odd feeling that she was being followed. She ignored it until the letter was safely in the pillar box and then looked about her to see that she was being trailed by Mary and Joey.

She smiled. 'Good morning to you both. Were you looking for me?'

They each nudged each other, Joey having more success as it was Mary who spoke. 'We was wondering if there was going to be any more school.'

Jemima sighed, because the answer to that was complicated. Now that her employment involved writing two serials but not the timetabled hours of working in a school, she could feasibly teach yard school in the mornings and write in the afternoons and evenings. But the problem now was the 'yard' part of it, because the weather was too bad to sit out of doors in an uncovered space, and the group was too big to be seated in anyone's house, even if the yard's housewives hadn't objected on the grounds of rags and dirt.

'It's something I would very much like to do,' Jemima explained, 'but it's just not possible until we can find somewhere indoors. I'll keep looking, and if and when I do start up the school again, I'll let you know.' She had no way of finding or contacting them, she realised. 'You can keep checking back, if you like.'

This wasn't the answer the children had wanted, but they brightened at not being rejected entirely.

They fell into step beside Jemima as she walked. 'We've got a new bruvver,' Joey volunteered. 'A baby.'

'That's nice for you, and I hope your Ma is well. What's his name?'

'He's called Alfie,' Joey continued. 'Which is strange, 'cos he don't look like our other Alfie.'

Jemima knew that many families used the same name again when children died, and she gave a small shiver at the thought that there might have been another Jemima Shaw, and that she might never find out either way.

Mary was speaking now.

'I'm sorry, my mind was wandering, and I didn't quite catch that.'

'I was just saying, how are we supposed to know which one we mean, now, if we say "Alfie"? And does it mean we have to forget about the other one? 'Cos . . .'

She sounded forlorn, and Jemima stopped walking so she could look at the child properly. 'It's all right,' she said, as softly as the street noises would allow. 'Loving your new little brother doesn't mean that you love your old one any less. It's perfectly all right to keep both of them in your heart.'

'Really?'

'Yes, really.'

Mary cheered a little. 'Well, miss, if you say so then it must be right. See, Joey? I told you she was the right one to ask.' She paused. 'And we can really keep checking, in case there's going to be more school?'

'Yes. And if there is, I'll be glad to see you there.'

They ran off through the puddles, and Jemima turned her mind again to the subject of school as she tried to keep dry on her way home. It was all a question of money, as so many other things were. Nobody was going to let her use a building or turn somewhere into a large classroom without wanting rent, but even her enhanced payments from Mr Grundy wouldn't cover something as expensive as that, on top of the more regular rent she was now paying the Whitings.

Still, there was always the hope that this Saturday's lecture would provide some useful information. She and Betty were both going to attend, because Henry had taken the trouble to walk up to the library during one of his dinner hours to ask specifically about whether the event was open to female attendees. He had brought back the welcome news that it was, because apparently there were many women involved in this Ragged School Union – which made sense, when Jemima thought about it – as teachers, volunteers and raisers of funds. Indeed, as far as the senior library clerk knew, the speaker was bringing his wife with him, so it was all very proper and acceptable.

All of this put Jemima's mind at rest on the score of her being either overtly thrown out or forced to leave via more subtle means, and by now she was actively looking forward to the lecture.

* * *

The three of them set out in good time on Saturday evening. To their surprise, they arrived at the library to find an almost empty lecture room, which was still only half-full by the time the talk started. 'Not everyone in Liverpool is as keen on teaching poor children as you, then,' whispered Betty to Jemima, leaning across in front of Henry, who sat between them. 'But at least we're not the only women.'

Jemima had no time to reply, because the speaker was beginning. Ragged schools – so named because most of the pupils came from families who could not afford proper clothing or shoes – provided free education to poor children, both boys and girls, who would otherwise be excluded from it. The Union had been established to support those schools already running and to promote the formation of more, especially in cities outside of London.

This was all a very good start, and Jemima felt invigorated to know that there were people throughout the kingdom who felt the same way she did about education for the poor.

'We have probably all heard,' continued the speaker, 'the common objection to such schools, usually voiced in a superior or condescending manner, that they will "simply result in a better-educated class of criminal".'

Jemima smiled, having heard precisely those words in precisely that pompous tone from Mr and Mrs Silverton.

'But I say to you – is it not better to *prevent* crime

from occurring in the first place, rather than punishing it after the fact? By giving these children an education, we keep them off the streets and provide them with the means of obtaining gainful employment, which will, in time, lower the crime rates.'

Jemima nodded, watching as Henry scribbled notes in a pocketbook.

A brief history of the movement followed, about how schools had been set up by tenacious individuals working in difficult conditions, teaching classes in all sorts of nooks and crannies, in attics and even under railway arches. Then the speaker moved on to the practicalities of how such schools might be established in Liverpool, and, as Jemima had expected, most of it came down to money. As she already knew, you could have the best will in the world, but it was difficult to teach if you had no equipment and no space to do it in. But it turned out that there were ways and means of raising what was necessary: petitions for funding and grants, and the solicitation of donations from wealthy individuals, and so on. Jemima watched Henry adding to his notes, and remembered that they were sitting in the William Brown Library – did Liverpool still contain rich men who were willing to put some of their fortune towards the public good? Surely it did.

The day-to-day details of how a school might run

were even more interesting. Many of them, the speaker explained, ran two separate half-days – morning and afternoon – so that children could attend either one or the other, and then still be available for paid work the other half a day if their families needed it. This had not occurred to Jemima before, but she thought it a good idea if it would enable more pupils to attend. Even if school were completely free, some families *still* couldn't afford to send their children, as they needed every penny of income they could bring in.

Lessons were, by necessity, generally restricted to the three Rs and Bible study, plus needlework for the girls, but as Ragged schools were not tied to the system of payment by examination results, they could in fact include whatever they thought would be most useful for their own pupils. They might also do further social good by providing food and clothing as well as education. Many of the teachers, predominantly women, were volunteers – *Women working for nothing?* thought Jemima, *There's a surprise* – but some of the more formally established Ragged schools were run by a salaried headmaster or were able to pay their teachers.

Despite the sparse attendance there were many questions at the end of the session, and it was late and dark by the time the three of them spilled on to the street, exhilarated by new ideas. Fortunately their route home was a reputable one, mainly along wide thoroughfares lit by gas lamps, so they were able to concentrate on their discussions. There must be a way to finance such a school that they could run between them, and tomorrow they would get started on ideas of how to raise the funds for it.

* * *

By Monday Henry was so enthused by the idea of teaching at a Ragged school, so full of the plans they'd spent most of yesterday discussing, that he could hardly bear to go to work. But that was unreasonable of him, he knew – he should be grateful to have such a steady and decently paid position when so many other young men didn't. Although, in teaching youngsters, might he not be ensuring that more of them could have steady positions in future, and therefore he would spread the good around a little more? There was an interesting discussion to be had there.

This thought occupied him until he and Matthew reached Brunswick Street, upon which they parted and Henry went to his desk. Matters of income and expenditure then engrossed him until dinnertime, at which point he and his fellow workers had an hour's leisure. This was one of the advantages of the position, he reminded himself; the time each day to take a break from work, stretch his legs and visit the library or the shops, and all with a little bit of money in his pocket now that more of the family were earning.

His trips to the library and his walks about town were not just for interest or study. He was slowly working his way through every Shaw listed in *Gore's Directory*, looking up their type of business and address, and then passing by it to see if he could discover anything that might help Jemima. She, of course, hadn't asked him to do this, or even given him permission to do so, but he persevered anyway, on the basis that if she ever did tell him she wanted to start looking, he would be able to cut down the number of her potential searches. Henry had given up as futile the idea of trying to trace the sister who, for all her unusual Christian name, could have any surname under the sun now, but the Shaw connection was merely time-consuming, so all he had to do was to keep working through the list.

It turned out that there was, in fact, a Shaw in his own company, and for a short while Henry was excited by the prospect that a miraculous coincidence might have occurred, and that this would turn out to be Jemima's brother. But the man was forty, and when Henry managed to engage him in casual conversation he revealed that he lived with an elderly father who had retired from a lifetime's work in a mill. So that wasn't the stroke of luck Henry was looking for, but he didn't give up hope. If Jemima was fated to find her family, something would turn up.

Fate was on Henry's mind as he left the office and turned up the collar of his coat against the sharp wind. Specifically, his fate and Jemima's. He knew by now that he had strong feelings for her, but the problem was that she didn't reciprocate them. This was not due to Rob; Henry had recognised some while ago that Jemima wasn't interested in Rob except as Betty's brother, so Henry had no need to be jealous. But the problem was that she also thought of Henry in the same way. 'You're our brother,' Betty had said, that day when she'd asked him to come up to the attic, and it was true, wasn't it? And Jemima's reluctance to go out to the lecture with him, although she had put it down to a different reason, was surely that it sounded too much like he'd been asking her to walk out with him. Which he would very much like to do, if he could ever pluck up the courage, and if he could be confident that he wouldn't be turned down. She would be nice about it, of course, and wouldn't humiliate him, but it would be rejection and a dashing of all his hopes nonetheless.

All of this was tied up in Henry's conflicting feelings about Jemima's own family, and whether or not she wanted to find them, and whether or not *he* wanted her to find them. If she did, she would surely want to be with them, see them constantly – live with them, even, and he would lose her. If, on the other hand, she didn't find them or chose not to look, she might well stay where she was. In that case he would at least continue to see her, even if it wasn't quite on the terms he would prefer, and who knew what might transpire in the future, if they continued to live in the same household?

And this was why he was taking such efforts to trace Jemima's family on her behalf: because it would be the most selfish act imaginable to want to keep her if it was not in her own best interests. And those interests could not be fully known until she was in possession of all the relevant information. If Jemima could find her brothers and sisters, she would know who and what she was, and could make her own decisions about her future life. Whether that future life included Henry or not was the point on which he agonised constantly, but if he truly loved her then he would support her in any path she chose to take.

He'd almost reached the top of Dale Street by now, without really noticing. Today, as it happened, he was not on a search for Shaws, but rather for tobacco. It was Pa's birthday later this week, and Henry had kept back the spending money that Ma allowed him out of his wages so that he could buy something a little finer than

Pa normally used. Dale Street was not the home of large, impressive department stores, but it was packed with smaller shops that sold all manner of items: just from here Henry could see a watchmaker, a musical instrument maker and a linen draper between him and the tobacconist he was seeking.

After taking advice and making his purchase, Henry came out of the shop and turned to make his way back towards Brunswick Street and the docks. About halfway down, he paused. There was a flower shop here – the property of F. AND D. MALLING, SUPPLIERS TO LIVERPOOL'S BEST HOUSES AND TO THE GENERAL PUBLIC, according to the sign over the door – and he hadn't spent all his money. Flowers always made him think of Jemima; partly because of the significance of her book about them, and partly, well, because one tended to think of flowers at the same time as one thought of the girl one admired.

Perhaps he should buy her some. It would be bold, but it would at least bring the matter to a head, and he'd have a clearer idea of her feelings one way or the other. He would give her a bunch of flowers, just as a gift for no reason, and he would watch her reaction very carefully. If he could discern the slightest indication that she understood or shared his sentiments, then that would be wonderful. If she showed nothing but a sisterly reaction, that would be terrible, but at least he would know, and he could give up and stop torturing himself.

Fate, he thought, as he pushed open the door.

Having never been in a flower shop before, he had no idea what sort of thing might be available in the middle of October, but there seemed to be quite a choice. He would have to ask for advice, or knowing him he'd end up buying something that was totally unsuitable.

The room was filled with a very pleasant scent, and the red-haired woman at the counter bore a welcoming smile. Encouraged, Henry moved forward and explained his need for guidance.

'Oh,' said the woman. 'You should know I'm not the owner, just her sister-in-law.' She had a soft Irish accent. 'I'm only minding the shop while she gets the children their dinner, and I'm no expert, but I'll fetch her.'

'Oh, please don't disturb—' began Henry.

'It's no trouble, sir, really, and I know she'd want to make sure you had exactly the right flowers for the purpose. Just wait there one moment.'

Henry watched as she moved to a door behind the counter, which he presumed led to living accommodation.

'You've a customer here who needs some advice,' the woman called. A pause, and no reply. She pushed the door open a little further. 'Did you hear me? Delilah?'

Chapter 17

It was wash day once more, in the never-ending round of household chores, but Mrs Whiting had told Jemima in no uncertain terms to sit down and get on with her writing instead of labouring over the tub. 'It's work, like Betty's or Henry's, for all you do it sat at the table rather than in a school or an office. And if you're being paid, you need to give it proper time and effort.'

Jemima did wonder how much of this was real solicitude about her writing, and how much was due to Mrs Whiting still not wanting a rank amateur under her feet while she had so much laundry to do, but she was happy to comply in either case. She'd already posted the instalments of both stories that were due tomorrow, and was now working up her rough draft of next week's. There were plenty of other matters on her mind, too, chiefly to do with the possibility of setting up a school, but there was no point in thinking too much about those until Betty and Henry got home. In the meantime she should put everything else to one side and concentrate on Stowaway Tom and the maids.

A burst of noise and action announced that the children were home, and Jemima was surprised to see that it was already gone half past four and that there were rather a lot of sheets of paper spread out in front of her.

'Which one have you been writing?' asked Maisie, peering over Jemima's shoulder in the hope of getting a clue to what might happen next for the maids.

'Ah, you'll have to wait and see,' said Jemima, cheerfully, sweeping up the sheets. 'Now, tell me all about what you did at school today.'

She listened as she began to chop up the ingredients for that evening's large pan of scouse – a household task she *could* be trusted with, while the soaking and exhausted Mrs Whiting was busy with the day's last load in the tub, aided now by Betty, who had arrived home too – and heard about how Maisie had been praised for being able to recite a long poem by heart, which she would repeat in front of an examiner in due course, to represent the school. She also heard how Maisie would have liked to discuss the poem's content, but that this was not allowed.

Jemima praised and sympathised in equal measures,

promising that the two of them would find time to talk about it as soon as they could, and determined that tomorrow she really would go and redeem Pa's books. Then there would be as many poems and as much Shakespeare as she and Maisie could wish for. Maisie read so well that Jemima even wondered if she might like to start on *Pride and Prejudice.*

She hummed as they set the table. Of the workers, Matthew was always home first; he generally ran all the way, with the boundless energy that ensured he was well thought of at his job, and also so he could get a good seat at the table ahead of tea, because he was always ravenous. Henry would arrive a few minutes later, and then Rob and Mr Whiting shortly after that, following their longer walk.

'Jemima!' Henry burst in, panting, with Matthew at his heels.

Alarmed, she turned. 'What is it? Is something wrong?'

Mrs Whiting and Betty hurried in from outside. 'Is it Pa? No, you shouted for Jemima—' Betty swallowed the rest of it, her gaze flicking from Jemima to the expression on her brother's face. 'It's not . . .?'

Henry was so out of breath he couldn't continue, so Jemima looked enquiringly at Matthew.

He shrugged. 'Said he had to get home as quick as he could 'cos he had to talk to you. He didn't say why.'

Henry remained for a moment longer with his hands on his knees, then he managed to take in enough air to stand up. 'I've found her,' he panted.

'Found who?' asked Mrs Whiting, but Jemima knew. A sudden chill swept over her, and she opened her mouth to find that no words would come out.

'Delilah,' he gasped.

'But who . . .?'

'Ma,' Jemima heard Betty's voice as if from a great distance. 'I'll explain it all later, but for now let's get on and leave them to talk. It's nothing bad, I promise.'

Jemima managed a whisper. 'But how do you know? How do you know it's her?'

'I heard the name . . .'

Jemima was shaking her head. 'I know it's unusual, but there might well be more than one of them in Liverpool. How can you be sure it's her?'

Her hands were trembling, and Henry reached out to take them in his own. 'Because she runs a *flower shop*.'

* * *

Jemima stood outside the flower shop for the third time that day.

It had been too late, the evening before, to come up into town. The shop would be closed, and Jemima didn't want to interrupt the family in the evening, and it was dark, and anyway she hadn't been sure her legs would take her that far. And she was scared.

Once the children had gone to bed she'd explained the whole story to Mr and Mrs Whiting, who had exclaimed, sympathised and encouraged her just as much as she might have expected from such loving parents. They had assured her that whatever happened she would not be alone, but as she'd left the house this morning Jemima had felt even more lost than usual, her sense of being adrift between two families greater than ever.

She'd reached the flower shop a little after nine, but it was far too busy for her to consider going in – there was a long queue of smartly dressed and liveried servants outside, taking their turn to enter and then emerge with their arms full of blooms to take back to the houses of their employers. Jemima had watched for a while, angry and annoyed at herself for having misunderstood Pa when he was trying to tell her. His insistence on flowers hadn't just been related to the book – he was trying to tell her that Delilah *sold* flowers. 'Find . . . ', he'd said. *Find the shop.* If only Jemima had understood this earlier, a great deal of confusion and heartache could have been avoided.

Delilah's mention in the letter that things were looking up had been no exaggeration, for it was clear that she owned the business and was not merely an employee of it. She must be the 'D. Malling' on the sign over the door – the 'F' presumably being her husband, which meant that he could not be the William who had written the letter – and the woman Henry had spoken to had referred to Delilah as the owner. A sister-in-law, she'd said, which meant that there was at least one other relative still living somewhere.

Jemima didn't want to loiter outside the shop for the whole morning while it was so busy; she would go away and come back later. The last thing she wanted was to meet her sister at a time when there were dozens of strangers around, and Delilah would need to concentrate on serving them. So Jemima took herself up to the library, where she was totally unable to concentrate on any kind of work. Instead she settled in the Ladies' Reading Room, first with some remarkably tedious magazines, and then with another novel by the author of *Pride and Prejudice*. There always seemed to be something pertinent in this collection of works, and this morning it was a young woman who was about to be reunited with a family she hadn't seen since she was a little girl. She wasn't 'addicted to raptures'; rather 'her happiness was of a quiet, deep, heart-swelling sort', and there were 'emotions of tenderness that could not be clothed in words'. Jemima wondered how these lines, written so long ago by an author living in a different world, could be so piercingly relevant to her now.

It was time to have another try; the morning rush would have subsided by now. But when she reached the shop again it was to find that it was closed for the dinner hour, and once again Jemima's nerve failed her and she didn't like to interrupt. Delilah had children, Jemima knew that from Henry's account of his visit, and they would no doubt be at home from school, just as they had been at the same time yesterday. A reunion and all the attendant explanations in front of children – nieces and nephews! – would be far too awkward.

And so Jemima walked around town, not really noticing where she went, until she heard the church clocks strike four. This was late enough to be a quieter time in a flower shop, and early enough that the children would still be safely at school.

It was time. What would Pa say? *You're my Jemima, and I believe in you.*

One thing Henry hadn't been able to tell Jemima was what Delilah looked like, because he'd fled from the shop as soon as he heard the name. As he'd eventually explained, there was no way he could have continued his original planned conversation with anything like calm, and he was afraid he would blurt something out when it wasn't his place to do so, and thus a swift retreat had seemed his only option. Jemima didn't know, therefore, whether the tall, elegant woman she could now glimpse through the window, as she stood alone in the shop rearranging what was left of the day's displays, was Delilah herself. But there was only one way to find out, wasn't there?

Clutching the flower book and Pa's handkerchief in her shaking hands for luck, Jemima pushed open the door.

She was met with a beautiful, welcoming smile. 'Good afternoon, miss. How may I help you?'

Jemima was overpowered. That hair, that voice . . . this was the bride at the wedding who had given her a flower from her bouquet, and it was also the woman who had been talking to Ma on that long-ago morning at home.

The tone turned to one of concern. 'Are you all right? Or have you come about the job? If so, there's no need to be nervous. Please, come in.'

Jemima stared blankly for another moment, then took a couple of faltering steps forward. She knew who she was addressing, but she had to say it out loud, had to hear it confirmed from her sister's own lips. 'Pardon me, ma'am,' she managed, 'but is your name Delilah?'

'Yes, it is,' replied Delilah, a little confused. 'But—' She gasped and stopped dead.

'And are you . . .'

But Jemima didn't need to continue. Delilah's eyes had opened as wide as saucers, and they were flicking from Jemima's face to the book and the handkerchief and back again. Then she turned pale and began to tremble almost as much as Jemima was. She opened her mouth and made a silent attempt to speak a word that began with *J*.

And then they were in each other's arms.

For a long while, neither of them could say anything. They simply held on as tightly as they could, as if each was afraid the other would vanish if she let go, while they cried hot tears of emotion and joy. Jemima wanted the embrace to go on forever. She was found; she was *wanted*.

Eventually Delilah pulled back a little, though she still kept her hands on Jemima's shoulders. 'And is it really you? Truly?'

Jemima nodded and made a futile attempt to wipe her eyes.

A door at the back of the shop opened and a girl of about twelve or thirteen appeared, carrying a toddler. 'Mummy?'

Delilah swung round. 'Daisy! Leave Andrew there and run to your Auntie Meg. *Run*, do you hear me? Tell her to drop whatever she's doing and come back with you, right now.'

The girl's face took on an expression of panic. 'Is something wrong? What shall I tell her?'

Jemima was pulled into another close embrace, and she willingly wound her arms around Delilah and buried her face in the hollow of her shoulder. 'Tell her,' came Delilah's voice, hoarse with emotion, 'that our darling Jemima has come home at last.'

* * *

Once Daisy had stopped staring and left on her mission, Delilah pulled herself together enough to turn the key in the lock and the shop sign to 'Closed', and then took Jemima's hand to lead her through the far door. Jemima found herself in a cosy room that was both kitchen and parlour, with a small range, a wooden table and chairs, a sideboard of various possessions and a neatly made bed over in the far corner.

There were two comfortable, upholstered chairs by the range, and they sat down. The toddler, unsure of what was going on, came over to investigate. He stared curiously at Jemima for a moment, then took his thumb out of his mouth, tugged at Delilah's skirts and said, 'That lady looks like Uncle Jem.'

Delilah's hand flew to her mouth. 'Oh! I was so . . . I

didn't see it at first... but of course... and it was the last thing that Ma...'

Jemima wasn't really taking any of this in.

'Tea,' said Delilah, more firmly. 'We both need a hot cup of tea with sugar. It's about time I lit the range, anyway.'

Jemima tried to calm herself while she watched her sister busying herself with coals and kettle. Her *sister*. And there were more. Auntie Meg and Uncle Jem, at the very least, as well as possibly the mysterious William.

Delilah sat down again. 'I've been dreaming of this day for so many years, I can hardly believe it's happened. I'm so happy, I can't—' she choked on a sob. 'I can hardly talk, and look at me, I'm making a complete fool of myself.' She took in a shuddering breath. 'There's so much to say, but the most important things are that you're here, and we love you, and we've never stopped loving you.'

Slowly, hesitantly, Jemima reached out to take her sister's hand. 'I know,' she said, 'And I know the sacrifice you made, all those years ago.' Jemima had been gripping the book all this time, she now noticed, and she held it out. 'It's all in here.'

Delilah's eyes grew wide again. 'But how did—?' She

shook her head. 'It's going to take me a while to understand all this.'

She's in even more shock than I am, thought Jemima. But, of course, that was only to be expected. She, Jemima, had known she was looking for her family, had known before she entered the shop that she was about to be reunited with her sister, but the whole thing had struck Delilah like a thunderbolt. No wonder she was in pieces.

Jemima was now able to think and speak the more clearly of the two. 'I'll give you the short version now, shall I? Just to give you an idea. Because we've got the rest of our lives to go through the details.'

'Have we?' asked Delilah, wild hope in her voice. 'Have we really?'

'If you . . . want me?'

'Oh, Jemima!' Delilah seemed on the verge of tears again but, with a huge effort, she controlled herself. 'Yes, please tell me something now.'

'I didn't know anything about you until a few months ago,' Jemima began. 'I always thought that Ma and Pa were my real – I mean, my—'

'They *were* your real parents,' said Delilah, in a tone that was a little bit stronger. 'They took you in, they brought you up, they loved you. Don't ever be ashamed of calling them your Ma and Pa.'

Jemima nodded. 'My Ma died when I was five.'

'Yes,' said Delilah. 'And that was when we really lost you. When I heard about it, I was going to come round and see James, to see if he needed anything from us. I could have done it just that once without you knowing, so it wouldn't really be breaking my promise. But then I went into labour – a bit earlier than I expected, maybe it was the shock of the news – and I was in bed for days. By the time I was well enough to walk down to Brick Street, you and he had moved out and nobody could tell me where.'

'I didn't understand at the time, but Pa just couldn't bear to live there without her. That was why we moved on so quickly, I suppose. Plus he couldn't look after a house and do all the cooking and laundry and go out to work, so we always lived in lodgings after that.'

Delilah hesitated. 'And . . . now? I did hear . . .'

'Pa died,' said Jemima, simply. And then she burst into tears.

'Oh, my darling girl!' Delilah knelt by her and held her in her arms. 'Your Pa was one of the finest men I've ever known. He was with me, you know, on two of the worst days of my life. But never mind that now. I'm just so sorry that you lost him.'

'He was ill – dying – for a long time,' continued Jemima, when she was finally able to speak again. 'And he kept saying confused things about me not being alone after he'd gone, about me having another family. I thought he was just rambling, but he said such specific things about me being given to him and Ma by neighbours when I was a baby, that I had to believe him. But he died – this was back in July – without being able to tell me everything, and he couldn't remember your name.'

'But where have you been since then? Still in the same lodgings? Or do you need somewhere to live? Anything we have is—'

'No, no, that's not why I'm here.' There was no need, just now, to go into too many details about what had happened. 'Like I said, I didn't know what you were called, so how could I look for you? I've been living with my best friend and her family, and they're lovely, and I just thought I'd never know, but then I found this, hidden in the book.' Jemima drew out the letter.

Delilah unfolded it with a soft cry. 'Oh! I remember when we wrote this. Dear, dear Ellen.' She looked up. 'Don't forget, I knew your Ma all my life, and she was my Ma's – our Ma's – you're right, this is going to get complicated – best friend for years before that. Whenever you want to talk about her, anything you want to know, just ask.'

Jemima was so choked that she could hardly reply,

but she was almost done. 'And this gave us some clues, so Betty and I – that's my friend – and Henry – that's her brother – started looking, and we didn't get very far because of— well, never mind all that – but yesterday he happened to come into your shop, and he heard your name—'

'Ah! Was he the young man who came in at dinner-time? Normally we're closed for an hour, but Bridget was here and said she didn't mind looking after the shop.' Delilah shivered. 'And I'm glad she did. Imagine if we'd been closed and he hadn't come in.'

'Bridget. Is that her name? She told him she was your sister-in-law, though I don't know whether that means she's your husband's sister or your brother's wife. *Our* brother's wife,' Jemima added, abruptly.

Delilah laughed. 'Both, as it happens. And thank goodness – or thank my parents, at least – for my unusual name. Is that what made him run out?'

'Henry was worried he'd let something slip, and it wasn't up to him, so he had to tell me first. And he had to sit at work all afternoon before he could come home and find me. And by then it was too late for me to come, so I waited until this morning, but—'

There was a sudden commotion as the back door was flung open. Two boys hurled themselves through it, each holding one hand of the smaller girl between them, and both talking at once, but they halted abruptly when they saw the stranger. 'Off you go and play in the yard,' said Delilah, 'and take Andrew with you for now.'

'Oh, but—'

'Either that or you can go and sweep the shop floor, but you can't stay in here, not while we're talking.'

The boys exchanged a look and went outside, pulling the two smaller children with them.

'You have rather a lot of nieces and nephews, I'm afraid,' said Delilah, smiling as she watched the door banging shut behind them. 'But we'll worry about those introductions later. In the meantime, I should tell you that we've been searching for you since July, since you ran out on Meg that time. That was the first we'd heard of you for years, and it sounded like you needed us, so it was time to put my earlier promise to one side and start looking.'

Jemima had no idea what Delilah was talking about, but before asking for an explanation there was one all-important question she needed to ask. 'How many brothers and sisters have I actually got? Pa never said.'

'You don't know?' Delilah sounded shocked. 'I'm sorry, if I'd thought, I'd have said something earlier. You have three brothers and three sisters.' She looked up at the sound of voices outside the back door. 'And this will be Meg, if I'm not mistaken. She was in despair not to have caught up with you that day, and she's been desperate ever since, just as much as me. Come in!'

The door swung open, and Jemima prepared herself to meet another sister.

And then she froze in the very act of rising from her chair, because the woman standing on the threshold was Mrs Hopkins, of Hopkins' tea room.

Chapter 18

Jemima felt her jaw sagging. How, what . . .?

'Delilah,' said Mrs Hopkins, 'how long has that kettle been boiling?'

Delilah exclaimed and jumped up to take it off the heat. Neither she nor Jemima had noticed that the room was half-full of steam.

Jemima was on her feet and Mrs Hopkins, without another word, stepped forward to embrace her. She was, as Jemima already knew, tiny, and now it was Jemima's turn to drop tears down on to the top of a sister's hair.

But she was still bemused when they stepped back. 'I don't understand, Mrs Hop—'

'It's Meg,' came the firm reply. 'Meg, your sister. Oh, if only I'd paid more attention, all this time! But I'm always busy in the kitchen, so I don't go out into the tea room much – Sally and Hannah do most of the serving.'

'But wait, wait. You're Mrs Hopkins. But I thought you must have been called Roberts before you married, not Shaw. How can you be my sister?'

Meg was puzzled for a moment, and then comprehension dawned. 'Ah – you thought Mrs Roberts was my mother?'

'Well . . . yes?'

'I'd be proud if she was. But no, she was the cook in the house where I was a maid in service, when I was younger. She looked after me and taught me everything I know. She's retired now, and lives on her own, so she likes to come to the tea room, and we couldn't be happier to have her there.'

'Oh, I *see*. And all this makes more sense about what you said' – she looked at Delilah, who was pouring tea – 'about running out.' Jemima turned back to Mrs Hopkins, whom she would remember to think of as Meg from now on, and realised that she'd got the wrong end of another stick as well. 'I heard that a sister had run away from you, and I thought it must have been Hannah, and I was upset thinking about all of you. But you meant me, didn't you?'

'Yes. You'd been coming to the tea room for some time, I knew that, but I'd never really seen you close up before. If I had I might have said something, because you *do* have a look of Jem about you. But when you spoke to Mrs Roberts that day, you told her your name. And after you'd gone, she told it to Hannah. But it wasn't until a few minutes afterwards that Hannah mentioned it to me, and I dropped a whole tray of jam tarts. How many other girls could there be in Liverpool, of the right age and called Jemima Jenkins? I ran out into the street and shouted for you, but it was crowded and I had no idea which way you'd gone.'

'And Meg told me about it,' broke in Delilah. 'But she also said you came in every week, so all we had to do was wait until the next Saturday afternoon. We were there, ready. But you never came back.'

Jemima was still floored by the fact that she had unwittingly been in the same building as one of her sisters every week for nearly a year. If *only* she'd known. It would have made dear Pa's final days a little easier if he'd been able to see them all reunited, secure in the knowledge that Jemima wouldn't be alone and lost.

Meg continued in a more practical tone. 'I know this is a huge shock all round, but those children are going to want some tea, Delilah, and so will Frank and Annie when they get home. No, you stay there – I'll do it. I can talk, listen and cook at the same time.'

Jemima was getting inundated with the mention of

all these names. 'Delilah, just before Meg came in, you were saying that I had three sisters and three brothers. Please, tell me who they are?'

'Sorry, yes. Three sisters: that's me, Meg and Annie. She's the youngest, only two years older than you, and she lives here with us. She'll be back from work soon. And the three boys are William, Sam and Jem.'

'And you've both said that I look like Jem?'

Delilah gave a sad sigh. 'Yes. It was the last thing that Ma – our Ma – said. She lived long enough to hold you in her arms, and she said, "She looks like Jem, bless her." Ellen told me so when she came downstairs with you. Ma hadn't said anything about a name, so I decided to call you Jemima, to remember her last words.'

'You've mentioned our Ma several times, but no Pa. Where was he?'

Delilah exchanged a glance with Meg. 'He's been dead a long time, and we're all better off without him.'

Jemima sat back. Delilah, Meg, Annie. William, Sam, Jem.

'I think we'll leave fetching the boys this evening,' said Delilah. 'Poor Jemima will be overwhelmed enough as it is. I know I am.'

'Not to mention the fact that between the six of us, we've got two husbands, one fiancé, three wives and eleven children,' said Meg, drily, from her place at the range. 'Thirteen if you count Hannah and Charlie as well.'

Jemima was almost too tired to exclaim over this.

The others noticed. 'You sit there and have another cup of tea,' said Meg, in a tone that brooked no argument. 'Delilah, I'll need to get back home soon, to feed George, but this just needs an occasional stir now.'

A babble of voices sounded outside the back door, including a deep male one, and after a few moments the owner of it put his head round. 'What's going on then, my darling?' He had an Irish accent. 'The children said there's a visitor and you told them to stay out the way, but it's getting cold for them out here, not to mention me and Annie, just home after a hard day.' He noticed Jemima. 'Ah, this will be the fair lady guest herself, no doubt.' He paused, looking at the smiles of Delilah and Meg, which were lighting up the room. 'What?'

He came in, dressed in a smart uniform of some kind, and was followed by a young woman who was surely Jemima's other sister.

Delilah stood. 'Frank, Annie: this is our sister Jemima.'

There was one moment of stunned silence, and then Annie shrieked and ran to hug Jemima. Being more robust than either of the older sisters, she swept her right off her feet, and Jemima laughed in delight.

Frank's initial response had been to do the same to his wife, but then he came over to Jemima. Rather unexpectedly and extravagantly, he took her hand and raised it to his lips. 'You're dear to me already,' he said, 'as a new sister. But on top of that, you've made my wife happier than she's ever been, and her life complete, and for that I can never thank you or love you enough.'

The children were by now crowding in, and the room was in happy family chaos.

'You are staying for your tea?' Delilah asked.

Jemima exclaimed. 'Tea! Oh my goodness, it was nine o'clock this morning when I went out – Mrs Whiting and everyone will be wondering what's happened to me. They'll be worried sick by now.'

'That's the family you're living with?' Delilah was already reaching for a shawl. 'They're good people, and the last thing we want to do is worry them. We'll walk you back now.' She paused. 'But please, come back to us as soon as you can. Tomorrow?'

Frank laughed. 'Give the girl a bit o' breathing space, my darling. She might not want to be drowning in Shaws quite so quickly.'

'Oh, I do!' said Jemima. 'I mean – yes, I'd love to, perhaps tomorrow evening after we've all finished work for the day?'

It was agreed that she would come round at five

o'clock, and stay for her tea; the first of what Delilah hoped would be many family meals together.

Annie hugged Jemima again, while listening to instructions from Meg about what was in tonight's pot. 'I can't tell you how glad I am not to be the baby any more,' she joked. 'And to have someone nearly my own age, among all these old people.'

'Oi!' said Frank, in a tone of mock-offence. 'I know I've got a couple of grey hairs these days, but really . . .'

They set off, and Jemima could still hardly believe she was walking with two sisters and a brother-in-law, chatting about herself and her work. It was a dream, surely, and she'd wake up any minute now.

'I'll ask the boys to come round tomorrow evening as well, shall I, if you think you can manage it?' Delilah asked.

Frank laughed. 'Boys! William's, what, thirty now? And the other two are in their mid-twenties.'

'They'll always be boys to me.' Delilah's tone was affectionate. 'But we'll leave all the other husbands, wives and children until Sunday,' she said to Jemima, 'if you can come.'

'Sunday?'

'You chose just the right week to come back to us. Once a month we all go up to Meg's for our Sunday dinner, because it's the only place big enough to hold us all.'

'And because the cooking is the best in Liverpool,' added Frank.

'And it's this coming Sunday,' finished Meg. 'Please do say you'll come.'

Jemima was floating on a cloud of happiness. 'I'd love to.'

'That's settled, then.' They reached Williamson Square, and Meg embraced Jemima once more. 'Until tomorrow.' Then, heedless of her dignity, she skipped like a little girl. 'Just *wait* until I tell Tommy and the others!'

The remaining three continued on their way, Jemima arm in arm with her oldest sister. When they got near to Back Colquitt Street, a small Albert-shaped figure appeared out of the shadows and dashed round into the yard. 'She's here! She's back!' Jemima also caught something about 'a woman, and a fella in a uniform'.

By the time they got to the door, there was a crowd around it. Jemima rushed forward to Mrs Whiting. 'I'm so sorry! I forgot I'd been so long, and I didn't mean to worry you.'

'You're safe now, pet, that's all that matters.'

In answer to the enquiring looks, Jemima turned to indicate her companions, feeling as though the glow of her heart should be lighting up the whole yard. 'This is my sister Delilah, and her husband Frank.'

Mrs Whiting exclaimed in joy and moved to take Delilah's hands in her own, almost kissing her in her excitement. 'Well, then! I'm that made up. And any friend or relation of Jemima's is always welcome here. Will you step inside?'

'Thank you, ma'am, no, we'd better get home to our children. But I'm so glad to hear from Jemima that she has such wonderful friends. I hope we'll get to speak to you properly soon, once we all know whether we're coming or going.' Delilah had one last embrace with Jemima. 'Tomorrow. Five o'clock. Please don't forget!'

'Forget? I wouldn't miss it for the *world*.'

Frank, who had been shaking hands most heartily with Mr Whiting and anyone else he could reach, tipped his cap at them all and ushered Delilah out of the yard. They paused for one last wave before disappearing around the corner.

'Now then,' said Mrs Whiting. 'You're just in time for tea, so come in and tell us all about it.'

* * *

Henry had known it was all over as soon as he saw the shining light in Jemima's eyes when she got home, and the rest of the evening only reinforced that fact in his mind. She had found her family and, more to the point, she had found that they loved and wanted her. It wouldn't be long before Jemima decided to move in with them, and then he would lose her. And the loss would be complete. Would this new family, these seemingly well-established and prosperous people, want to encourage Jemima to open a school for poor, ragged children? Surely not. And he wouldn't even have the tenuous connection of her being a colleague of Betty's at St James's, with the hope that he would run into her from time to time on that basis.

In a further blow, Henry recognised that he would now also lose the very relationship that had been troubling him, but which, ironically, he would now seize upon eagerly as a crumb of comfort. Jemima would have no need to see him as a brother now she had three of her own.

But he had no regrets about what he'd done. None. Just look at how *happy* she was, as she told everyone about her day and its discoveries! That was more important than anything, and Henry could rejoice for her, even in the depths of his own sadness.

Betty's astonishment was so great at finding out that Mrs Hopkins, of Hopkins' tea room, was one of Jemima's sisters that she almost wouldn't believe it, even when Jemima assured her several times that it was true. That meant that Jemima also knew of a brother-in-law, even though she said she hadn't seen him this evening: Mr Hopkins, the kindly grocer. Henry was already losing track.

The livelihoods of the others were discussed, although Jemima admitted she'd been so dazed that she hadn't really asked. Delilah had the flower shop, which Frank seemingly didn't work in, even though his name was over the door. Pa chipped in here to say he thought the uniform might be something to do with the railway, and Henry privately agreed, although he didn't speak out loud. Jemima didn't know what the third sister did, except that it must be a job that didn't involve living in anywhere, so she wasn't a maid – perhaps she worked in a different shop, or a factory? And she could only speculate as to the brothers. She would find out tomorrow when she met them all and had more of an opportunity to talk. Although there were so many, she didn't know how she would get used to it.

There was some gentle amusement around the room at the idea of a family of three brothers and three sisters being considered 'large', but, to be fair, the dozen or so nieces and nephews would certainly make up the numbers. Jemima had seen five that evening, she said, and she looked forward to meeting the others.

As this subject was mentioned, Henry saw in the shadows that he had a fellow sufferer: Maisie, already looking bereft at the idea of Jemima having so many other children to know and love. He promised himself that he'd be extra kind to her as time went on, helping with her schoolwork and talking to her about anything she liked. He wouldn't let his little sister feel Jemima's loss as keenly as he would.

In the meantime Henry sat back and watched Jemima, revelling in her joy even though it had come at the expense of his own.

* * *

Jemima spent Wednesday morning and afternoon at the table trying to write, but never had she found it so difficult to concentrate. By half past four she'd crossed out so many lines and paragraphs and crumpled so many sheets that she would need to go out tomorrow and buy more paper.

The hands of the little clock on the shelf moved with aching slowness, but eventually it was time for Jemima to leave. She asked Mrs Whiting not to worry if it was late by the time she got back, and agreed to the older woman's instruction that she would ask one of the men in the family to walk her home. 'Or

I can send Pa or Henry or Rob to meet you, if you prefer.'

'No, please – let them put their feet up when they get home, and anyway, I don't know exactly what time I'll be leaving, and I wouldn't want them to have to wait around for me. I'm sure one of my brothers' – how she thrilled at the word! – 'will see me back.'

Jemima tried hard not to run all the way. This was so different to her previous nerves, for now she knew she was to receive a hearty welcome. She was going to a place she was wanted, and that thought was both a spur and a warm blanket of comfort.

She was faced with a slight dilemma when she reached Dale Street. Should she knock? Or simply enter the shop, as she had done yesterday? The other members of the family had entered the house via the back door, reached by a lane off the main road and then a private yard, and this was the way Jemima had left it. But she didn't feel that she should consider herself quite so much at home, at least not until she was invited to do so.

She needn't have worried. Two of Delilah's children, the older boys, were playing with some others on the pavement in front of the shop, and at the sight of Jemima the larger of the two ran inside, shouting 'She's here!' while the younger scampered excitedly forward to take her hand and almost drag her into the shop. 'I'm Billy,' he said. 'And that's Joe. And the others are—'

Delilah came through from the back room. 'Manners, now! What did I tell you all?'

The eldest girl followed her in, hand in hand with the two smallest, and then she organised them all into a neat line in age order. 'Ready, Mummy.'

Delilah assumed a laughing mock-formality. 'This is Daisy,' she said. 'My eldest, and I don't know how I'd manage without her.'

Daisy held out her hand. 'How do you do, Auntie Jemima.'

Jemima took it and smiled. 'I'm very well, thank you, but goodness! I'm not sure how I feel about being called "Auntie" by someone who's only – what, three or four years younger than me? Perhaps we can be friends.'

Daisy beamed.

'Joe,' continued Delilah, 'and Billy.'

Jemima shook hands solemnly.

'And Eliza, and little Andrew.' Delilah paused and then added, impishly, 'Jemima is a schoolteacher.'

Joe gave an almost comical start, but he bravely held his ground even against such distressing news.

Daisy elbowed him to one side. 'Well, I *liked* school, when I was there, and the mistress. I've left now,' she explained, 'but I still like to read. Uncle William lends me books.'

'I like reading, too,' replied Jemima. 'And I even have a membership at the public library. If it's all right with your parents, perhaps we could go there together one day?'

Daisy gulped and looked pleadingly at Delilah, who threw her head back and laughed with joy. 'Oh, you're going to fit right in. Come on through, now, and sit down while we wait for the others. They all said they'd get here as quickly as they could after work, so it'll be just after six, I expect.'

Jemima spent a wholly pleasant hour, wondering how it was that she could be so relaxed and comfortable with someone she'd only met the previous day.

At five minutes past six there was a shout of greeting from outside the back door, and it opened to admit three men who could hardly have looked more different from each other if they'd tried. The first and eldest was tall, and wearing a suit with a starched white collar and tie. The other two, a few years younger, looked about the same age as each other and were both dressed for manual labour; one was a great bull of a man, while the other was smaller than either of his brothers, lithe and agile.

Jemima stood up, her mouth suddenly dry.

'Our brothers,' said Delilah, simply. 'William' – she indicated the tall one – 'Sam' – this was the giant – 'and Jem.'

There was a moment of awkwardness similar to the one Jemima had experienced earlier, as she didn't quite know how to greet them. They were her brothers, but they'd only just met. What was appropriate?

William stepped forward and took her hand in both of his, pressing it affectionately. 'You don't know what this means to us, truly. I'm so glad to meet you. Or to meet you again, I should say.'

Sam brushed him aside, threw his arms round Jemima, picked her up and twirled her round with a loud crowing noise, then set her on her feet again and gave her a smacking kiss on the cheek. '*That's* what it means to us.'

Jemima laughed in delight and turned to Jem. He didn't say anything, but instead gazed at her with soft, kind eyes and made a series of gestures. His hands were so ingrained with coal dust that she could see it in every line, even though he'd evidently scrubbed them.

'Jem's deaf,' explained Sam. 'So he don't speak, and he can't hear you. But if you look at him while you talk, he can see what you're saying by watching your lips. He says he's very happy to meet you, and he knows everyone else is as well.'

'I'm happy, too,' she said to Jem. Then she turned back to Sam. 'Which one of those signs meant "happy"?'

He demonstrated.

Jemima faced Jem again. She pointed to herself and then attempted to imitate the sign as she spoke. 'I'm very *happy* to be your sister.'

His smile grew wider, and he leaned in to peck her lightly on the cheek.

Frank, Annie and Meg arrived in due course, and a crowded and happy meal was eaten. Then there was more time for talk, with many questions and answers on both sides. Jemima toned down the events immediately after Pa's death, because there was no point in accusing Mrs Lewis when she could provide no proof, and there was nothing anyone could do about it. But she did mention her pain at having to take Pa's books to the pawn shop on Pitt Street. 'I was actually planning to redeem them yesterday, but events overtook me! I'll go back soon.' She smiled, watching Sam sign something rapidly to Jem. She must learn this language as soon as she could, as it seemed everyone else in the family was proficient.

'Oh, William,' said Annie, cheerfully. 'How does it feel to finally have another scholar in the family?'

William hadn't spoken much, and Jemima looked at him with interest. Of course, the collar and tie indicated that he worked at something other than manual labour, but he hadn't said what it was. 'Do you like reading? And, sorry, I haven't asked you yet what you do for a living.'

Sam guffawed. 'Reading? Him? You can't hardly get inside their house for all the books in it.'

William smiled. 'I've been trying to decide whether to say this or not, but I think you already know where I work.'

Jemima looked at him blankly.

'In fact,' he continued, 'if the description I received was accurate, I believe you've actually been there.'

She still didn't understand.

'You asked for me, and I wasn't there, but you didn't leave a message. You said you'd call back another time, but you never did. And I remembered about what Meg had said about knowing you were somewhere around in town, and I wondered and wondered if it might have been you.'

For the second time in as many days, Jemima was so taken aback by the vagaries of fate that she could hardly speak.

'Shaw,' she whispered. 'Hughes and Shaw? The printers and bookbinders?'

'Correct. It used to be just Hughes, but I've been working there for so long that I was offered a partnership, hence the change of name.'

Jemima made a strangled noise. 'But I've been walking past there every few days for *months*.' It was yet another missed opportunity, missed because she hadn't had the wit or the courage to take action.

But then she knew that it didn't matter. Not any more. What mattered was that she was here now, with her family around her. Lost and found, and never to be lost again.

Chapter 19

It was a busy few days at the Whiting house.

The usual household tumult went on around Jemima, and she was also trying to keep herself occupied in order to take her mind off the intense disappointment of Thursday afternoon. Everything had been going so well recently that she was beginning to believe life had no more bricks to throw at her, so it had come as a nasty shock when she had entered the pawn shop to find that Pa's books had all been sold – and that very morning, too. She was late with coming back with the money, she admitted that, so the pawnbroker was within his rights, but she'd truly believed that the books would still be there. They were, after all, something of a luxury item when compared with the clothes, shoes and blankets that everyone needed, so they were less likely to be bought. But bought they had been, and there was nothing Jemima could do about it except dash away a tear as she left the shop.

She therefore threw herself into other matters, attempting – still with little success – to get on with some writing, but also to move forward with plans for the Ragged school. She, Henry and Betty had been eagerly enthused in the immediate aftermath of the lecture, but of course this fervour had subsequently taken a back seat to all the other excitement, and Jemima was aware that this was her fault. The sight of Mary and Joey peeking into the yard almost every day was also a regular reminder that she had promises to keep, so she got back to it. During the daytimes, while the others were at work, she sat calculating how much money they would need to raise and what they would need in terms of space and equipment, and drafting letters of application for funding, and then she discussed it with the others in the evenings.

This turned out to be harder than Jemima had anticipated, and at first she couldn't work out why. It wasn't until Saturday evening that she realised the entire conversation was being continued by herself and Betty, and that Henry had almost completely withdrawn from it. He'd been quiet on the previous evenings, too, but Jemima had just assumed he was tired after his day in the office. Now, though, there was no mistaking his lack of enthusiasm.

Jemima sincerely hoped that Henry hadn't gone off the idea of the school, but of course it wouldn't be terribly surprising if he had. His position at the grain merchants' office was a good one and he'd spent all that time getting his accounting certificate – could she wonder if he preferred to concentrate his energies on developing a career there?

Betty didn't seem to notice anything amiss. She was still extremely keen, on the basis that if they found enough money to pay an infants' teacher then she could finally hand in her notice to Mrs Silverton, 'and tell her where she can put it, an' all, after the way she treated Jemima'. Jemima hoped that such funding could be found, and if it was then Betty could certainly have it, as she herself was happy to work as a volunteer. But it would be such a shame to have the school without Henry. Jemima would say nothing to him for now, in the hope that he might come round again in due course.

* * *

Sunday dawned and with it Jemima's excitement at the prospect of seeing the remaining members of the family she hadn't yet met. And this, of course, was to take place at Hopkins' tea room, where she was now to be a guest rather than a customer.

When she arrived, the place was so packed that at first she wondered if she could possibly have mistaken the day and turned up when the tea room was open to the public. But no, it couldn't be, could it, not on a Sunday? And, on closer examination through the window, Jemima could see faces she recognised.

There was surely no need to knock here, so Jemima simply took a moment and then went inside.

A warm welcome awaited her, along with a plethora of new introductions. Fortunately, Jemima's three sisters-in-law were as different from each other as their husbands, so she was able to make notes to herself. William's wife, Bridget: bright red hair, Irish accent. She was very friendly with Frank, and Jemima remembered something that Delilah had said on that first day – they were brother and sister. How two pairs of siblings had come to marry each other Jemima didn't know, but there was no doubt a story behind it somewhere. Jem's wife, Amy, had rosy cheeks and an infectious smile. She was also deaf, and so signed her greeting; Jemima recalled the gesture for 'happy', used it with a smile of apology and said out loud that she would do better next time. Clara, meanwhile, was dwarfed by her husband Sam, but was a no-nonsense type of woman juggling a toddler and a baby. Jemima knew little of such things, but the infant looked very young, certainly quite a lot smaller than Tilly Whiting. She stroked his little hand.

'Ah, there you are, my dear.'

The voice came from behind Jemima, but she recognised it straight away as that of Mrs Roberts and turned eagerly. 'Oh, ma'am! I've been thinking of you all this time, and I'm so grateful to you for being so kind to me that day, that last time I was here. And I'm so sorry if I seemed odd, I was in a bit of a state, and—'

Mrs Roberts cut her off with a few kind words and a squeeze of the hand.

Meg was there too, her own child in her arms, though Jemima wasn't quite sure whether to classify him as a baby or a toddler. Again, her only point of comparison was with the Whiting family. Younger than Benjy, older than Tilly, perhaps halfway in between them . . . about a year and a half in age? Anyway, he was called George, and both his parents were besotted with him.

Meg smiled at the older woman. 'Mrs Roberts has kindly agreed to come out of retirement for today, to let me have more time out here with you and the others, and Sally and Hannah will help her.' She nodded at Sam. '*Now* you'll see some cooking.'

He grinned. 'Can't wait.'

'Well, I'd best get back to it,' said Mrs Roberts, though she paused a moment longer. 'I'm truly sorry about your father, my dear, but I'm also truly glad that you've found dearest Meg and the others.'

Jemima was watching Mrs Roberts head off in the direction of the kitchen when Clara elbowed Sam. 'Did you give them to her yet?'

'Not yet. Jem's got them, anyway.' He waved across the crowded room and then signed something.

Jem came over with a large parcel wrapped in brown paper. He stood next to Sam and gestured for him to speak.

'Well.' For such a large man Sam looked improbably awkward. 'The thing is. We're not reading men, Jem and me, but from what you said the other day, we knew these were important to you. So we went to fetch them back, before anyone else got to them. Fella in the shop said he knew which ones we were talking about, so I hope he was right.'

Jem handed over the parcel, and Jemima unwrapped it to find Pa's books.

'Oh!' She had a lump in her throat and a stinging sensation in her eyes.

There was a short pause. Then, 'Sorry, Jem, I will learn this sign language, but I don't understand it yet.' She looked at Sam. 'What's he saying?'

He grinned. 'He says, he'll take that as a yes.'

'Thank you,' she said, simply and sincerely, as she

wiped away a tear. 'And you're right, they are important to me.'

'Good,' replied Sam. 'That's that, then.' Jemima must have made a slight movement towards her bag, which contained her purse, because he added, 'Don't even *think* about it. We've missed out, all these years, on giving you presents. We need to catch up, little sister.' His tone was affectionate. 'And I'll carry them home for you later, so they're not too heavy for you.'

Jemima took the parcel over to a table in the corner and placed the books down carefully. They hadn't suffered from being in the pawn shop – no creases, tears or missing pages – so they were just as Pa had last touched them. Or, rather, just as she'd picked them up from the floor after they'd been scattered by a rough and uncaring hand that was only after money.

This was in sad contrast to the flower book, with its cracked spine. Sighing, Jemima pulled it out from her bag; it had seemed right, somehow, to bring it with her today. She and Delilah had managed to work out the history of the volume during their private chat on Wednesday evening, before anyone else had arrived – a story put together from Delilah's memories and some of Pa's last words. When Delilah had first started out selling flowers – from a basket she carried round the street, long before she had a shop – she hadn't actually known the names of each different type. A friend had said that Pa was keen on self-improvement and could probably find her a book on the subject, which he had. It had been a library copy, which she had studied and then given back, but Ma had liked it too, and had always associated flowers with both Delilah and Jemima, so Pa had managed to buy an identical copy, which he had given to Ma as a present. And then she'd put the letter in it, and he'd kept it hidden after she'd died as he couldn't bear to look at it.

Jemima came out of her reverie to find that both Delilah and William had come over to sit with her.

'Books,' he said, pointing. 'I did wonder what Sam and Jem were up to. But this one looks like it's been in the wars. May I?'

She handed over the flower book.

'Hmm. It's actually not as bad as it looks. If you'll let me borrow it, it'll be as good as new in no time.'

'Really?'

'Jemima,' he said, trying to hide his smile, 'where do I work?'

She felt foolish but he brushed it off, saying that it was hardly surprising she couldn't remember everyone's name, age, job and shoe size, with the number of new people she'd met recently.

His mention of work reminded Jemima of something

else, and she addressed Delilah. 'Did you say, when I first came into your shop, that you had a job going?'

'Yes. As well as the shop, I have a couple of girls who go out with baskets, selling buttonholes, little posies to couples in the park, that sort of thing, and one of them has handed in her notice.' She frowned. 'Why. Do you want it? I thought . . .'

'Oh no, not me. But I do know someone who could do with a new job, and what you've just said makes it even more suitable – she loves being out and about. She's a maid-of-all-work at the moment, for a hard mistress, and I'd like to see her getting away.' Jemima paused. 'Of course, I can't ask you to take her on just on my say-so, but if she came to see you about it, would you at least talk to her?'

'Of course I would. It's tiring work, but' – Delilah glanced towards the kitchen – 'if she's a maid, she'll know all about that, and being on her feet all day. Why don't you bring her to the shop next time she has an afternoon out? And in the meantime I'll take the card out of the window.'

Jemima hugged herself at the thought that her own good fortune might extend to Sarah as well.

It wasn't too long before they were all called to dinner. Nearly all of the tea room's tables had been pushed together to make one big one, and Jemima had never sat down to a meal with so many people in her life. Twenty-eight of them, altogether! Fifteen adults and thirteen children, if she counted herself as the youngest adult, and Daisy and Hannah as the oldest children. Even the Whitings would have to consider that an impressive number.

Jemima found herself seated with Delilah on one side and, as luck would have it, a young man whose name she couldn't recall on the other. Not Frank, and not Tommy – as she must now remember to call Mr Hopkins – but the one who was engaged to Annie. Think, now. His name was . . .

'Jack,' he said. 'And don't worry that you didn't know. I'm the next newest around here apart from yourself – well, you know what I mean – and it took me an absolute age to get used to it. It was only ever my Ma and me before I met Annie, and this was all rather . . .' he gestured vaguely at the room.

'Overwhelming?'

'Yes.'

'I think I have all the adults sorted out now, but the children might be another matter.'

'Ah,' he said. 'I might be able to share some of my tips with you there. The trick is to be scientific and methodical.'

She laughed. 'Please do.'

'Rosie and Maggie' – he pointed at two girls of about ten and eight, who both had flaming red hair – 'are quite obviously William and Bridget's. When trying to differentiate, always start with them.'

'Very well. And I know Hannah and Charlie already, from having been in here and in the grocer's shop before, but I can't work out how they fit in. Mr and Mrs – I mean, Meg and Tommy – don't look old enough to be their parents.'

'They're adopted,' Jack explained. 'Long story, we'll save it for another time.'

'All right. Who's next?'

'Anyone else older than about five belongs to Delilah. She's the eldest, and she started having children first.'

Jemima located Daisy and the others. 'That makes sense. But what about all the smaller ones?'

He shrugged. 'That's where my system falls down, I'm afraid. Science has no answer, and they blur into a mass of tots and babies, not helped by the fact that most of the Shaw family seem to be determined to name their children after each other. Sam's daughter is called Annie, and Jem's son is called Sam . . . I'd just give up there if I were you, and call all the small ones "my dear" or something.'

Jemima laughed again, determined that she would learn the names of all the nieces and nephews she'd been so suddenly blessed with, though perhaps it didn't need to be right now.

The dinner was delicious, a treat of baked meat, potatoes, vegetables and gravy such as Jemima had never encountered, and the quiet around the table while everyone savoured the meal was taken as a compliment by Mrs Roberts and her assistants in the kitchen. And this was followed by some of Meg's finest cakes and confections, until even the children – and Sam – declared themselves full.

'Don't you dare!' called Meg to Jemima, from a couple of places away, as Jemima began to stand up and stack plates after the meal.

'And not you, neither,' said Mrs Roberts, taking a similar pile out of Meg's hands. 'You're not to set foot in that kitchen for the rest of the day.' She bustled off, shepherding the older children and a few more willing volunteers on the way, while the younger ones got down so they could romp about the place with Charlie's dog.

'Tsk,' said Frank, teasingly, 'is that the great Meg Hopkins, being thrown out of her own kitchen?'

'I couldn't disobey an order from Mrs Roberts if I tried,' was Meg's simple reply, before a mischievous grin appeared on her face. 'But there's nothing stopping *you* from helping with the washing up.'

Frank was suddenly very busy talking to Tommy on

his other side, and Meg laughed. 'Come on, then, sisters all, let's take advantage of our unexpected holiday.' She led the way over to the corner table, where it was quieter, with Delilah, Annie and Jemima following.

They all sat down, and then there was a moment of silence as each of them seemed to feel the profound nature of the occasion. 'I never thought . . .' said Delilah, taking Jemima's hand.

'Nor did I,' said Annie. 'And nor did any of us, though we did all hope, remember?' She took Jemima's other hand. 'Do you know, I only found out that you existed about two or three years ago. And now here you are. Here *we* are.'

'And I always wanted a sister!'

Jemima heard the catch in her own voice and felt the danger that this was all about to become too emotional, so she was glad when Meg cleared her throat and took an interest in the pile of books. 'These were James's? I mean, your Pa's?'

'Yes.' Jemima had touched on the subject with Delilah a few days ago, but she thought she ought to mention it again to the others. 'I hope you don't mind me still calling him Pa, because—'

Meg was already shaking her head. 'You absolutely should keep doing that. You won't hear this from the others, because Annie doesn't remember and Delilah doesn't like to speak ill of the dead, but our Pa was a violent drunk who didn't care two farthings for any of us. He nearly killed Sam once, and he hurt the rest of us too.' She was almost glaring, as if defying the others to contradict her, but they didn't. 'So, although you had such a tough time of it, and you grew up not knowing about us, in that particular respect you were better off.'

'I know,' said Jemima. 'But now, having met you all, and knowing you're my family, I just feel . . . I don't know. Guilty? Stuck between two places?'

Delilah squeezed her hand. 'That's only natural, but you mustn't worry. We're all sitting together now, but we've all got here by very different paths, and we have other families, whether they're related to us by blood or not. You can care for everyone at once – love isn't a cake that you can only slice into so many pieces, as my rather wise daughter once told me. You can love a new family *and* an old one, and that's perfectly fine. And in your case, I don't just mean your Ma and Pa, but also those wonderful people you're living with. You don't need to feel guilty towards anyone.'

Jemima was struck by the resemblance to what she herself had told Mary and Joey about their baby brother. *Loving your new Alfie doesn't mean you love the old one any less.*

Delilah was continuing. 'You also don't need to feel

obliged to anyone, least of all us. I would love nothing more than for you to come and live with us, and stay with us always, but I have to recognise that you have your own life and your own ties. I've learned my lesson about being overprotective and smothering, and I'm not going to do it to you. You are your own person, and you have to find your own way.'

Jemima listened, and, in that moment, she finally gave the permission that was needed for her to be *herself*. A unique person with a unique history, one who was not lost but who was making her own path. Friend and honorary family member at the Whiting house; sister and aunt to the Shaws; friend and perhaps almost-sister to Sarah; and yet still the daughter of dearest Ma and Pa. She was Jemima Jenkins, but she was also Jemima Shaw, and she could hold all of this in her heart at the same time.

'A cup of tea!' Sally had appeared with a tray, and was happily unloading it without the slightest notion of what she was breaking into.

Her arrival did serve to lessen the tension and the emotion, and the four sisters smiled at each other. 'Speaking of family,' said Meg, fondly, 'Sally isn't related to me, but she's as much my sister as anyone, and my life would be much the poorer without her.'

Annie was looking through the books. 'Oh, Jack would

like this one on engineering. But what's this? Was this one of your Pa's too?' She held up *Pride and Prejudice*.

'Yes,' said Jemima, 'it's different from the others, but he used to read it out loud to Ma. She liked it so much that we kept it and we used to read it to each other after she'd gone.'

'What's it about?'

There were many answers to that, but Jemima settled for, 'It's a story about a family of sisters, as it happens, who end up making their fortunes by marriage.'

'Fairy tales,' said Meg. 'Hard work and determination is what gets a girl through life.'

Jemima agreed, but in fairness she did feel herself obliged to point out that the book had been written some time ago. 'There are lots more opportunities for women now, in the modern age.'

'There are,' said Annie, 'and I'm glad of it.'

'Mind you,' said Delilah, indulgently, 'there's a lot to be said for marriage, too, if you find the right man.'

Jemima was amused to see that all three pairs of eyes immediately sought out the object of their own affection. 'Well then,' she asked, light-heartedly, 'seeing as you all know so much about it, what advice would you give me in that regard?'

'Find a man who wants you to follow your own dreams, not his,' said Delilah.

AN ORPHAN'S DREAM

'Find a man you can trust,' said Meg. 'Everything you own will be his if you're married, so marry one who respects you as a person in your own right.'

'Find a man who'll always stand by you, no matter what,' said Annie. 'Oh, and one who likes children.'

'But, most importantly of all,' added Delilah, her tone a little distant as she looked fondly at Frank, 'find a man you can love.'

Jemima laughed. 'And where will I find such a shining example of manhood? I don't suppose they grow on trees. A man who wants me to follow my own dreams, who will stand by me, who respects me and likes children? A man I can trust and love? Why—'

She stopped.

She swallowed.

She blinked in disbelief.

All this time, she had been walking round with her eyes closed.

But now, finally, she could see.

Chapter 20

Memories flooded back, threatening to carry Jemima away. Henry, supporting her quietly and thoughtfully through the day of Pa's funeral. Pushing himself in between her and the ruffian near the workhouse, heedless of whether the man might have been armed with a weapon. Bouncing his baby sister on his knee, looking after his little brothers, helping Maisie with her schoolwork and boosting her spirits, teaching with such joy at the yard school. Henry, who roundly condemned the man who'd belittled Jemima in the newsroom, and told her she was better than that. Who'd encouraged her in her job applications and her writing. Who shared her dream of a school. Dreams, support, respect, trust . . . *love*.

Henry.

Jemima tried to collect herself, but the other three were sharing such knowing smiles that it was pointless.

Delilah put down her teacup and patted Jemima's arm. 'I'd tell him, if I were you.'

'Oh, I can't. I don't think he'd see me in the same way – he thinks of me as just another sister.'

'Is this by any chance the young man who came in the shop that day?'

'Yes.'

'The one who took such pains to help you find your family, who cared enough for you to do that?'

'Well, yes, but . . .'

Delilah merely raised her eyebrows.

Jemima felt a little detached from all conversation after that, but it wasn't long until the party broke up in any case. There were excited children to calm and take home, and there would be work and school tomorrow.

'Listen,' said Delilah, as she gave Jemima a final hug. 'I meant what I said about not interfering in your life, and I'm not going to be coming round to check on you every five minutes. But that doesn't mean that I don't want to see you, that I won't be *delighted* to see you, whenever you want. You know where we are, and I hope you'll come and see us very often. Our home is your home, regardless of how many other homes you have.' She pulled back, a twinkle in her green eyes. 'Or will have, in future.'

Jemima had a great deal on her mind on the way

home, and in the days that followed. She couldn't pluck up the courage to say anything to Henry, wanting first to get a better idea of what his reaction might be, and sensing that he continued to draw back from what had previously been an easy intimacy. She tried not to be upset by this, forcing herself to concentrate on her writing, and also spending as much time as possible with Maisie and the books they loved to share. Henry, of course, had also been helping Maisie out with her education, so this was something that did bring them together a little more, but it was still awkward. Jemima didn't know whether she was acting differently because she'd come to her stunning realisation, and that this was what was putting him off, or whether in fact he was acting just the same as usual and she was seeing it all differently because she was looking more carefully. In any case, she couldn't bring herself to speak of her feelings.

Delilah held off from asking anything about it, on the couple of occasions Jemima saw her that week, for which she was grateful. Outwardly she'd agreed with her sister that they shouldn't be in each other's pockets all the time, but in truth she wanted to see her new family as often as possible, and had to restrain herself from running over to Dale Street every day. She kept it to twice over the week, once on Wednesday evening and once on Sunday afternoon, plus she and Betty made a happy and triumphal return to the tea room on Saturday afternoon. Jemima had savoured her chocolate and her macaroon, and wondered if Sarah might by now feel confident enough to come here, or whether she would still feel it was 'too good for the likes of her', as she'd said before.

Jemima was eager to tell Sarah about the possibility of a new job, but she had to wait until Sarah's next afternoon out, which wasn't until the first Thursday in November. The day eventually came, however, and Jemima set off in high spirits. She was sure that Sarah and Delilah would like each other, and that Sarah would prefer the job selling flowers to being Mrs Lewis's maid-of-all-work. It would mean moving out of the boarding house, of course, but Jemima would be able to help her find somewhere else, and maybe they could even find a room to share somewhere. They were single girls, with all the difficulties that entailed, but Jemima now basked in the enormous advantage of having respectable brothers and brothers-in-law who would be taken seriously by society. William making enquiries at a boarding house and saying he was looking for somewhere safe and reputable for his sister and her friend to live would be a very different matter from Jemima knocking on the door by herself. And the wider family might even know of someone themselves who was looking for a lodger.

As Jemima turned on to Pitt Street, she could see a crowd and a commotion further down. At first she couldn't place exactly where it was, but as she got closer she could see that it was outside Mrs Lewis's boarding house. Alarmed, she quickened her pace.

'What's happening?' she asked a woman at the back of the group of onlookers, as she strained to see over the many heads.

'The police are here,' came the reply.

Jemima's heart gave a lurch. She wouldn't put anything past Mrs Lewis, and the horrible thought occurred that the landlady might have managed to blame some of her crimes on poor Sarah, who would have nobody to fight her corner. Well, she did have someone, and that someone was Jemima, who began to force her way through the crowd. Sarah would not be left alone to face this.

Just then, the front door opened and a police constable emerged. He was handcuffed to, and leading, another person, and Jemima prepared to throw herself forward, so that Sarah could see her and she could find out where they were going. But then the constable jerked his arm to bring his prisoner into full view as they started down the steps: it was Mrs Lewis herself.

There was half a ragged cheer from the onlookers. 'Been robbing her tenants,' came a voice from Jemima's left. 'For years, apparently.'

'Aye,' replied another. 'And always widows and women and children, who had nobody to protect 'em.' Jemima heard the sound of someone spitting on the ground. 'Deserves all she gets.'

Jemima was dumbfounded. This was too good to be real. Mrs Lewis arrested? The truth spoken openly? And the landlady would never be able to cheat and steal from her tenants again?

These pleasant thoughts were interrupted by the sight of a second constable appearing at the door, with Sarah beside him.

Oh no. No, no. Surely not.

Jemima's heart hit the ground again, and she attempted to surge forward. She was prevented, however, by a large woman with an even larger basket who would not give up her place at the front of the audience, and thus she was still on the pavement, reaching helplessly forward, when the constable spoke. 'And this here is the heroine of the hour,' he said, indicating Sarah. 'You good people on this street need to know that she had nothing to do with her employer's crimes. In fact, it's her bravery and cleverness that's brought the woman to justice. So you look on her kindly, if you please.'

Another, heartier cheer sounded, and some calls of 'Good for her!' and the like. This was followed by jeers as Mrs Lewis was put into the back of a police vehicle and the horse was set in motion. A couple of small boys chased after it for a while, but the show was over, and people began to disperse and get about their own business.

Jemima ran up the steps and flung her arms around Sarah. 'Oh, I'm so happy to see you. And what's happened? How did . . .?'

'Are you a friend of this young lady, miss?' asked the constable, a solid man of middle age with grey muttonchop sideburns.

'I certainly am. Oh, and I'm also one of the people Mrs Lewis robbed, if you need any additional witnesses.'

'Ah,' he said. 'I'll take your name, but you might not be needed, so we'll spare you the courtroom if we can.'

'Because of Sarah? But . . .' Jemima clutched Sarah's hand. '*I* know she's telling the truth, but if it comes to court, won't it just be her word against Mrs Lewis's? And won't they be more likely to believe Mrs Lewis?'

'Ah,' said the constable again, this time beaming with an almost paternal fondness at Sarah. 'That's what was so clever. When she saw it happening herself, she called on others to witness, including a couple of gentlemen – gentlemen boarders here with very respectable jobs – who also saw what was going on. And when we were arresting the landlady, she let slip a couple of things what implied she'd done this before. We have ways of tracing stolen goods and so on, to find out who was selling them on. My sergeant, he says he's confident she'll be found guilty.'

Jemima gave her name and the Whitings' address. Even if she moved out of there before any court case, they would be able to provide her new directions.

'Well, I'll leave you to it,' said the constable, putting away his notebook. 'You get yourself a cup of tea, young lady, and congratulate yourself. I don't know what'll happen next – whether someone else'll take this place on, or it'll shut down – but you've got your good name, and I'm sure you'll find something else if you need.' He shook his head. 'Who'd have thought it, eh? A little maid unmasking a criminal. You're about the same age as my youngest daughter, and I'm going to tell her all about you this evening.' He nodded and made his way down the street.

The girls stood on the step for a few moments, until Jemima noticed that Sarah was shivering. 'Come on, let's go down to the kitchen, and I'll put the kettle on and you can tell me all about it.'

Once Sarah had some hot liquid inside her and her

teeth had stopped chattering, she could speak. 'It was partly you,' she began.

'Me?'

'Yes. I remembered how you acted funny when I said about the widow lady, and then I remembered it was nearly the same as what happened to you, and then I remembered that things like that had happened before.'

'That was clever.'

'But to start with I didn't know what to do, or what to say – I couldn't say anything to her, could I? I'd have been out on my ear.'

'So how did you . . .?'

'That was partly you again,' continued Sarah. 'I remembered what you said, that day, about how I wasn't useless. And your Pa had said I was a good, hard-working girl. But what really made me do it was this.'

Sarah went over to the bed in the corner of the kitchen and drew out a crumpled piece of paper from under the pillow. 'I thought, if they could do it, so could I.'

Jemima smoothed the sheet out on the table to find that she was looking at a copy of episode six of *The Maids of Maddox Place*. She closed her eyes for a moment until she was sure she could steady her voice. 'I've seen this, too. The clever maids who foiled a crime.'

'Yes. And, like I said, if they could do it, then so can I.'

Jemima stood up and went round the table to hug Sarah. 'You're the cleverest, bravest girl I know.'

'That's kind of you to say.' Sarah heaved a heavy sigh. 'Though I'll have to start looking for a new job. I don't want to stay here, not even if someone else takes it on. But that policeman said I had a good name, so, maybe if I ask up and down the street, someone might have something.'

Jemima clasped her more tightly. 'That's what I was coming to tell you. I haven't had the chance to say it yet, because of all that excitement.'

'Tell me what?'

'I've got some good news for you.'

Chapter 21

Jemima hummed as she sat at the table with her pen and paper on Saturday afternoon. Delilah had already been expecting to see Sarah the previous Thursday, so Jemima had taken her straight up to Dale Street once both of them were calm enough to walk. Each had liked the other immediately, Delilah's kindness as a prospective employer and Sarah's willingness to work hard being evident mutual attractions. And it was even better than that: Delilah happened to know from Meg that Mrs Roberts, who lived on her own, had been thinking about taking in a lodger, so she would make enquiries. 'And in the meantime,' she'd added, 'you're welcome to stay here if you don't mind sharing with Annie or with the girls.' Sarah was almost overcome, but Delilah only said, firmly, that 'Any friend of my sister's is a friend of mine.'

AN ORPHAN'S DREAM

And so, Jemima thought, as she considered what on earth the maids might do to top their existing achievements, her own good fortune had been shared, and that was the best thing about it. Now she needed to continue and grow her own career so that the Ragged school could move from dream to reality. She decided that the maids would do something cheerful next, something that would please her readers. *Let other pens dwell on guilt and misery.*

A knock at the door proved to be the postman with a letter for her, which Mrs Whiting took and laid on the table. Assuming it would be something from Mr Grundy, Jemima left it for a few minutes while she finished the paragraph she was in the middle of, but when she paused and glanced at the letter again, she laid down her pen.

As it was addressed to 'Miss Jemima Jenkins', it could not possibly be from Mr Grundy. Thank goodness, he'd never found out that his valuable author was a girl, or Jemima's job and earning power would come crashing down around her ears. The envelope was also, she now noted, of a much better quality than the ones Mr Grundy used, the paper thick and creamy. Intrigued, she opened it, to find an equally high-class sheet inside with a crest as the letterhead. She began to read.

Jemima's exclamation attracted the attention of the

others in the room: Mr Whiting, Betty, Henry and Rob. Mrs Whiting was out at the market with the week's wages in her hand, and the children were all outside, it being a mild day for November.

'What is it?' Betty put down her sewing and moved to the table. 'Not bad news?'

'I . . . I'm not sure what kind of news it is, except that it's astonishing.'

Henry also came over. 'Are you all right?'

'I just . . . Sorry, this has taken me by surprise.' Jemima saw that they were both worried, and she attempted to pull herself together. 'Do you remember, months ago, when I wrote all those letters asking about teaching positions at schools?'

'Yes,' said Betty. 'They all said no, except that one place you went where they didn't give you the job. More fool them,' she added.

'No,' said Henry. 'There were two who never got back to you at all, I remember you saying. The two girls' boarding schools.'

'Yes. And I didn't really expect them to reply, because they were so far above me that I thought they'd think my application was a joke.'

'And is that . . .?' Henry pointed at the letter.

Jemima looked once more at the polished handwriting. 'They apologise for not replying sooner, but my letter was mislaid during a refurbishment of the headmistress's office over the summer and has only just come to light. As it happens they *do* have a vacancy for a junior schoolmistress to work with their younger girls, aged ten to thirteen, and they are offering it to me first as it means they might not need to advertise.'

She frowned as she went on. 'I don't mention in my own letter whether I can speak French or play the piano, but it doesn't matter in either case as they have specialist masters and mistresses for that. There would be some history and geography but it would mainly be English – spelling, grammar, literature and poetry.' She gave a nervous laugh. 'I did mention books and reading in my letter.'

'What else?' asked Betty.

Jemima scanned the later part of the letter again, hardly able to believe what she was reading. 'As they're a boarding school, the position comes with accommodation in a set of rooms, and there would be an expectation of pastoral work, looking after the girls as they're away from home. And the salary they're offering is . . . well.'

She pointed to the relevant line, and Betty whistled.

'Well, now,' called Mr Whiting, from where he was puffing his pipe in the corner. 'That's just what you've always wanted, isn't it? And good for you – you deserve every success.'

'A proper schoolmistress, in a proper school. I'm so made up for you!' exclaimed Betty. 'Just you wait, Pa, she'll be "Miss Jenkins, headmistress" before you know it, and have the whole place under her thumb.'

'It's certainly the offer of a lifetime,' said Henry, more neutrally. His eyes met Jemima's.

She looked away. 'It *was* what I wanted . . .' she began. 'But—'

Despite the riches and the distinguished career being dangled in front of her, two other thoughts were uppermost in Jemima's mind. The first was the Ragged school, and the chance she had to bring education to children who would otherwise never get any. The girls at this boarding school would receive instruction no matter who took the job there, and they would all have comfortable homes to go back to. But the others, the children Jemima thought of particularly as her *own* little pupils . . .

The second thought, and the one she was trying to push behind the other one so as not to have to face it just now, was that schoolmistresses were required to remain single and never marry.

Jemima stood in silence, not realising that she was staring at Henry.

'Pa,' said Betty. 'Why don't you and I go out and get a nice bit of air, while the sun's out? You too, Rob.'

'Eh?'

'Just shut up and come outside, the both of you.'

The door closed behind them.

'As I said,' Henry's voice was almost a whisper as he stared at the floor. 'It's the opportunity of a lifetime.'

'So . . . you think I should take it?'

There was a long, long pause. 'I think you should do whatever is best for you. You had a dream, and you should follow it.'

Find a man who wants you to follow your own dreams, not his.

'But what if my dreams have changed?'

He looked up.

Jemima saw the hope in his eyes, and it finally gave her the confidence, the push, that she needed.

'This' – she waved the letter – 'is not me. Not any more. Not since—'

He waited.

She collected herself. 'Once, a job like this would have been my dream. But now, I want a different kind of school, with a different kind of pupil. I've got my writing to support myself, so I don't need the salary they're offering – I'd rather do something worthwhile, something to help. What's the point of having good fortune if you don't share it around?'

'It's the school, then. You believe in the school that we— that you want to set up.'

Jemima took a deep breath. *Now or never.* 'It is that. But it's not *only* that. I want to set this school up with Betty, and with you.'

'You mean . . .'

Now she'd started, she had to keep going, even if it meant interrupting him, otherwise she might never finish. 'And when I say with you, I don't mean only as a fellow teacher. I know that you probably think of me just as another one of your sisters, but even if that's true then I have to tell you it's different for me. I have to be honest, because I can't keep it in any more. Because that's definitely not how I see you. When I look at you, when I think of you, what I'm thinking is . . .'

'A sister?' His voice was incredulous. 'You think I see you as a sister?'

'Oh.' Jemima's fervour burst like a bubble. 'Oh dear. I've made a fool of myself. Is it not even that? Am I just Betty's friend? I've said too much.' She screwed up her eyes for a moment. 'But I'm not sorry. I'm not sorry I said it, because I just wanted you to know, even if you don't feel the same way. I have to be honest. You're a wonderful man, Henry Whiting, a clever man, a kind man, one who loves his family and wants to do some good in the world, and – and . . .' She couldn't go on, although she wasn't sure whether she'd run out of breath, words or courage.

'Oh, Jemima,' he said. 'My dearest Jemima.'

She revived a little at the sound of the word *dearest*, and risked raising her eyes to his.

His emotion was palpable. 'You honestly thought I'd been thinking of you as a sister? When all this time I've been worried that you only thought of me as a brother? What a fool I've been.'

'*You've* been a—' The implication of his words sank in. 'You mean . . .?'

He nodded, apparently now hardly able to speak himself. 'I should have been as honest with you as you've just been with me, but I was too scared. An amazing girl like you? Why would you be interested in someone like me?'

'Someone like . . . but you're the most wonderful man in the world.'

He laughed. 'I never thought to hear that, not from anyone. And to hear it from you? My life is complete, school or no school.' He reached forward, stopped, started again, and then gently took her hand. 'My dearest Jemima, would you consent to walk out with me? To be the girl I think of, that I'm *allowed* to think of, now, as being the one for me?'

'Yes, Henry, yes. I'd like that very much.'

The door burst open. 'I wasn't listening!' lied Betty, running in and flinging her arms around both of them.

'But I'm that glad.' She gave each of them a hefty thump on the shoulder. 'I was wondering how long it was going to take, and whether I was going to have to poke the both of you with a sharp stick.'

Jemima felt a moment's awkwardness, but Henry was still holding her hand, and she could do nothing but dissolve into a smile. 'Well, I'm glad we haven't let you down.' She looked at Henry and squeezed his fingers. 'Oh, and when you said "school or no school"? It's definitely going to be "school". We'll find a way, and we'll find it together.'

* * *

The following day, Jemima and Henry took a leisurely Sunday walk around St James's. Their conversation was probably not what most people would expect a courting couple's to be, but it was their own and on subjects dear to their hearts. They spoke of themselves, and their own foolishness in not speaking out earlier, but this was interspersed with hard practical details about the setting up of a school and the funding it would need. At the very minimum, if the school were to be taught only by Jemima, they needed a room, a blackboard and sufficient slates and chalks. This was the most probable scenario, and was already vaguely possible given Jemima's income from writing. They would only need some fairly modest donations, and the talk at the library had given them some ideas on how to ask for them and whom to approach. If they were to think more ambitiously, however, they needed a greater amount. Enough for dinners for the children, for more and different equipment, and to provide a salary for Betty, and possibly also for Henry as well. All of this would require some rather significant investment, but it was not impossible. Nothing seemed impossible now.

They were in a cheerful mood as they returned to the house for dinner of beef and pudding, which was dished up in copious amounts by a beaming Mrs Whiting.

After dinner the room remained crowded, as it had started to rain and the children were waiting to see if it would stop before they went outside to play again. The noise level rose even as the washing up was being done, and by the time it was finished Mr Whiting was starting to say that it must have stopped by now, and in any case a bit of wet wouldn't hurt them, especially when he and Ma wanted to take the weight off their feet in peace for five minutes.

Matthew got up to check, with some of the others crowding round. He opened the door only to find that there was a man standing outside, his hand raised as though he was just about to knock. 'Pa,' he called. 'Someone here. A gent.'

All the adults turned in surprise, and Mr Whiting heaved himself out of his chair. 'Can I help you, sir? Out the way, children.'

They stood back and the visitor could be seen properly. He was a small, dapper man, just past middle age, in a smart suit and bowler hat, and he peered over the top of a pair of half-moon spectacles. Who could he be? 'Probably got the wrong house,' said Mrs Whiting to Jemima, settling back in her chair. 'Pa'll set him on the right road.'

The man raised his hat. 'Good day to you, sir, and my apologies for interrupting your Sunday. My name is Robert Grundy, and I'm looking for the author of the penny-paper serials entitled *The Adventures of Stowaway Tom* and *The Maids of Maddox Place*.'

'Oh,' interrupted Matthew, cheerfully, pointing into the room. 'That's our Jemim—' He stopped in horror and clapped his hands over his mouth.

Slowly, very slowly, her mouth dry and her heart in her throat, Jemima stood up. She knew she'd been the recipient of far too much good fortune recently. And this was how that run of luck was going to end. It wasn't just the wrenching idea of giving up her writing; it was the humiliation that this interview was going to entail, and the disaster for their school plans.

Mr Whiting hadn't noticed anything amiss. 'Come in, sir, and welcome.' He allowed Mr Grundy to pass him, and then belatedly saw the expressions on several faces, and Jemima's most of all. 'Er. Well. Jemima, lass, this gentlemen is here to see you, but if you don't want to talk to him then I'll ask him to leave again.'

It was too late for that. Might as well face it here and now. 'Thank you, but it's fine,' she said, through numb lips that would hardly move.

'Well, then – would you prefer to speak to him in private? We can all go—'

There was an exclamation from Henry, but it was Mrs Whiting who got to Jemima's side first. 'No,' she said, resolutely. 'If this gentleman has anything to say to Jemima then he can say it to me too. And' – she cast a fierce glance at Mr Grundy – 'if he's got anything bad to say, that she doesn't want to hear, then he'll have me to deal with.'

Mr Grundy opened his mouth, but Mrs Whiting was in full flow. 'You're the gent what publishes her writing, I remember your name now. Well, she sits there day after day, and she works hard at it. I didn't used to hold with education for girls, but our Jemima's proved me wrong, and she deserves every bit of success she's had. And if you want to take that away from her, then I for one—'

He held up his hands in a placatory gesture and managed to get a word in. 'Please, madam – am I addressing Mrs Jenkins? – your sentiments are admirable, but I can assure you they're not needed. That's not why I'm here.'

'You'd best sit down,' said Mr Whiting, indicating the table and taking a seat himself. Mr Grundy did likewise, and they were joined by Mrs Whiting, Jemima and Henry. Betty stood behind Jemima and put a hand on her shoulder in solidarity.

Mr Grundy began again. 'For the avoidance of any doubt, I'm not here to cancel your commission. In fact I would like to speak to you about the continuance of both serials once our present agreement ends. But I do admit' – his eyes gleamed from behind the spectacles – 'the reason why I've come in person rather than writing is so that I could satisfy my curiosity.'

'You suspected I was female?'

'For some while now, yes. I confess that the thought didn't cross my mind, when you first wrote to me about *Stowaway Tom*, that you were anything other than male – but this only testifies to my own regrettable narrow-mindedness. But an idea of it stole upon me when you suggested writing a serial aimed at girls, and that idea grew when I read the instalments. No man could have produced such work, nor made it so popular with our rapidly growing female readership.'

'So that was what gave it away. But . . . I suppose it doesn't matter now, if you want to continue?'

'Ah, that was what made me *more* certain. But the final clue was contained in your latest letter.'

Jemima frowned as she tried to remember what she'd written. She hadn't given anything away, surely?

Mr Grundy took a sheet of paper from the inside pocket of his coat. 'Nothing too overt, my dear, but you apologised for not having received my letter. *Apologised*, for something that was in no way your fault, and should have been blamed either on myself or the good men of the Post Office. I have noticed this trait in other women, and my sister reminds me often that girls are brought up to be self-effacing and modest, to take up as little space in the world as possible.'

Jemima caught Henry's eye.

'Not round here, they're not,' murmured Betty.

Mr Grundy heard her and beamed. 'I can certainly see that. Mr and Mrs Jenkins are much to be congratulated.'

Jemima felt that she had to correct him. 'These aren't my parents, Mr Grundy. Now that other things are in the open, I might as well be completely honest. I'm an orphan, the daughter of a dock worker who never went to school and who taught himself everything he knew. But he made sure I had a proper education, and after he died' – she surprised herself with the steadiness with which she could now say those words – 'I thought that using that education was the best way to honour his memory. I intend to open a Ragged school, along with my friends, to teach poor children for free.'

She cast a glance around the small room, so different from what Mr Grundy would be used to himself. 'And it was the luckiest day in my life when Mr and Mrs Whiting invited me into their home.' She stared at him in defiance, waiting for the negative reaction she was sure to see now that she'd dismantled her own respectability one blow at a time.

He paused for a moment and then smiled once more. 'My dear, if you think any of that is going to put me off, you're sorely mistaken. My sister and I grew up in a house just like this one, and it was thanks to parents who worked hard and valued education that I have reached the position I'm in today. And, I may add, our mother and father valued education for girls just as much as for boys. My sister, I am proud to say, is a keen scientific investigator, though sadly a continuing prejudice against females prevents her from becoming a Fellow of the Royal Society.'

Mr and Mrs Whiting were by now looking a little dazed at having such eminence under their roof, but Mrs Whiting recovered sufficiently to react in the time-honoured fashion. 'Well, we don't often have bosses or employers here, sir, but would you care for a cup of tea?'

'Nothing would suit me better, dear madam.'

Mrs Whiting went to put the kettle on and to fret about which teacups might be considered the best china.

'Please,' said Mr Grundy to Jemima, Henry and Betty, 'do tell me more about your plans for a Ragged school. I've heard of such things.'

Little by little, over several cups of tea, they told him the whole story, and after a while Mr Grundy took out a pocketbook and pencil and began to make notes. 'Admirable. Yes, yes, you would certainly need . . . let me see . . .'

When the tale was finished and the cooling teapot nearly empty, Mr Grundy's eye caught the clock, and he started. 'My dear Mrs Whiting, please accept my apologies for trespassing on your hospitality for so long. But your young people here are so determined, and their plans of such interest, that I couldn't help myself.'

'You're very welcome, sir, I'm sure. And yes, they are. I'm proud of them all.'

'And quite right, too. Now, I address myself to you all equally, but especially to Miss Jenkins, which is not meant to cast any aspersion on you, sir,' he said to Henry.

'It's all Jemima's doing, Mr Grundy. It's quite right you should speak to her.'

'Well then, Miss Jenkins, I offer you a bargain. If you will keep writing your serials for me, and delivering instalments of both stories every Tuesday without fail, I will be happy to make a substantial donation to your school in addition to your regular payments. And, moreover, I undertake to canvass the subject with my fellow printers and publishers.'

Jemima felt as though the breath had been knocked out of her, a sensation not improved by Betty's sharp elbow in her ribs when she failed to answer. 'She means yes, sir, if you please.'

'Yes,' whispered Jemima. 'Yes. And thank you so much; it's so generous of—'

He waved away her gratitude. 'Generous? Possibly. But it's also a sound business investment.'

'Investment?'

'Yes, of course. Surely I don't need to remind you that it is very much in the interest of a publisher of penny papers to increase the literacy of Liverpool's general public.'

'Oh, of course!'

'They are by no means great literature, but not everybody wants great literature. Reading anything is better than nothing, and if children are encouraged to enjoy reading by means of tales of adventure in penny papers, I say so much the better.'

'That's exactly what I've always thought!'

'Well then, we are, as it were, on the same page. I bid you farewell for now, but I hope we might all continue this conversation soon, perhaps in my office when I've managed to assemble some other interested parties.' He was at the door and putting on his hat. 'For now, good day to you all.'

After he'd left there was a moment of stunned silence, and then Jemima, Henry and Betty all joined hands and danced around the room in exultation.

* * *

Over the next few weeks the excitement only grew. Jemima could hardly wait to tell Delilah and the rest of her family about her good fortune, and when she did their joy was as great as hers, just as she'd known it would be. Mr Grundy was true to his word, and it turned out that he really had meant it when he said his donation would be 'substantial'. Between that and the contributions of his fellow publishers, there would be sufficient funding to enable Jemima, Henry and Betty to think even more ambitiously than they had before. A large room would be affordable, once they could find one, and fully furnished with desks and benches so the children wouldn't have to sit on the floor. There would be ample supplies of paper, slates, pencils, chalks, and a number of maps and prints for the walls to display the alphabet and multiplication tables. Back copies of penny papers would be available in abundance for reading practice, as a change from standard primers.

But the information that really gladdened three hearts was that there would be money for teacher salaries. Jemima stuck to her original promise of working as a volunteer, because she intended to keep up with her writing, but the funding group undertook to match Henry's and Betty's current wages, and both were happy to hand in their notice before the end of the year. Betty was grinning from ear to ear on the day she came home after giving Mrs Silverton the news. Henry was glad in a quieter way, worrying that he'd passed his accountancy examination for nothing, but the others were very happy to say he could be in charge of the school finances. He was further pressed to take on some smaller jobs on an occasional personal basis, including checking the account books for Hughes and Shaw,

Hopkins' tea room and grocery, and Malling's flower shop.

Everybody – publishers, Shaws, Whitings and friends – came together to help. The first key point was that a location for the school needed to be found, and this problem was solved when a certain news office went out of business almost as quickly as it had sprung up. ('Too superficial and unreliable,' William had said. 'Nobody wanted to use them.') The owner of the building, faced with the prospect of it lying empty again, was only too pleased to have someone wanting to take over the lease straight away. The upper floor was to be the regular schoolroom, while the front shop and back rooms downstairs were eventually to be used for practical forms of education, and the provision and exchange of food and clothing. A tiny kitchen area was pronounced by Mrs Roberts to be capable of improvement and possible use for cooking lessons. Meg knew a seamstress and Jem a cobbler; Mr Whiting and Rob would organise visits by friends in the various building trades, so the pupils would be able to benefit from all sorts of practical teaching.

The school was to open in January, so November and December passed in something of a rush. However, amid the flurry of cleaning, organising, taking deliveries of desks and equipment and lesson planning, Jemima didn't forget the most important people associated with the school: the children. Mary and Joey skipped for joy when she told them the good news, and they and all the Whiting brood promised to tell their friends. Maisie had begged to be allowed to transfer to this new school, but Mr and Mrs Whiting had turned her down for now, on the basis that she would either have to call her brother and sister 'sir' and 'miss', or she'd be setting a bad example to the other children by calling teachers by their first names. 'You've got to have proper discipline,' said her father, though this was softened by, 'But we can always think on it again later,' from her mother. Jemima, who had heard this exchange, promised Maisie work as an assistant teacher once she was old enough, and Maisie was happy.

Jemima, meanwhile, was thoughtful. Any school did indeed need discipline, she knew that. But there was discipline and there was discipline: there would be no cane in her classroom, and rulers would only be used for their proper purpose. She would do things differently.

She was busy explaining all of this to Sam and Jem on Christmas Day, as they sat in the overcrowded tea room. Incredibly, nearly all of the Whitings had been squeezed in along with the extended Shaw family; and, even more incredibly, Mrs Whiting had been persuaded to sit down and be waited upon for the day. Jemima had felt some guilt on Meg's part when she had heard of all these arrangements, but Meg had dismissed them by saying that it was no more than she catered for on a daily basis; besides, Mrs Roberts had so much enjoyed her day out of retirement back in the autumn that she'd insisted on doing it again, and had basically taken over Meg's kitchen single-handedly.

Meg had been holding two boxes while she said all this, and she passed them over to Jemima. 'These are for the two sisters who work as maids.' Harriet and Anna Whiting had not been able to attend the gathering, because of course they were expected to work so that their employers could enjoy their Christmas Day. But Meg sympathised, and the boxes turned out to be full of some of her very finest pastries, as well as some biscuits and sweets from the grocery.

The whole place was a joyous whirl, but Jemima managed to catch a few odd moments for quiet chat. One such interlude was with Sarah, happier than Jemima had ever seen her, and also, if she was not mistaken, a little plumper. She was living with Mrs Roberts, working for Delilah, and enjoying both situations immensely. 'I've got my own bedroom, not sleeping in the kitchen, and Mrs Roberts has tea ready for *me* when I get home!'

It would take Jemima a while longer to master the

language of signs used by her family, but she had already made enough progress to understand Jem saying *Good* when she told him and Sam about her determination not to hit any children who attended her school. He followed up with *Amy . . . me . . . happy . . .* and something else she didn't catch.

Jemima grimaced, but Sam came to the rescue. 'He and Amy were happy that nobody hit them at school.' They both watched Jem again. 'They learned better like that.'

Yes, signed Jemima. *Children . . . happy.*

'I'm not so sure, though,' rumbled Sam. 'What if you get any bad boys that play you up?'

'Surely they wouldn't even bother coming to school? Nobody's going to make them attend if they don't want to.'

'Still,' said Sam, 'you don't know some of the lads in this city, the likes of the ones I see down at the docks sometimes, trying to steal anything that's not nailed down.'

Jemima remained doubtful that any such children would be among her pupils, but they ended by agreeing that Sam would come in at some point and talk to the boys about his time in the army. He hadn't mentioned it himself, but Jemima had recently found out from Annie that Sam was the very ex-soldier, the same Shaw, that

Betty and Henry had once mentioned as being in the news. He'd fought in a war, been a hero and won a medal; even the wildest boy would respect him.

Jemima had introduced Henry to her brothers and sisters. They all liked him very much, and Delilah whispered into Jemima's ear, 'Does he by any chance want you to follow your own dreams?' before she dropped a kiss on Jemima's blushing cheek.

Chapter 22

The new year of 1865 dawned.

It was a harsh, frosty morning when Jemima made her unsteady way to the school alongside Henry and Betty. She had, in fact, been out once already, taking a dawn walk down to the churchyard to see Pa. As she'd gazed at the fine new cross bearing his name, dates of birth and death and the words BELOVED HUSBAND AND FATHER, she'd whispered, 'This is it, Pa. Today's the day. I hope you'd like what I'm doing. I know you would. And I know you love me. I love you, too.'

And now it was time to begin the rest of this momentous day. Jemima was unsteady on her feet not because of the icy pavement, but because she was nervous. Why was she so anxious? She kept telling herself that she had no need to be – everything was ready and waiting, everything had been prepared properly and thoroughly, and this was, after all, the culmination of her ambitions.

But what if it all went wrong? What if she found herself unable to teach after such a long break from it? And, most terrifyingly, what if it turned out there was no desire for such a school? What if Mr Silverton and Mr Greenaway were right, and education for the poor was of no use or interest?

What if no children turned up?

By the time they were in the schoolroom, Jemima had half a mind to run away. But Henry was calm and Betty was confident, and she couldn't let them down. She reached into her bag and touched the repaired flower book for luck.

Footsteps were heard on the stairs, and they all turned in surprise at hearing anything so early. But the three people who appeared were not pupils: they were Delilah, Meg and Annie.

Jemima ran to them.

'Annie's part of the factory is shut today for maintenance,' explained Delilah, 'and so Meg and I thought it was a good opportunity to delegate, so we could all come and support you together.'

'Sally and Hannah are perfectly capable of starting the day without me,' explained Meg, 'and Bridget and Daisy are at the flower shop.'

Jemima's gratitude made it difficult to speak, but Delilah took her hand. 'It's a special day,' she said, 'and we're here to support you. Today, and always.'

'It certainly is,' added Henry, who was standing a little way off the family group, in response to the first part of Delilah's speech. 'And it's all thanks to Jemima.'

Jemima was about to disclaim modestly, but then she remembered what Mr Grundy and Henry had both said on different occasions, and she caught the glint in Delilah's eye. 'Thank you,' she said, simply. 'But exactly how special the day turns out to be remains to be seen.'

Betty was standing by the window that looked out over the street. 'Jemima.'

'Yes?'

Betty merely smiled and pointed. The others all joined her, and were thus able to see the large groups of children converging on the building from every direction. Boys and girls, some with shawls and coats and some without, some shod and others barefoot, and in varying degrees of cleanliness, but all happy and excited. Mary looked up, spotted Jemima and waved.

Henry's hand touched Jemima's, and he murmured close to her ear, 'Special.'

* * *

Jemima faced the packed schoolroom. Her worries had all vanished as more and more children arrived, squeezing themselves on to the benches, and she had no doubts that she would be able to address them properly. She was enveloped in the warm and joyous support of the people she loved most in the world; and, more than that, she had confidence in herself.

'Good morning, children,' she said, smiling as she heard the somewhat hesitant, straggled reply.

'Before the day starts, I just wanted to welcome you all. We don't mind where you live, what you're wearing, what sort of family you come from or whether you've ever been to school before. None of that matters. What we care about is that you've come here because you want to learn, and we're glad that you did. We think you're important, that you matter, and that your education matters.'

The astonishment on the children's faces was quite some sight to behold, but not one of them interrupted.

'Now, let's introduce ourselves. My name is Miss Shaw-Jenkins.'

Out of the corner of her eye, Jemima saw the triple start of surprise, and then Delilah wiping her eye.

'But you can call me Jemima.'

That was daring, and she could hear the general surprise. But this was a different sort of school for a different sort of pupil, and she might as well start as she meant to go on.

'There are three teachers at this school, including me, and we will be helped out from time to time by other people who value your education as much as we do. These are the other two teachers, who will introduce themselves in a moment.' She indicated Henry and Betty, and then took a deep breath.

A breath and also a pause, so that she could savour the words she was about to utter. The precious, triumphant words that she'd never thought to hear herself speak, and that meant so much.

Jemima closed her eyes for a moment and then opened them wide, so that her happiness could blaze out across the room as she looked at Annie, Meg and Delilah.

'And these,' she said, 'are my sisters.'

Read on for 'behind-the-scenes'
research by Judy Summers.

Dear Readers,

Thank you for joining me in the world of the Shaw family for this fourth and final time! You're most welcome to be here, regardless of whether *An Orphan's Dream* is your first encounter with the Shaws, or if you've read any or all of *The Forgotten Sister, A Winter's Wish* and *A Daughter's Promise*, my earlier books focusing on Meg, Delilah and Annie.

For me, creating this book was slightly different from writing the others in the series. Partly this was because I had to bear in mind that some readers were meeting the Shaw family for the first time, while others already knew them well (and were also aware of more of the backstory of some of the other characters, like Mrs Roberts, Hannah and Charlie), so I had to make sure I was talking to all of you while also not giving too much away. And then there was the fact that Jemima herself doesn't realise, to start with, that she *is* a Shaw, and only discovers her background through a gradual process. I hope you agree with me that she still exhibits plenty of the qualities that we've come to know and love in the other members of the family, combining a compassionate nature with a steely determination to make the best of herself.

Part of the way in which Jemima wants to make the best of herself is in getting an education, and it will probably come as no surprise to any of us that the sort of education you might get in Victorian Liverpool, and indeed Victorian England as a whole, depended very much on your sex and your social class. The best was reserved for wealthy men, while women and the poorer classes had to make do with a very inferior product, if they could access anything at all. Those quotes from magazines and school advertisements that Jemima reads during the course of *An Orphan's Dream* are all real, as was the widespread belief that women were 'totally unsuited to intellectual labour', and I honestly don't know how they coped with being so continually belittled and patronised.

While upper-class girls of the 1860s might be able to scrape together something approximating an education (albeit one that focused more on the 'accomplishments' that would gain them a husband rather than anything too academic), the poor were denied even that. Partly this was because they tended to be sent out to work at very young ages, and thus had no opportunity to do anything else, but it was also because there was no national provision. The schooling available in any given area depended very much on the whims of local churches and philanthropists, and what they thought was suitable for the labouring classes. If poor children were lucky, they might attend Sunday school once a week to learn some basic reading and writing, but the number of marriage certificates that had to be signed 'X' by both bride and groom unable to write their name shows that even this was far from universal in Liverpool in the nineteenth century. At the time *An Orphan's Dream* is set, literacy rates in England as a whole hovered around the fifty per cent mark, with the poor being markedly less likely to be able to read and write than the rich, and women less likely than men.

In 1870, a few years after the events we depict, partially state-funded Board Schools were set up to provide some primary education, but such schools were not compulsory, and, as they still charged a fee, attendance was low. Schooling finally became obligatory for children aged between five and ten in 1880, and the Free Education Act of the following year did away with the cost, meaning that they were at last open to all. Jemima would have been thirty-three when this happened, and I like to imagine her and Henry celebrating the passing of the act together, after all their years of hard work, as a victory for all.

Daily life in a Victorian school was more or less as I have described it here. I'd just like to clarify that I'm not quite old enough to have experienced that era myself (!) but the cane was still in use when I was at school, and I recall older generations of my family talking about how they were forced to hold pens in their right hands even though they were left-handed, and being hit when they did not. Humiliation and violence were classroom tools employed far too frequently.

The 1860s was a period of growth for the so-called 'Ragged schools', again along the lines depicted in *An Orphan's Dream*. They were designed for the poor and destitute, those children of such low condition that they might not even be allowed into Sunday schools. The London Ragged School Union had actually been established a little longer than I have portrayed here, having been founded in 1844; although focused primarily on London, it produced publications that were sent across the country to help spread its ideas and practices. Ragged schools declined in number with the passing of the national education acts that made them redundant, but by the time they disappeared at the end of the nineteenth century they had helped hundreds of thousands of children.

Liverpool was one of the most forward-looking places in the country in terms of promoting widespread education, with philanthropists often making substantial donations to good causes. One of these was Sir William

Brown, who (as Jemima would probably be interested to know) was a merchant, banker and Liberal MP who spent the then-enormous sum of £40,000 establishing a free library for the city, which was opened in October 1860. The free educational lectures that James Jenkins attended before his illness were also a regular feature of Liverpool life, although, inevitably, they were aimed at the improvement of the *male* working class.

* * *

The questions of what was and was not 'suitable' for women, in terms of activity and education, and what counted as 'proper' writing, were subject to the usual Victorian types of snobbery. Forms of writing that were considered to be non-standard (for which, read: not written by upper-class men for an educated male readership) were looked down upon, and these included the so-called penny dreadfuls. These pamphlets were all the rage in the mid-nineteenth century, an early sort of mass popular culture. Naturally this meant that they were derided by the upper and educated classes, but they did contribute to the rise of literacy among those lower down the social scale. However, they really were aimed at men and boys: unfortunately I've had to invent the idea of one being written about female characters.

The disparagement of penny dreadfuls is echoed in the criticism of 'lowbrow' literature today, which includes the very sort of saga fiction that *An Orphan's Dream* represents. Who could possibly think that a large female readership might like stories about women that reflected the reality of their own lives? Not the literary establishment, certainly, who call it by dismissive terms such as 'chick lit', which isn't all that far removed from their ancestors branding mass-market fiction penny dreadfuls.

Even Jane Austen, one of the greatest writers of English literature, was not immune from this sort of patronising nonsense. Austen is by a long way my favourite author of all time, as you might guess by reading *An Orphan's Dream* (I've quoted directly from three of her novels, but there are also some other, more subtle, allusions to her works scattered about – did you spot any of them?). I have always loved her books, having re-read them all multiple times, and I would certainly encourage you to *read* them as well as watching the film and TV adaptations. Although many of these adaptations are very good in their own way, they just can't get across the sheer joy and wit of Austen's writing.

Austen (whose name, incidentally, did not even appear on the title pages of the early editions of her work) was underestimated, overlooked and even criticised for being a female author writing about women's lives and their domestic concerns. This offended many of those who felt that Great Literature could and should only be written by Great Men focusing on Important Subjects. But they were wrong. Firstly, why shouldn't the domestic life of female protagonists be the subject of novels? Why is an event or an emotion significant to narrate if it happens to a man on a battlefield and unimportant if it happens to a woman in her own home? And, secondly, Austen is much more than that anyway, having a great deal to say about the social position of women.

Jane Austen retaliated against her critics in the best way possible, by skewering their pomposity in her novels – especially in *Northanger Abbey*, with its running sardonic commentary about women and reading. She also highlighted the very real lack of choice afforded to women in her own day, and the unpalatable decisions with which they were often faced. If you think her books are all bonnets and fluffy romance, read carefully the section of *Pride and Prejudice* in which Charlotte Lucas justifies to herself why she is marrying the odious Mr Collins. It's enough to make you weep with frustration, though Charlotte does eventually learn to make the best of her lot, just as the Shaw sisters do.

* * *

The Shaw family, and all the other characters in *An Orphan's Dream*, are fictional. Some of them do represent certain types: there were undoubtedly schoolteachers around in the 1860s who resembled Mr and Mrs Silverton and Mr and Mrs Greenaway, and some landladies who acted in a similar fashion to Mrs Lewis. And it definitely wasn't uncommon for single girls who had no male protector to be taken advantage of in various unpleasant ways. However, there were also many genuine counterparts to Mrs Roberts, Mr and Mrs Whiting and Mr Grundy, not to mention real-life Jemimas, Henrys and Bettys who demonstrated kindness and a sense of community.

Jemima, as we have seen, survives her troubles and finds happiness, both in being reunited with her sisters and brothers and also in founding the school she has dreamed of. And that triumph, dear friends, marks the end of the tale of the Shaw family of Liverpool. I hope you've enjoyed reading it as much as I've enjoyed writing it – and, if you have, then please be assured that there are plenty of other stories still to be told about women of the Victorian era.

Yours truly,
Judy Summers

About the Author

Judy Summers is an avid reader, historian and mother of three. Her forebears – some of whom probably entered England via Liverpool in the Victorian era – were miners, labourers and domestic servants. She finds these lives far more interesting than those of the upper classes.

Judy lives in the English countryside with her family and is a keen baker and gardener.